MW00468817

LONG

TIME

GONE

Books by Charlie Donlea

SUMMIT LAKE

THE GIRL WHO WAS TAKEN

DON'T BELIEVE IT

SOME CHOOSE DARKNESS

THE SUICIDE HOUSE

TWENTY YEARS LATER

THOSE EMPTY EYES

LONG TIME GONE

Published by Kensington Publishing Corp.

CHARLIE DONLEA

LONG TIME GONE

KENSINGTON
PUBLISHING CORP.

www.kensingtonbooks.com

This book is a work of fiction. Names, characters, businesses, organizations, places, events, and incidents either are the product of the author's imagination or are used fictitiously. Any resemblance to actual persons, living or dead, events, or locales is entirely coincidental.

To the extent that the image or images on the cover of this book depict a person or persons, such person or persons are merely models, and are not intended to portray any character or characters featured in the book.

KENSINGTON BOOKS are published by

Kensington Publishing Corp.
900 Third Avenue
New York, NY 10022

Copyright © 2024 by Charlie Donlea

All rights reserved. No part of this book may be reproduced in any form or by any means without the prior written consent of the Publisher, excepting brief quotes used in reviews.

All Kensington titles, imprints, and distributed lines are available at special quantity discounts for bulk purchases for sales promotion, premiums, fundraising, educational, or institutional use. Special book excerpts or customized printings can also be created to fit specific needs. For details, write or phone the office of the Kensington Special Sales Manager: Attn. Special Sales Department, Kensington Publishing Corp., 900 Third Avenue, New York, NY 10022. Phone: 1-800-221-2647.

Library of Congress Control Number: 2023952647

The K with book logo Reg. US Pat. & TM Off.

ISBN: 978-1-4967-2718-3
First Kensington Hardcover Edition: June 2024

ISBN: 978-1-4967-2722-0 (ebook)

10 9 8 7 6 5 4 3 2 1

Printed in the United States of America

"Photographs open doors into the past
but they also allow a look into the future."

—Sally Mann

Cedar Creek, Nevada

July 13, 1995
9 Days After . . .

A BLACK-TAILED COOPER'S HAWK WITNESSED THE DEATH OF SHERIFF Sanford Stamos.

The majestic bird glided down from the heavens and landed on the front of the police cruiser, perching like an ornate hood ornament. It squawked once during the battle that took place inside the vehicle, fanning its wings as the car rocked. When the scuffle ended, the hawk folded its wings into its body as Sheriff Sanford Stamos sat in the driver's seat and looked his killer in the eye. The sheriff's icy glare came not from an intense determination to lock eyes with the man who was about to kill him, but rather from the paralytic drug that coursed through his body and prevented even his eyes from moving.

He wanted to do a thousand things other than gawk at the man next to him. His training told him to either engage his attacker or put distance between them. He wanted to escape his vehicle, to draw his gun, to call for backup. But the needle hanging from his neck had robbed him of the ability to move and brought on a profound weakness that infected every fiber of his body. The drug finally stole the function from his eyelids and they fell shut. Sitting behind the wheel of his squad car, Sandy's chin slumped to his chest. The odd angle brought on a raspy snore when he breathed. Sandy had no doubt he was about to die. The things he had discovered during the last few days of his investigation into the missing Margolis family guaranteed it.

He heard the passenger-side door open and close as his killer exited the vehicle. Sandy's door opened next, and he felt the shirt-sleeve of his left arm being tugged upward. A tight band cinched the skin of his bicep before a sharp pinprick on the inside of his elbow jolted his eyelids open. There wasn't much there besides brightness. His vision was blurry, like someone had smeared Vaseline into his eyes.

A localized burning assaulted his arm as the syringe was emptied into the vein. A moment later he felt something else entirely. Something foreign and exotic and more sensational than he'd ever felt before. A cloud of euphoria descended over him, or perhaps he rose up into it. Either way, Sheriff Stamos forgot about the confinement of his vehicle. He forgot about his inability to move or talk. He worried not about his killer, but instead relaxed into the bliss that filled his body and mind. His soul, too? Was his soul being touched?

"You're just another Harrison County junkie now."

Sandy couldn't tell if the voice was his own or someone else's. If it originated from inside his head or was spoken to him. But he didn't really care. A second syringe was emptied into his arm before the door to his squad car slammed shut and another level of ecstasy took control of his faculties. So powerful was the pull of the drug coursing through his system that it disengaged Sandy from his body. He floated above the scene in a way that allowed him to see where he was and what was happening. Seated in his squad car with the seatbelt tight across his chest, he watched from his elevated perch as his vehicle rolled down a shallow hill toward Cedar Creek. Just before the patrol car speared into the water, the Cooper's hawk that was balanced on the hood took flight. Two strokes from its powerful wings lifted the bird into the air until the creek breeze allowed the hawk to hover overhead, wings outstretched. The car continued until the hood sunk beneath the water. The slow creep persisted and Cedar Creek eventually swallowed the automobile, ingesting it fully until only the taillights peeked from the surface.

A foggy comprehension told Sandy he was submerged under the surface of Cedar Creek, but the feeling of euphoria and exhilaration that ran warm through his veins brought with it a weighty apathy that was impossible to overcome. He cared little about the water rising up his chest and lapping at his chin, threatening to crawl up his face and over his head. Instead, he was anxious to fly into the stupor that waited somewhere off in the by-and-by. He was mesmerized by the brightness he saw in the distance. He ignored the scene of his body trapped beneath the surface of Cedar Creek, and instead followed the black-tailed Cooper's hawk as it soared toward the light. He flew and flew and flew, until the brightness absorbed him and ushered him away.

PART I

Genealogy 101

CHAPTER 1

Raleigh, North Carolina
Monday, July 1, 2024

SLOAN HASTINGS WALKED INTO THE OFFICE OF THE CHIEF MEDICAL Examiner fifteen minutes prior to the 9:00 a.m. start time that marked the beginning of her forensic pathology training. She and three other fellows were about to embark on a challenging two-year fellowship that would culminate with each of them being crowned a medical examiner. That was, of course, if they could handle the trials and tribulations that waited for them. Sloan was sure she could. Becoming a forensic pathologist was all she'd ever dreamt of doing.

A Duke graduate with a dual degree in criminology and forensic science, Sloan had cruised through medical school before completing a four-year anatomical and clinical pathology residency. Now, she was twenty-nine years old, and all that stood in the way of accomplishing her dream were two intense years of fellowship. The first of which was a grant-sponsored research year that required Sloan to explore an area of forensic pathology, advance the subject in some meaningful way, and write a thesis paper on the topic. After her research year, she would embark on a twelve-month clinical program at the Office of the Chief Medical Examiner studying under the renowned Dr. Livia Cutty. There, she would perform hundreds of autopsies on her way to becoming a medical examiner. She was anxious. She was excited. And she was hungry.

Dressed in a sleeveless black blouse that showed off her CrossFit-built athletic frame, white slacks, and high heels, Sloan showed her new ID card—which proclaimed her to be one of four first-year fellows as of 9:00 a.m. that morning—to the woman at the front desk. The door adjacent to the desk buzzed. She walked through and headed for "the cage."

Inside the OCME, and to new fellows in particular, the cage was infamous. Closed in by chain-link fencing and filled with rows and rows of forward-facing chairs, the cage was where fellows presented their cases each afternoon. Standing before the attending physicians and bathed in the glow of the SMART Board was like standing in front of a firing squad. Rumors and folklore ran rampant of fellows being crucified as they squirmed at the front of the cage while they stumbled through their cases and fielded questions from the wizards they were training under, who caught every misstep, highlighted every oversight, and corrected every misguided thought. It was a place Sloan feared, and couldn't wait to conquer.

Sloan knew the morgue was located in the basement, that the attending physicians' offices were located on the second floor, and that the cage was somewhere on the first floor. She wandered only for a moment before she found it, walking through the entrance at the back of the room and taking an aisle seat. Thirty or so folding chairs lined the room, each facing a screen that captured light from a projector that hung from the ceiling and greeted Sloan and her colleagues:

Welcome First Year Fellows!

The other fellows soon arrived, introductions were made, and conversations started about where they had each completed their residencies and what they thought they were in for during the next two years. At exactly 9:00 a.m., a woman wearing green scrubs and a long white coat walked into the cage.

"Good morning, newbies," Dr. Livia Cutty said as she made her way up the middle aisle and took a spot in front of the SMART Board. "Good to see all of you again."

Dr. Cutty had interviewed every candidate that applied to her prestigious forensic pathology fellowship, and had handpicked the four who sat before her.

"It seems like a lifetime ago that I was sitting where you are today—as a first-year fellow nervous and excited about what lay ahead. In reality, it was only seven years ago."

Dr. Livia Cutty was the youngest physician to ever chair the fellowship program at the OCME in Raleigh, North Carolina. The former chairman and Livia's mentor, Dr. Gerald Colt, had aggressively recruited her when he retired the previous year. In less than a decade since she'd completed her training, Livia Cutty had crafted a storied career as a medical examiner. For the last few years she had worked as the Chief Medical Examiner in Manhattan and had thrived in New York. Over the years Livia had been involved with several high-profile cases, and had served as the medical advisor for multiple television networks including FOX, CNN, and NBC. Her current side gig was dishing about forensics for HAP News during her frequent appearances on the hit newsmagazine show *American Events*.

"Since I'm not too far removed from where you are now," Livia started, "know that I will not only understand what you're going through during these next two years, but I will empathize with you as well. I'll be hard on you, just like my mentors were hard on me. But I'll be fair. We all have the same goal, which is to mold each of you into the best and brightest medical examiners this country has to offer. My pledge to you is to provide the tools and the opportunities to get you there. What I ask from each of you is that you give me your best effort. Deal?"

"Deal," Sloan said in unison with her colleagues.

Sloan was, she admitted, star struck as she stared at Livia Cutty. She'd seen the woman so many times on television, either discussing high-profile forensic cases or offering expert testimony and analysis on *American Events*, that it was surreal to be sitting in front of her now. Even harder to comprehend that she would be training under her.

For most of her life Sloan had ranked as the best and the brightest in the endeavors she took on, whether that was leading her debate team in high school, mastering the maze of cranial nerves in anatomy lab, or cranking out burpees with her CrossFit buddies. She always rose to the challenge and was determined to do the same during her time studying under Livia Cutty.

CHAPTER 2

Raleigh, North Carolina
Monday, July 1, 2024

Dr. Cutty spoke for thirty minutes, giving Sloan and the other first-year fellows the lay of the land and reviewing what would be expected during their research year. The twelve months were not entirely void of morgue time. In addition to their research, each of them would be paired with a second-year fellow and would be required to observe five postmortem examinations each month during summer. Ten during winter. The final three months would require them to not only assist with the postmortem exams, but also present the cases to the attending physicians and subspecialty pathologists that made up the staff at the OCME. The second year of fellowship would throw them fully into the morgue, promising each fellow two hundred fifty to three hundred autopsies by the time they finished their training.

"Any questions?" Livia asked.

There were none. Livia checked her watch.

"Okay, for the rest of the morning I'm scheduled with each of you for a thirty-minute session to discuss your research topic. Sloan, you're up first."

Sloan smiled and stood.

"We'll talk in my office," Livia said. "Feel free to grab coffee," she said to the other fellows. "And while you're waiting, walk around and get to know this place. It's going to be your home for the next two years."

Sloan waved goodbye to her new colleagues and followed Dr. Cutty out of the cage. They walked down the hallway and into Livia's office.

"Have a seat."

Sloan sat in front of the desk while Livia slid into her chair and began typing at her computer.

"The staff here at the OCME has chosen four topics unique to forensic pathology, and we randomly assigned each of our fellows to one of them. Ready to hear what the next year of your life will revolve around?"

"Ready," Sloan said.

The two-year fellowship opportunity under Dr. Livia Cutty was unique compared to other forensic pathology fellowships across the country, which were each made up of just a single year of training. The extra year with Dr. Cutty promised a stronger résumé for those seeking positions tangential to criminology and law enforcement. Sloan's dream was to work side-by-side with a major homicide unit, and she had set her sights on Livia Cutty's program the day she started residency four years earlier.

"Your area of interest," Livia said, "will be forensic and investigative genealogy."

Sloan raised her eyebrows and nodded. "Okay," she said slowly.

"Not familiar with this area of forensics?"

"I think we covered it in one of my college courses, but that feels like a lifetime ago."

"A lot has changed since then. It's a constantly evolving specialty. Forensic genealogy is the science behind the breaks in more than a few high-profile cold cases that have been in the news over the last few years. The most well-known is probably the Golden State Killer case. Do you know the case?"

"I know *of* it," Sloan said.

"During the seventies, a guy went on an extended spree of rape and murder in Northern California. Each incident was a middle-of-the-night home invasion. From a few of the scenes, police were able to secure the suspect's DNA. There was no national DNA database back then, so the DNA went unidentified but was preserved as evidence. The guy continued his reign of terror into the early eighties, and then abruptly stopped. His DNA remained unidentified for decades until really smart investigators decided to tap into online genealogy databases in an effort to identify the source of the old crime scene DNA."

"Like Ancestry dot com? The online sites where people submit their DNA to create family trees and learn about their heritage?"

"Correct," Livia said. "Ancestry dot com, Twenty-Three and Me. There're dozens of them, and they contain a treasure trove of genetic information. Bigger than any database law enforcement could ever create."

"But no serial killer is dumb enough to submit their own DNA to one of these sites."

Livia shook her head. "The killers don't, but their unsuspecting relatives do. Cold case detectives working the Golden State Killer case took a chance and submitted the killer's DNA, which had been sequestered from one of the crime scenes and preserved for decades, to GEDmatch—a free service that allows users to upload and analyze their DNA sequences—and hoped for a hit. Low and behold, the killer's DNA showed a genetic link—a match, they call it—to a man who had uploaded his DNA sequence and was identified as a second cousin to whoever the Golden State Killer was. Then the investigative work began. A genealogist working with detectives tracked down the cousin and worked backwards to create a family tree. Second cousins led to first cousins. First cousins led to aunts and uncles. And so on down the genetic line. Detectives researched every relative to see if any of them lived in the areas where the crimes had taken place. After some legwork, they narrowed their list down to just a couple of names. Then they did some stakeout work and waited each week until these potential suspects wheeled their garbage cans to the curb. A DNA sample taken from a used tissue in one of the suspect's garbage bins was an exact match to the DNA sequestered from the crime scenes. An arrest was made and the decades-old case of the Golden State Killer was solved."

"Fascinating."

"I'm glad you think so, because you're about to spend a year of your life researching this topic and finding a way to advance it."

Livia slid a three-ring binder across the desk.

"This contains everything that will be required to complete the project. Of course, your research will culminate in a thesis paper that you will present at the end of the year. Information about 'Presentation Day,' as it's called, is also in the binder. The presentation must fill four hours, broken into two two-hour segments. There are benchmarks that you'll be expected to meet throughout the year, and they're aimed at keeping you on schedule. We'll meet to review your progress every three months. And, of course, you'll be required to keep up with the second-year fellow you've been assigned to and also reach the milestones laid out that will prepare you for the second, clinical, year of fellowship."

"Understood," Sloan said.

"I've given you a lot of information this morning. Take a day or two to review and process all of it. If you have questions, find me. I'm always available. And I'll give you a little bit of advice my mentor gave me: Procrastination is the devil's way of stealing your time. Avoid it at all costs. Get busy and stay busy."

"Yes, ma'am."

CHAPTER 3

Raleigh, North Carolina
Tuesday, July 2, 2024

SLOAN GRABBED HER MAIL FROM A ROW OF BOXES BEFORE SHE WALKED up the steps of her apartment—a one-bedroom in Trinity Circle. Inside, she popped open a Diet Dr. Pepper, her beverage of choice and the secret weapon, along with her obsession with CrossFit, that had helped her survive both medical school and residency. At the kitchen table she flipped open her laptop. She'd spent the previous day reading through the information contained in the giant three-ring binder Dr. Cutty had given her, making notes, and outlining the approach she would take to researching, dissecting, and somehow advancing the field of forensic and investigative genealogy.

The first thing she'd have to do is find a case that had been solved using DNA profiles stored on databases of online ancestry sites. She knew better than to consider the Golden State Killer case. It was too well known, too mainstream, and completely unoriginal. She made a list of people she needed to get in touch with. It included homicide detectives, genealogists, and maybe a reporter or two who had covered true crime and could tip her off to a less well-known case involving forensic genealogy.

She took a sip of Dr. Pepper and got busy on her laptop, deciding that contacting a genealogist would be the easiest of the three. A quick search brought up a website for the Association of Professional Genealogists. Sloan paged through scores of profiles until she found a genealogist named James Clayton located in North

Carolina. The profile included an email address, so she ripped off a quick message to him.

> Dear James,
> I'm a fellow in forensic pathology at the Office of the Chief Medical Examiner in North Carolina. I'm researching forensic genealogy and looking for a genealogist to give me a "Genealogy 101" lesson. I located your name from the Association of Professional Genealogists online. I'm in Raleigh, just like you. Please let me know if you'd be willing to answer a few of my questions.
> —Sloan Hastings

She included her phone number and logged out of her email. She spent the rest of the morning researching homicides that had been recently solved using online genealogy databases. She made a list of the ten that looked promising and spent three hours after lunch reading and printing articles on each of them. It was mid-afternoon when her phone buzzed with a text message. She didn't recognize the number but saw when she opened the message that it was James the genealogist.

Hi Sloan, thanks for reaching out. I'd love to talk. Yes, I'm also in Raleigh and can meet anytime.

Sloan typed her response.

SLOAN: Anytime? Is tonight too soon?

JAMES: Not at all. Meet you at The Daily Drip at 9PM?

SLOAN: See you there!

Procrastination is the devil's way of stealing your time. She didn't plan to waste a minute. Just two days into her fellowship and Sloan was already out of the gate and running. Where she was headed would be the greatest shock of her life.

CHAPTER 4

Raleigh, North Carolina
Tuesday, July 2, 2024

T HE DAILY DRIP WAS ITS USUAL BUSTLING SELF, EVEN AT NINE AT night. The city, it seemed, lived on caffeine, and its residents took in large quantities at all times of day and night. Sloan sat at a tall table in the middle of the café, within easy sight of the entrance. There had been no image of James the genealogist on the website where she found him. She expected a middle-aged man with glasses and a pen protector, but instead, at just past 9:00 p.m., a man in his early twenties walked into the café and looked around, lifting his hand in a subtle wave and mouthing her name. *Sloan?*

Sloan smiled and nodded.

James she mouthed back.

The man nodded and walked over.

"James Clayton."

He reached out and Sloan shook his hand.

"Sloan Hastings," she said with a crinkle to her left eye. "You don't look like a genealogist."

"Really? What's a genealogist supposed to look like?"

"I don't know. Older, I guess. More studious?"

"You mean nerdy?"

James sported an I-work-from-home scruff and a frat-boy hairdo. He looked much more like a college student than someone who studied family trees for a living.

"It's okay," James said. "I get that a lot. Everyone expects a seventy-year-old dude with white hair and glasses. But don't worry, I know what I'm doing."

"I trust you. Thanks again for meeting so quickly."

"Sure thing. Most of my work is done online or over the phone. It's rare that I actually meet a client in person. When you said you were in Raleigh, I jumped at the chance to get out of my apartment and talk face-to-face with a client."

A few minutes later they each had a cup of coffee in front of them.

"So how can I help?" James asked.

Sloan opened her computer.

"I just started my fellowship in forensic pathology."

"What's that mean? You're a medical examiner?"

"Not yet. But I will be in a couple of years. My first year of training is a research year. My topic of interest is forensic and investigative genealogy, and I need someone in the know to guide me through the ins and outs of the topic."

James smiled. "I can do that."

"I need to learn how online genealogy databases and the genetic information they contain are being used to solve years-old cold cases. The Golden State Killer was offered as an example."

James pulsed his eyebrows. "The Golden State Killer was the first. At least, the first case that went mainstream. And it set a precedent."

"Okay," Sloan said, tapping on her keyboard and taking notes. "Let's start there. Tell me how it works. Explain how the guy got caught forty years after he committed the crimes, simply from a family member submitting their DNA to an online site."

"Sure," James said. "How much do you know about the case?"

"My department chair gave me a quick rundown yesterday, but I'm looking for a deeper explanation on the inner workings of forensic genealogy."

"Got it. Stop me if I wander too far into the weeds."

Sloan nodded and tapped away at her computer as James spoke.

"The Golden State Killer was a serial rapist and murderer who terrorized Northern California for several years in the seventies and eighties. Back in the seventies, DNA technology was not what it is today. Still, investigators knew enough to preserve DNA-laced evidence for future use. In the case of the Golden State Killer, that DNA evidence was in the form of rape kits."

"So rape kits were done on his victims, and those kits were stored in evidence for decades?"

"Correct. It was 2017 when cold case detectives kicked their investigation into overdrive. That meant the rape kits had been preserved for close to forty years before DNA was pulled from sperm cells sequestered in them."

"Amazing." Sloan tapped away. "Talk me through the process. How did the killer's DNA, which authorities had in their possession for decades, suddenly lead to the killer being identified forty years after he committed the crimes?"

"In 2017, with the Golden State Killer case ice cold, a clever investigator decided to submit the killer's DNA—taken from one of the rape kits—to a genealogy website and create a 'fake' genetic profile. Fake in the sense that the DNA did not belong to the detective creating the profile. From there, the investigator attempted to match that DNA profile to other online users who were innocently looking to build family trees and delve into their heritage. Any match that came back would obviously be from a relative of the killer."

"Ah, now I see."

Sloan continued to type.

"The investigators jumped through a lot of legal hoops, and ultimately had to convince the executives of the genealogy site to allow them access—although there is still much debate about whether what this particular investigator did was ethical, let alone legal. Anyway, the genealogist ultimately matched the killer's DNA to a distant relative—a second cousin—who had submitted their DNA and created their own profile, for the sole purpose of looking into his ancestry. Once the authorities identified the killer as a descendent of a particular family, they investigated all the men who could possibly be related to that second cousin. Eventually, they settled on one suspect."

"How did they narrow their search down?"

"Geographically, at first. Out of all the relatives, only one lived in

Northern California at the time the crimes were committed. But also, the detectives knew from the DNA profile that the killer had blue eyes. They searched DMV records and driver's license info to confirm that the man they had in their sights also had blue eyes. It was enough to secure a warrant. Then they quietly worked with the waste management company that collected the suspect's garbage, and picked through the man's trash until they found a good source of DNA. When they ran it, it was an exact match to the DNA from the rape kit. Case closed."

Sloan tapped a few last keystrokes. "You mentioned ethical or legal issues with the way authorities handled the case."

"Right. One argument is that it's an invasion of privacy for authorities to tap into these online databases of the public's DNA, since the people submitting their DNA are not openly giving permission to law enforcement to use their profiles. The Golden State Killer case caused many of the online genealogy sites to change their privacy policies, and some have even restricted law enforcement from accessing their databases. It's turning into an ugly fight and I'm sure there will soon be legislation around it."

"Okay," Sloan said, looking over her notes. "I need to understand how these online genealogy sites work. If I wanted to create a genetic profile myself, or build a family tree, how would I do it?"

James nodded. "First thing you'd do is register online with one of the genealogy websites, pay whatever fee they charge, and then they'd send you a kit in the mail. The kit requires you to submit your saliva—basically, they send you a test tube, you spit into it several times, and send it back. Then the company extracts your DNA from the saliva sample. Once you have a DNA profile, you log into your account and see what other relatives, close or distant, you match with. From there, you start building your family tree. There's a lot more to it, and really, the best way to demonstrate this would be for you to actually submit a sample and let me guide you through the process of building your family tree."

Sloan hesitated. "Um, yeah, I'm not sure I want to go that far."

"It's no big deal. You just spit in a test tube. I'll do the rest."

"It's not that. It's just . . ."

Like a semitruck materializing out of nowhere and passing in

the dead of night, headlights off and speeding in the opposite direction, Sloan's realization was jarring and abrupt.

"Is something wrong?" James asked.

"I'm adopted," she finally said. "I guess I hadn't thought this out
fully, but I wasn't planning on tracking down my biological relatives."

"Oh." James cocked his head to the side. "I work with lots of
adopted clients. It could be fun. I'd facilitate the whole thing and
walk you through the results."

Sloan considered the offer, and whether there might be ways to
learn the ins and outs of online genealogy other than by creating
her own DNA profile.

"Assuming I go ahead with this, what's the turnaround time after
I submit my DNA?"

"The first step would be to create a profile online. That would
take no time at all. You could do that today. Then, it would typically
take a week to receive the kit, and maybe six to eight weeks to have
a DNA profile up and running."

"Two months?" Sloan asked with wide eyes.

"That's if you go through the normal channels."

Sloan raised her eyebrows. "You have a way to get around the
normal channels?"

"Of course. It's what I do. I'm one of the lead genealogists for
Your Lineage dot com."

"How does that help me?"

"I can expedite things for you. We could have your DNA profile
up and running in, say, a week. And then I can walk you through
the whole process of how you create a family tree, use your DNA
profile to connect with distant relatives, and trace your lineage
back to the days of yesteryear."

Sloan pouted her lower lip, thinking of her parents and what
they would say about her digging into her ancestry and locating
her birth parents. Then she thought of Dr. Cutty, and her warning
about procrastination. She finally nodded.

"Okay, I'm in."

CHAPTER 5

Raleigh, North Carolina
Wednesday, July 3, 2024

THE FOLLOWING MORNING SLOAN STOPPED AT HER PARENTS' HOUSE before she was due at the morgue to meet the second-year fellow she had been assigned to. She parked in the driveway and walked through the front door.

"Hello?"

With an orthodontist for a father and a dentist for a mother, both in the same practice, her childhood mornings had always been controlled chaos. The breakfasts Sloan saw on television growing up, of bacon and eggs served in the kitchen nook, while dad drank coffee and read the paper, were nonexistent in the Hastings home. Those picture-perfect television mornings were replaced instead by a quick bowl of cereal or a breakfast bar as Sloan scooped up her backpack and climbed in the back of her parents' SUV for the ride to school before Dr. and Dr. Hastings hustled off to the office.

"Hello?" she yelled again from the front foyer.

"In the kitchen, honey," she heard her mom say.

"Hi," Sloan said as she walked through the doorway.

"What are you doing here?"

Dolly Hastings stood at the kitchen counter and buttered a piece of toast. She wore green surgical scrubs. There had never been ties or blouses or scenes of her mother hurriedly slipping into high heels on the way out the door. In the Hastings home all Sloan ever remembered her parents wearing to work were scrubs and gym shoes. From day to day, the color changed but not much else.

"Just thought I'd stop by to say hi."

"My BS radar is going off," her dad said on the way down the back staircase. Todd Hastings, too, wore scrubs—although his were light blue and covered with braces and teeth.

Drs. Dolly and Todd Hastings, of Hastings Family Dental & Orthodontics Center, were not shy about their disappointment that Sloan hadn't followed them into dentistry.

"Your first week of fellowship, and you stopped by to say hi?"

Sloan smiled. "Yep. *Hi* Dad."

"You haven't just 'stopped by' since medical school. You only come over when you want something. Money? I thought this forensics fellowship paid you decently."

"It does not. But I don't need money."

"Ignore your father," her mom said. "He's overly pessimistic since we've become empty nesters."

"That was, like, ten years ago."

"It hasn't gotten any better."

"I looked it up," her dad said. "Fellows make about seventy grand a year. You'd be making three times that by now if you'd joined the practice straight out of dental school."

Sloan smiled. "Oh, Dad, you keep forgetting. I didn't go to dental school."

"Don't remind me. But you could've at least gone into oral surgery. We could use a good surgeon on staff. Do you have any idea how much business we refer out to the local oral surgeon?"

Dolly slapped Todd on the shoulder. "Leave my daughter alone. Can I get you a cup of coffee, sweetheart?"

"Doesn't coffee stain your teeth?" Sloan asked.

"Soda is worse," her father said. "You would have learned that in dental school, and probably wouldn't have such an addiction to Dr. Pepper."

"Diet," Sloan said. "*Diet* Dr. Pepper."

"The carbonation ruins your enamel."

"Will you two please stop," Dolly said.

The ribbing would go on for her whole life, Sloan was certain.

Her mother had gotten over it, but she was sure her dad would never fully embrace the idea that his thriving dental practice would someday be sold to someone outside the family.

Sloan sat at the kitchen island and her mother delivered a steaming cup of coffee.

"Really, sweetie," her mother said, checking her watch. "Is something the matter? I've got patients at nine."

"Kind of," Sloan said.

Her parents waited for her to continue.

"So here's the thing. I received my research topic and . . ."

"And what?" her mother asked.

"It's just . . . it has to do with forensic genealogy, and it's going to require me to take a deep dive into those ancestry websites."

"So what's the problem?" her mother asked in a balanced voice.

"I just . . . the best way for me to start the research and see first-hand how the websites work is to submit my DNA. I submitted my DNA already, actually, and the genealogist I'm working with is going to create a DNA profile for me. I guess I didn't want either of you to think I was doing it on my own or behind your backs."

"Sweetie," her father said. "You had me worried that there was something wrong."

"So you're okay with me looking into my family tree?"

"Of course. We know very little about your birth parents," her dad said. "We met your birth mother on two occasions, but your birth father was not part of the process. So anything you learn would be just as foreign to us as it is to you. We don't mind if you track down your biological parents. No matter what you find, you're our daughter, plain and simple."

Sloan's childhood—the perfect, unblemished childhood experience—flashed through her mind in random highlights. Family vacations to Florida, neighborhood block parties that marked the rare time her dad had a drink, her years on the high school volleyball squad with her parents cheering from the bleachers. She remembered fishing with her dad, being too scared to touch the fish she caught, and smiling as her dad held the fish for the camera. Sloan had the unique experience of going through the awkward phase of high school braces with her father as her orthodontist.

She remembered the summer of road trips she and her mom had taken as Sloan looked at colleges up and down the East Coast. It was as normal an upbringing as she could imagine. She'd known about her adoption from an early age but had never thought of Dolly and Todd Hastings as anything other than her mom and dad.

"I'm not planning to track my biological parents down. I just need to see how the whole thing works. How these vast DNA databases are being utilized by law enforcement to track down killers in cases that have gone cold."

"We understand, Sloan," her mother said. "Maybe, I don't know, you'll share what you find with us. If you *do* find them, we'd . . ." Dolly looked at Todd. "We'd like to know, too. We've wondered over the years."

Sloan slowly nodded. "I guess it depends what I find. There's no guarantee that submitting my DNA will lead to my birth parents. My profile might not match to anyone on the site. I just wanted to let you know that I'm starting the process."

Her father nodded. "So you really *don't* need money?"

"Dad, you're such a . . ."

"He knows, sweetie. He knows."

CHAPTER 6

Raleigh, North Carolina
Wednesday, July 10, 2024

SLOAN STOOD NEXT TO DR. HAYDEN COX AND WATCHED AS HE closed the Y incision, which ran from each shoulder of the corpse before meeting at the breastbone and then descending past the navel. Dr. Cox was the second-year fellow she had been assigned to. He used thick, ugly staples to bring the incision together, a sight that would turn a plastic surgeon's stomach. But since the next stop was a casket, where the body would be fully clothed and the ragged incision never seen again, aesthetics were not considered at this stage of the game.

"All done," Dr. Cox said, snapping off his surgical gloves. "Get him in the cooler and then we'll do our write-up."

Sloan had just observed the first autopsy of her fellowship. With help from two autopsy technicians, Sloan transferred the body onto a gurney and wheeled it to the row of freezers at the back of the morgue. She made sure the body was properly tagged, and then slid the gurney into the freezer. In the hallway she looked back into the morgue through the viewing window. Other than the table she and Dr. Cox had just finished at, which stood empty and isolated, the rest of the stations were full. Fellows, residents, and attendings huddled around each autopsy table and stared down at the bodies lying on them. Overhead lights illuminated the workspaces, and Sloan imagined herself there the following year—performing her own autopsies and discovering the clues every body left behind that explained how death had come.

In the locker room, she dropped her scrubs in the laundry bin and changed into her street clothes. Her phone buzzed from the top shelf of her locker. She checked the caller ID. James the genealogist. It had been just over a week since Sloan submitted her DNA. A nervous flash of energy flushed through her system, followed by a pang of guilt. Her adoption had been something her parents discussed openly since the time Sloan was a young girl, which diffused any desire to look for her biological parents. Slowly, though, over the last several days, an unfamiliar anticipation stirred in her gut at the thought of discovering who had given birth to her and why they had decided to give her up.

Sloan lifted the phone to her ear. "Hi James. Everything come back okay?"

"Yeah, well . . . that's why I'm calling. I found something . . . weird with your DNA profile. Let's meet so we can talk. I'm free later tonight. The coffeehouse again?"

Her hands grew clammy, and a flush of warmth burned her cheeks and neck.

"How about you come to my place. Or I can come to you, whatever's easier."

"I'll come to you," James said. "Text me your address. I'll be free at eight."

"James," Sloan said before the call ended. "Is it bad?"

There was a long pause.

"I'm not sure yet. I'll see you tonight, Sloan."

CHAPTER 7

Raleigh, North Carolina
Wednesday, July 10, 2024

S LOAN WAITED ANXIOUSLY AS THE CLOCK TICKED AWAY. SHE TRIED TO finish her write-up on the autopsy she had scrubbed in on that morning, but her mind refused to focus on the details of the overdose patient, the toxicology results, the weight of the spleen, or anything other than what James had discovered about her DNA profile. At 8:30 p.m. her doorbell mercifully rang.

"Hey," she said when she opened the door. "Thought you got lost."

"Sorry, running late."

"Come on in. Want a beer or something? You're old enough to drink, aren't you?"

James smiled. "Do you need to see my ID?"

"I trust you."

Sloan closed the door to her cozy one bedroom, which consisted of a small kitchen with a breakfast nook, a living area, and her bedroom.

"We can work at the kitchen table."

Sloan rummaged through the fridge as James unpacked his laptop and a few papers from his rucksack.

"I've got Coors Light or a hard seltzer."

"Coors, thanks."

She handed James a can of beer and popped the top on her Lover Boy, sitting down across from him.

"Your phone call got me pretty anxious, I'm not going to lie," Sloan said. "What did you find?"

James opened his laptop and quickly typed his password before looking at Sloan.

"I usually start consultations by asking questions about a client's family. Since you were adopted, we don't have access to that background info. That's not a problem. I work with lots of adopted clients looking for their birth parents. But in your case . . ."

"Yes?"

"Your DNA profile," James said, tapping on his laptop, "tells an interesting story."

"Interesting, how?"

"Let's start with what we know for sure. You're adopted. Part of my services includes confirming this fact by doing a quick match of your DNA against your adopted parents and any Hastings family members. I don't have access to your adopted parents' DNA, but you gave me enough information about them to do some good research on the Hastings family in general. I created a partial family tree, and I can tell you for certain that you have no ancestral connections to the Hastings family."

Sloan nodded. "We knew that, so what's got you so concerned?"

James took a deep breath. "After I created your DNA profile and started matching it to users on the database, I found something . . . odd."

James turned his computer so that Sloan could see the screen.

"My search shows that you're a descendent of the Margolis family. My review and search for your biological relatives, combined with the matches that came up to your genetic profile, suggests that your birth name was Charlotte Margolis."

Sloan squinted her eyes. "My *birth* name?" She shook her head. "What are you saying? My biological parents named me before giving me up for adoption?"

"I wish it were that straightforward." James pointed to the screen. "Look, here's how this works. I send your DNA profile out into the database to see if you match to any family members who are users of the genealogy website. Sometimes we get a hit to a distant relative like a third or fourth cousin, other times we hit pay dirt and match directly to your birth parents. In your case, your profile matched to Ellis and Nora Margolis. Ellis Margolis is your biological uncle. His wife, Nora Davies Margolis, is your aunt through marriage. So that makes Ellis your biological father's brother."

Margolis. Margolis. Margolis.

The name echoed in Sloan's mind as if someone had rung a bell close to her ear.

"Nora Margolis," James continued, "is very active on the online genealogy site. She's made her profile public and has created an extensive family tree of both her own biological family and the Margolis family, which she married into."

"Okay," Sloan said, shaking her head. "So my DNA profile matched to Nora and Ellis Margolis. From there, you found my biological parents?"

"Correct. Your biological parents are named Preston and Annabelle Margolis."

Sloan swallowed hard. *Preston and Annabelle.* She was entering a portal to her past she had never intended to explore and couldn't fully comprehend the emotions that came with discovering her birth parents' names.

She blinked several times to corral the tears that had welled in her eyes.

"But . . . so, how did you come to the conclusion that my *birth* name was Charlotte Margolis?"

"I did some digging into Preston and Annabelle Margolis, as well as their daughter. Charlotte was born May 11, 1995, in Cedar Creek, Nevada. Harrison County records have a copy of Charlotte Margolis's birth certificate, listing Preston and Annabelle as the parents. A social security number was also on file."

Sloan shook her head. "I don't understand. If my biological parents gave me up for adoption, why would they have named me first? And why would they have registered me with the county, or whatever it's called, to make it legitimate that I was their daughter? That makes no sense if they were giving me up for adoption."

"That's just it. Your parents didn't give you up for adoption, Sloan."

A brief spell of vertigo sent Sloan's head spinning.

"Then how did I end up being adopted by my parents?"

James looked at her. "I don't know. But according to Nora Margolis's family tree"—he pointed again to his computer screen—"Preston, Annabelle, and their two-month-old daughter, Charlotte, disappeared on July 4, 1995."

Sloan pulled the computer closer. "Disappeared?"

"Correct."

James ran his finger across his monitor, where Nora Margolis's family tree was displayed. Sloan followed his finger until she saw the names of her birth parents.

Preston Margolis = Annabelle Akers

|

Charlotte
(Family Missing, presumed dead, 1995)

"Presumed dead?" Sloan looked up at James.

James nodded. "Preston and Annabelle Margolis, along with their infant daughter, disappeared almost thirty years ago. According to every bit of information I've been able to get my hands on, they're still missing today. And you're their daughter."

CHAPTER 8

Raleigh, North Carolina
Wednesday, July 10, 2024

AS MIDNIGHT APPROACHED, SLOAN SWITCHED FROM LOVER BOY TO Diet Dr. Pepper as she and James dug into her lineage. Her small kitchen table was littered with pages they had printed off the Internet as they scoured websites looking for information about the Margolis family that went missing in 1995. The family's disappearance had been front-page news throughout the country, and cover-worthy fodder for every grocery store tabloid.

"*Baby Charlotte*," James said as he stared at his laptop. "The tabloids called you baby Charlotte. Look at this."

On James's monitor was an old image from the cover of *Events Magazine*, one of the country's most popular publications. On it was a photo of Preston and Annabelle Margolis holding their infant daughter, Charlotte. Sloan's stomach dropped when she looked at Annabelle Margolis. The resemblance to herself was shocking.

The headline read:

Up and Vanished
Where Are Baby Charlotte and Her Parents?

Sloan went back to her own computer. She, too, had pulled up photos and articles from 1995.

"It wasn't just *Events Magazine*," she said. "The Margolis family was on the covers of *People*, the *National Enquirer*, and *The Globe*, to name just a few I see here."

"Your adoptive parents never mentioned anything like this to you?"

"No, of course not," Sloan said. "When I told them I was doing a genealogy search, they were all for it. They even asked me to share whatever information I found about my birth parents." Sloan looked up from her computer. "How accurate is the type of DNA search you did, by the way?"

"Very. There's a ninety-nine point nine percent chance you are a descendent of the Margolis family."

They both went back to their laptops.

"It wasn't just the tabloids, either," James said. "The story also made it onto the covers of legitimate papers like the *New York Times, Chicago Tribune, LA Times,* and the *Washington Post.*"

James turned his computer so that Sloan could see the front pages of the papers he'd found. She pulled his laptop closer and clicked on a link to a *New York Times* article.

The Mysterious Disappearance of the Margolis Family
July 7, 1995

CEDAR CREEK, NEVADA—The mystery surrounding the disappearance of Preston and Annabelle Margolis, along with their two-month-old daughter, Charlotte, continues as the investigation enters its third day. Nevada state investigators, as well as the FBI, have been brought in to assist the Harrison County Sheriff's Office in the search for the missing family.

"We are following several leads at the moment," Harrison County Sheriff Sandy Stamos said. "And we are using every possible tool available to us to search for this young couple and their daughter."

The last time the Margolis family was seen was on the Fourth of July during the "Split the Creek" Independence Day gala in Cedar Creek. Three days later and there are still no clues to what happened to the family or where they might be.

"We saw Preston and Annabelle at the gala," Nora Margolis, Preston's sister-in-law and well-known Cedar Creek photographer, said.

"They were getting ice cream with Charlotte and stopped by my studio. I have a large outdoor display each Fourth of July. We spoke briefly and then they were on their way to enjoy the festivities."

Preston Margolis is a member of the prominent Margolis family of Harrison County, Nevada, and an attorney at the family's law firm, Margolis & Margolis. According to a marriage certificate filed at the Harrison County courthouse, Preston and Annabelle had recently married on May 30. Baby Charlotte is just two months old.

The Harrison County Sheriff's Department, the Nevada State Police, and members from the FBI missing persons division have provided few details about the investigation. Adding another layer of mystery to the story, the New York Times has learned that Annabelle Margolis is a person of interest in the hit-and-run death of a local Cedar Creek man earlier in the summer. Annabelle Margolis's car was found abandoned near the scene of the accident, fueling speculation that the family is on the run to avoid prosecution.

"The hit-and-run accident from earlier in the summer is being treated as a wholly independent investigation, unrelated to the disappearance of the Margolis family," Sheriff Sandy Stamos said. *"That case is still open, and we have not taken any resources away from the investigation as we search for the Margolis family. We are confident that someone in Cedar Creek has information that will lead us to the family. Anyone with knowledge about the whereabouts of Preston, Annabelle, or baby Charlotte Margolis is encouraged to contact the Harrison County Sheriff's Office."*

This is an ongoing investigation.

Sloan looked up from the computer.

"This can't be real."

"I wouldn't have brought this to you if I wasn't sure about it."

They both went silent for a moment.

"Look, Sloan, I've discovered some interesting bits of history for my clients, but this whole thing we've stumbled over is bigger than me. It's bigger than the genealogy site I work for. I think . . . I mean, you need to talk with someone about this. I think you need to go to the police."

"I think I'll start with my parents."

Sloan's research assignment faded into the far recesses of her mind. She was wholly consumed with the mystery of what happened to her birth parents, and how baby Charlotte ended up as Sloan Hastings.

CHAPTER 9

Raleigh, North Carolina
Thursday, July 11, 2024

S HE TOLD HERSELF TO WAIT UNTIL THE END OF THE DAY, UNTIL HER parents were home from work, but the nervous energy that buzzed through her body would not allow it. She walked into her parents' dental practice, smiled at the staff behind the reception desk, and headed to her mother's office. Her dad's office was on the other side of the building, the orthodontic side, which had its own entrance and a second reception desk. Sloan's backpack hung from her shoulder and contained copies of everything she and James had learned the night before about Preston and Annabelle Margolis, and their infant daughter, Charlotte.

Sloan was in the process of removing a few of the items—the covers from *People* and *Events Magazine,* both of which showed the once happy family of three. In the *Events* photo, baby Charlotte lay cradled in her mother's arms while Preston and Annabelle stared down at their infant daughter. The photo looked to have been professionally taken, perhaps in celebration of Charlotte's birth.

"Sweetheart?" Dolly Hastings said as she walked into her office. She wore her usual green scrubs with dental loupes hanging from her neck.

"Hi Mom."

"What are you doing here?"

"I've got something I need to talk with you and Dad about."

"Right now? We both have waiting rooms packed with patients."

"I know. I don't mean to mess up your day, but I need to show you something."

Sloan offered enough urgency in her tone to cause her mother to slowly close her office door. Dolly Hastings sat behind her desk and picked up the phone.

"Hi," she said. "Can you please ask Dr. Hastings to come to my office? Thanks." Dolly looked at her daughter. "Your dad's on the way."

Sloan nodded. "Thanks."

It took only a minute for her father to arrive.

"What's going on?"

"Sloan has something she needs to talk with us about."

"Sorry to barge in during a busy morning," Sloan said. "But this can't wait."

"What is it, sweetie?" her father asked.

"My DNA profile came back."

Dolly and Todd Hastings looked at each other. Then Sloan's father asked, "You found your birth parents?"

Sloan nodded and pulsed her eyebrows. "Sort of. My DNA profile matched to a family from Nevada named *Margolis*. Does that name mean anything to you?"

Dolly and Todd Hastings looked at each other again and shook their heads.

"No," Dolly said.

"We had only limited contact with your birth mother," Todd said. "We never met your biological father. We were told he was out of the picture. But your birth mother's last name was Downing, not Margolis. Wendy Downing. We've got the paperwork if you need it."

"What else did you find?" Dolly asked.

Sloan pushed the *Events Magazine* cover across the desk so that it was in front of her mother. She handed the *People* magazine cover to her dad.

"Those are my biological parents," Sloan said. "Preston and Annabelle Margolis."

"Up and vanished?" Todd Hastings said, his words turning the magazine headline into a question. "I remember this story."

"I remember it, too," Dolly said. "It swept the nation. The family disappeared without a trace."

"What are you telling us, sweetie?" her dad said. "Your DNA profile suggests that these people are your biological parents?"

"Not just that," Sloan said. "I'm the baby they're holding."

CHAPTER 10

Raleigh, North Carolina
Thursday, July 11, 2024

T HE HASTINGS CANCELLED THEIR SCHEDULES FOR THE REST OF THE day and drove home with Sloan. The three sat at the kitchen table with all of Sloan's research spread around them—tabloid covers, newspaper articles, and the detailed family tree James had constructed. Although Sloan had never seriously considered that her parents knew any more about her origins than they had already told her, the astonishment in their faces as they paged through Sloan's findings was enough to remove any morsel of doubt that might be hidden in the shadowed corners of her mind.

"How accurate are these DNA sites?" her father asked.

"I asked James the same question. His answer was ninety-nine point nine percent accurate." Sloan held up another image of baby Charlotte in her parents' arms. "So this girl is me. Or I'm her, or whatever." Sloan tossed the picture onto the table in frustration. "The adoption agency you went through, can you get all my records?"

Sloan saw her parents offer each other a nervous glance.

"We have paperwork," her father said. "But it's not from an adoption agency. We were initially connected with an agency, and we were on their list, but after a few potential matches fell through we decided to go outside the agency."

"*Outside* the agency? What does that mean?"

"Private adoption," her mother said. "We were still on the list with the agency, but it had been such a long and laborious process with lots of leads that ended up in disappointment, that we started to look for other options. We'd heard of other couples finding birth parents on their own and working directly with them instead of going through an agency. Many of those stories had happy endings, and the process of private adoption was much faster when the middleman was removed."

"So if it wasn't through an adoption agency, how did you find me?"

"This was back in 1995," her dad said. "The Internet was new and just taking off. The World Wide Web and cell phones and texting and instant communication with anyone around the world is all *you* know, Sloan, but when we started the adoption process the Internet was this new and foreign thing. With the broad use of the Internet came an urgency among the adoption community to get in on the ground floor of this new technology. To not miss out on the chance to eliminate the middleman of an adoption agency, streamline the process, and meet birth parents online who wanted to find adoptive parents directly. It was like the Gold Rush. Once word spread about successful matches, everyone flocked to the Internet to try private adoptions themselves. We had been working with the agency for three years by then and hadn't been placed with a birth mother, so we decided to use the Internet. We met your birth mother pretty quickly. Two months later, we signed the papers and you were ours."

"Did you meet her?" Sloan asked. "My birth mother?"

Dolly nodded. "Of course."

Sloan held up the picture from the cover of *Events Magazine*, pointing at Annabelle Margolis. "Was this her?"

Sloan saw her parents glance at each other again before her mother shook her head. "No."

Sloan took a deep breath. "My God, what the hell is happening?"

"We have the paperwork," Dolly Hastings muttered to herself.

Sloan took a deep breath. "So either my DNA profile, which is statistically impossible to be incorrectly matched to this family, is wrong, or something really shady happened when you adopted me.

Like, this Wendy Downing woman who claimed to be my birth mother kidnapped me, or something. Christ, I don't know!"

Her dad came over and rubbed her back. "It's okay, sweetie. We're going to figure this out. But I think . . ." Todd Hastings glanced at his wife. "With everything you've discovered, I think we need to call the police."

CHAPTER 11

Raleigh, North Carolina
Friday, July 19, 2024

IT HAD BEEN A WHIRLWIND OF A WEEK.

Day one had started with a patrol officer stopping by the Hastings residence to listen to Sloan's story and take a formal statement. Day two involved a detective from the missing persons division of the Raleigh Police Department. Day three held a visit from the same detective, plus an FBI agent associated with the National Center for Missing and Exploited Children. Accompanying the FBI agent was an evidence technician who asked Sloan to sign a consent form before he swabbed the inside of her cheek and took a vial of blood. Proof that the FBI worked faster than even James the genealogist, two agents from the FBI's Criminal Investigation Unit arrived at the Hastings home seventy-two hours later with confirmation that Sloan's DNA, indeed, matched the DNA sample from Charlotte Margolis, which had sat undisturbed in an evidence locker at the Harrison County Sheriff's Office in Cedar Creek, Nevada, for nearly thirty years.

The next three days saw FBI agents politely but formally interview Dolly and Todd Hastings. The initial questions centered around how, exactly, the Hastings had adopted Sloan in November of 1995, four months after baby Charlotte Margolis went missing. After preliminary inquiries, the agents separated Dolly and Todd and asked more probing questions. Sloan had holed up in her childhood bedroom during that first day, when the Hastings home became an interrogation center. The following day, her parents had been whisked away to answer questions at the North Carolina State Bureau of Investigation headquarters in Raleigh, leaving Sloan to nervously pace her apartment as she waited. On Friday, the third day of questioning, Sloan's parents were escorted to the FBI headquarters in Charlotte, two and a half hours away. Sloan tried to tough it out, but the walls of her apartment began to close in, and she felt a desperate need for space.

Looking to distract her mind and escape the obsessive thoughts about her parents, the questions they were answering, and the FBI's suspicions about their role in her disappearance decades earlier, she decided work was the best place to be. She grabbed her keys on the way out of her apartment and headed to the morgue.

As she turned out of the parking lot of her apartment complex, with her mind racing and preoccupied, she was oblivious to the SUV that pulled into traffic behind her.

CHAPTER 12

Raleigh, North Carolina
Friday, July 19, 2024

Wʜᴇɴ ꜱʜᴇ ᴀʀʀɪᴠᴇᴅ ᴀᴛ ᴛʜᴇ ᴏꜰꜰɪᴄᴇ ᴏꜰ ᴛʜᴇ ᴄʜɪᴇꜰ ᴍᴇᴅɪᴄᴀʟ ᴇxᴀᴍ-iner, Sloan swiped her ID to open the door next to the reception area. She rode the elevator to the basement level, smelling formaldehyde even before the doors opened. She was told that the scent of the morgue—a combination of gross anatomy lab and hospital sterility—would eventually go unnoticed. It was the end of her third week of fellowship and her olfactory senses were still on high alert.

She had texted Dr. Cox on her way over to the OCME to ask if he had a case that day. He did, a suicide. The postmortem was scheduled for 11:00 a.m. Required to scrub in on five autopsies during her first month of fellowship, this would be Sloan's second. She had lost the last few days tied up in the revelation of her DNA profile and was behind schedule.

In the locker room, she changed into scrubs, pulled a surgical cap over her head, and tied a mask across her face before entering the morgue. The high-pitched buzzing of a bone saw filled her ears as she opened the door. The noise was coming from Dr. Cox's table as he sawed through the patient's breastbone to gain access to the chest cavity.

"Take that, will you?" Hayden asked, handing Sloan the saw as she approached the autopsy table.

Sloan placed the device on the surgical tray with the other instruments as the smell of burnt bone drifted in the air.

"Forty-six-year-old female. Suspected suicide," Hayden said. "Swallowed a bottle of Valium."

Sloan looked at the body on the cold, metal table. Naked as the day she was born, the woman's skin carried a dead, blue tone.

"Toxicology is key in suicides," Hayden said. "We'll draw blood from various areas—femoral vein and heart for sure. We'll also test the urine. We'll measure the drug's concentration throughout different parts of the body, determine how fully it was metabolized, and if the victim mixed the Valium with other drugs or alcohol. We'll also take tissue samples and send them along so the forensic toxicologist can paint a fuller picture. What are the four areas we should sample?"

Sloan quickly blinked away the fog of the last few days and righted her mind.

"Liver, brain, kidney, and vitreous humor."

"Nice job."

Sloan watched as Dr. Cox placed a scalpel to the woman's left shoulder and started the Y incision.

"The full tox report will take days or longer to come back. To present my finding in the cage this afternoon, we'll run a Quick-Tox. Results are less complete, but we get them in an hour or so."

"Got it," Sloan said.

"Diazepam depresses respiration. Taken in high enough dosages, it can stop breathing altogether. The process is accelerated if it's mixed with other depressants like alcohol. First, we'll remove and dissect the lungs to inspect the air sacs and look for signs of suffocation."

Twenty minutes later, Sloan was assisting Dr. Cox with the removal of each lung, which they weighed and photographed before they began the dissection. She had come to the morgue to get her thoughts away from her parents and what they were going through at FBI headquarters. It was working.

An hour and a half later, Sloan pinched the Y incision closed with staples. She stored the body in the freezer and headed to the locker room. Back in her street clothes, she spent an hour typing up her notes about the autopsy, which she attached to an email and sent to Dr. Cutty. Sloan was certain Dr. Cutty did not read lowly first-year fellows' autopsy write-ups. That distinction likely went to an assistant. Or maybe the summaries were never read at all but simply accrued in a graveyard of unread documents that existed only to make sure newbies followed the rules.

It was just past three o'clock and she figured she had another few hours to kill before her parents would be finished with the FBI. She pulled out of the parking lot of the OCME, turned onto District Drive and then onto Blue Ridge Road. After being confined in the morgue for the morning, the CrossFit gym would be her next distraction. She glanced into the rearview mirror and saw a Toyota SUV behind her. Something pinged in her mind, a subtle warning that might have gone unnoticed had the last few days not put her nervous system into overdrive. Sport utility vehicles were everywhere, and she worked to figure out what made the one behind her stand out. It was a late-model silver Toyota 4Runner that should have blended in with the hundreds of others that made up the Raleigh area traffic. Yet something about the vehicle caught her attention.

Sloan made a turn and approached the entrance to Highway 40. At the last second she swerved onto the on-ramp and merged into traffic. In her rearview mirror she watched the 4Runner follow her onto the highway and pass a few cars to keep pace. She slid into the middle lane and aggressively passed a few cars before jumping into the left lane, where she gunned the engine and flew past an eighteen-wheeler semitruck. Once clear of the big rig, she cut across all three lanes of traffic to narrowly catch the exit ramp. The reckless maneuver drew a cacophony of horns. As she exited the highway, she watched the silver Toyota continue on in the middle lane wholly uninterested in her lunacy, continuing north on Highway 40 as if it were any other vehicle on the road.

Sloan caught her breath and turned at the end of the exit ramp. The last few days had her on edge. She doubled back to the gym, changed into shorts and a tank top, and laced her shoes tight for the brutal AMRAP workout—As Many Reps As Possible—that was listed on the gym's chalkboard as the workout of the day. It was exactly what she needed. A popular CrossFit routine, it condensed a full-body workout into a small window of time. Music blared from speakers, the coach bounced on his toes to get everyone going, then counted down—three, two, one—and the workout began. Along with ten other CrossFitters, Sloan began on the rowing machine, worked through wall-ball shots and cleans, and finished with a brutal cycle of muscle-ups until her body was drenched with sweat, her lungs burned like hell, and her shoulders and arms were engorged with blood and lactic acid. She took a cold shower, changed into jeans and a blouse, and checked her phone for messages from her parents. None.

Outside she surveyed the health club's parking lot and noticed nothing out of the ordinary. Ten minutes later, however, she spotted the Toyota parked under a maple tree across the street from her apartment. As Sloan slowly passed the SUV, she finally understood what had caught her attention about the vehicle. It was the license plate. Absent was the typical "First in Flight" North Carolina plate. Instead, the 4Runner sported colorful mountains running along the bottom of the plate, and NEVADA stenciled across the top.

CHAPTER 13

Raleigh, North Carolina
Friday, July 19, 2024

As SLOAN PULLED PAST THE TOYOTA SHE NOTICED IT WAS EMPTY. SHE turned into the parking lot of her apartment complex, slid into a spot, and looked around. Several options ran through her mind. The first was to get the hell out of there, drive to her parents' house, and wait for them to get home. Or, she could go back to the OCME and bide her time there. Hell, she could drive to FBI headquarters and tell the agents that someone with Nevada plates was following her. *Nevada.* As in Cedar Creek, Nevada, where she and her birth parents disappeared from.

In the end, she got out of her car and hustled to the steps of her apartment, still feeling the burn in her quads from her workout. She lived on the third story. She raced up the steps and turned the corner to find a man standing next to her front door. Leaning against the stucco wall, with one leg crossed over the other, he casually scrolled through his phone. But the man's unimposing body language did nothing to staunch her fear. Sloan's eyes went wide, and a rush of anxiety took control of her body, momentarily paralyzing her. After a couple of seconds, she managed a step backward as she fumbled for her purse.

"Sloan?" the man asked, pushing away from the wall and slipping his phone into the front pocket of his jeans. He took a few steps toward her. "Sloan Hastings?"

With shaking hands, Sloan unzipped her purse. She tried to

scream but her lungs were void of air from hyperventilating. The man was another step closer, and then another, before Sloan found the bottle at the bottom of her purse. She looked up just as the man was reaching into the breast pocket of his jacket. In one swift movement Sloan raised the can of pepper spray and delivered a powerful stream to the man's face.

So forceful was the aerosol that the pepper spray ricocheted off the man's face and directly into Sloan's eyes. The man went down in a heap, moaning as he clawed at his eyes. It took just a fraction of a second for Sloan to feel the burn in her own eyes. She dropped the can and also fell to her knees. Just before her eyelids spasmed closed, she saw what the man had removed from his breast pocket. It had fallen onto the ground in front of her apartment door. It wasn't a gun or a knife, as she had imagined. It was a police badge.

CHAPTER 14

Raleigh, North Carolina
Friday, July 19, 2024

ALTHOUGH THE MAN HAD CLEARLY TAKEN THE BRUNT OF THE PEPPER spray, he came to Sloan's aid after the ricocheting mist sealed her eyes shut. He helped her into her apartment and turned on the shower. Sloan held her face under a stream of cold water. The man went to the sink while they both groaned and coughed.

"Here," Sloan said after a few minutes. "Switch. The sink is too small for you. I think I'm good. Or at least better."

The man happily traded spots and thrust his face under the showerhead, using his fingers to peel his eyelids open. It took thirty minutes before either was able to open their eyes, another thirty before their noses stopped running. Now, an hour after Sloan had pulled the trigger on the pepper spray, she and the man sat at her kitchen table with blood-red eyes, raw cheeks, and sore throats.

The man held a plastic bag filled with ice over his right eye.

"I had no idea you were a police officer," Sloan said. "I'm really sorry. I thought someone was following me."

When the man did not answer, Sloan felt the need to explain.

"I saw this truck with Nevada plates . . ." She shook her head. "It doesn't matter. I'm really sorry. I'm an idiot."

"No," the man said. "*I'm* the idiot. I should have shown my badge right away. Hell, I shouldn't have followed you in the first place. It's my Toyota."

Sloan narrowed her swollen lids.

The man nodded. "I knew you were onto me when you pulled your little NASCAR trick on the highway. I needed to speak with you, so I figured I'd wait at your apartment, but before I had the chance to explain who I was, well . . . like I said, I'm an idiot. Really stupid to follow a woman and then wait for her outside her apartment. Trust me, I got what I deserved. I'm just sorry you got a little bit of it, too."

Sloan smiled. "The instructions don't mention ricochets."

They both shared a laugh.

"What the hell was that? Bear spray?"

"Nope. Just regular old Mace. I bought it online. I guess it works, besides the back-at-you part."

"I'm a walking testimonial. We had to get pepper sprayed during police training and I don't remember it being this bad."

"I'm pretty sure I hit you directly in the eye."

"Yep, bull's-eye."

The man's other eye was a warm caramel brown that matched his dark hair and tanned skin. He had an athletic build, and it wasn't hard to imagine him as a police officer.

Sloan lifted the man's badge.

"Okay, *Sheriff Stamos,*" she said, reading his name from his ID. "Why were you following me?"

She slid the ID and badge across the table.

"You dropped them when I . . . anyway, I grabbed them when you were rinsing your eyes."

"Thanks." He took the badge and hooked it onto his belt, then slipped his ID into his breast pocket. "Eric Stamos. I'm the sheriff of a small town in Nevada called—"

"Cedar Creek," Sloan said, finishing his sentence.

"Correct."

"So this is about my online DNA search."

Eric removed the bag of ice from his eye. "I don't know anything about an online DNA search. I only know that the FBI showed up to my office a few days ago asking about a cold case involving a family that went missing from Cedar Creek almost thirty years ago. A couple and their daughter. The feds wanted any and all information my department had on the old case because there had been a break in the investigation. They said that the girl, who was an infant at the time of the disappearance, had resurfaced in North Carolina and was going by the name of Sloan Hastings."

Sloan offered a here-I-am smile. "That would be me. So why did you come all the way from Nevada to track me down?"

"The FBI told me next to nothing. I'm looking for information about the case."

"So you came all the way to North Carolina for information?"

"I did, and I'd be happy to fill you in on my motives if you'd be willing to share what you know."

"About what?"

"The missing Margolis family."

Sloan nodded slowly as she contemplated the sheriff's quid pro quo offer.

"I don't know much, but the way this whole thing started was that I did one of those online ancestry searches for a wholly different reason than finding distant relatives. My DNA profile came back indicating that I'm a missing kid from 1995. Once we figured out how big of a deal this whole thing was, my parents . . . my *adoptive* parents and I called the cops. The cops called the missing persons detectives. The detectives called the FBI. Now, here we are, about a week or so later. My parents are on their third day of interrogations, the FBI is chasing down old case files, and a sheriff from Cedar Creek, Nevada, is sitting in my kitchen."

Eric cocked his head, took a deep breath, and put the bag of ice back over his face. "That answers a few questions for me."

"Your turn. Why did you come all the way from Nevada to track me down?"

Eric leaned forward, keeping the ice pressed to the right side of his face. "My father worked the Margolis case when he was sheriff of Harrison County. His name was Sandy Stamos."

Sloan remembered the name from the articles she had read.

"Your father investigated . . . my disappearance?"

Eric nodded. "He started to, but . . . he died under suspicious circumstances just after you and your parents went missing."

"What happened?"

"The official line?" Eric sat back in his chair. "My dad was high on heroin, drove his cruiser into Cedar Creek, and drowned."

"That's . . . terrible."

"It's also complete bullshit. My father was no junkie. Christ, the man never took a sip of alcohol in his life. I don't believe for a second that he was a heroin user."

"So . . ." Sloan chose her words carefully. "You think his death was something other than an accident?"

"I think he was killed."

Eric took the ice away from his face again.

"I think my dad was close to figuring out what happened to Charlotte Margolis and her parents. Someone didn't want the truth to come out, so they killed him and made it look like a heroin overdose."

Sloan searched for a question to ask but too many ran through her mind. She finally settled on the most obvious.

"Why do you think that? I mean, do you know something about my birth parents disappearing?"

"No. And until just recently, I never thought much about my father's death. I was nine years old when he died, and I never really understood any of it at the time. When you lose your dad that young, you sort of tune out the rest of the world. I certainly never explored too carefully *how* he died, I only knew that my dad was gone. I come from a long line of law enforcement. My father was the sheriff of Harrison County, and my grandfather was sheriff before him. It was my grandfather who started me down this road of looking into my dad's death. My grandfather never believed the official narrative about what happened to his son."

"Wasn't there an autopsy? I'm a pathology fellow and my first thought is that your dad had to have had a postmortem exam."

"He did."

"Was there heroin in his system?"

"There was. But I don't believe any part of that autopsy report."

"You don't believe an *official* autopsy report?"

"Not for a minute."

"So you think the autopsy was incorrect?"

"I think it was manipulated to show what those in power wanted it to show."

"Who has the power to do that?"

"The Margolis family. Look, my grandfather was ninety-two years

old when he died last year. He had spent nearly thirty years searching for answers about what happened to his son. He never found
any. When the end was near and my grandfather knew he wouldn't
be able to keep looking, he told me about his suspicions and gave
me everything he'd collected over the years about my father's
death. A lot of that information contains details about my father's
investigation into the missing Margolis family. Just before he
passed, my grandfather made me promise to keep looking after he
was gone. I've been rooting through the case for the last year, and
the first clue that's come along is news that baby Charlotte Margolis turned up alive and well in Raleigh, North Carolina."

"So you came looking for me."

"I did."

Sloan squinted her eyes as a thought dawned on her. "Why drive?"
she asked. "Why *drive* all the way from Nevada just to talk with me?"

"Because airline tickets leave a trail, and it's important that no
one knows I came to find you."

"Who'd be interested?"

"The Margolis family. And none of them can learn that you and
I have met."

CHAPTER 15

Raleigh, North Carolina
Friday, July 19, 2024

IN ADDITION TO INCINERATING MUCOUS MEMBRANES AND CAUSING endless rhinitis, Sloan decided an additional side effect of oleoresin capsicum, the active ingredient in pepper spray, was hunger. She and Eric headed to the pizza joint on the corner to continue their conversation, ignoring the sideways looks from the waitress who stared at their beet red faces and bloodshot eyes with a combination of fear and disgust. They promised they were neither dying nor contagious, and ordered a large pepperoni. Eric gulped water and refilled his glass from a pitcher the waitress left.

Even with a swollen right eye and bright red cheeks, Sloan noticed that Eric Stamos was a handsome man. She did the math according to the information he'd provided and knew that he was thirty-eight years old. His solid build and angled jaw made him look younger.

"Are you sure you're okay?" Sloan asked.

Eric nodded as he crunched on an ice cube. The swelling to his right eye had plateaued, leaving a thin sliver that allowed partial vision.

"I'm getting there, just trying to rehydrate. You?"

"My eyes are starting to burn again, but I have no room to complain. Your right eye looks like it's about to bleed."

"I'll be fine. No one ever died from pepper spray." Eric took another sip of water. "It must've been a shock when your DNA profile came back."

"I'm still trying to process it. You said you were nine years old when my birth parents and I disappeared?"

"Correct. And I still remember how big the story was back then."

"Because your father was part of the investigation?"

"That was part of it, but also because the case was everywhere. You couldn't check out at the grocery store without seeing baby Charlotte and her parents on the tabloid covers. And to know that the whole country was focused on our little town was crazy, even for a nine-year-old. But for sure, I had more of a front row seat because of my dad. When I was a kid I never really thought of my dad's job as solving crimes as much as just making sure everyone in town felt safe. Then, during that summer, my father was faced with this huge, nationally known missing persons case. I was too young to comprehend what he was going through, but my grandfather has since filled me in on the details. He told me that my dad more than held his own during the investigation. Then, he died. Once my dad was gone, the state police took over."

"I guess what I'm struggling to understand is why you came all the way to Raleigh to find me. As sheriff can't you just request all the old case files and talk to the investigators who were involved? They'd have more information than me."

"In any other part of the country, maybe. But not in Harrison County. It's a tricky place to be sheriff."

"Tricky how?"

"The Margolis family is powerful. They own everything and run *most* everything in the county. For decades they have managed to place family members in critical places. Not just on the boards of influential companies, but in prominent political positions as well. The District Attorney's Office is fully under the control of the Margolis family. The chief prosecutor is a Margolis. One of the two Nevada senators is a Margolis. The head of the Nevada State Police is a Margolis. From local levels of government to some of the state's highest positions, the family has people in place to help them control everything that happens in our little county. So, anytime my dad had to run an investigation that crossed paths with the Margolises, either directly or indirectly, he had to tread carefully. Just like I do today."

"So the family runs everything, but they haven't found a way to infiltrate the Sheriff's Office yet?"

Eric smiled. "Not yet. If the Margolises want one of their own as sheriff, they'll have to find a way to get their candidate elected. And, trust me, they've tried. Every four years the family spends millions backing a new candidate for sheriff, but it's almost as though the folks of Cedar Creek and Harrison County know that the Margolis family is already too powerful, and the last thing the town needs is for the Margolis family to control local law enforcement. My dad was sheriff for nearly twenty years—reelected four times. And, like I said, my grandfather was sheriff before him. I'm on my second term."

"Your dad is mentioned in some of the articles I've read about the disappearance of . . . my biological parents and me."

Eric smiled. "Good ole Sandy Stamos. He's been gone longer than I ever knew him. He was the quintessential small-town sheriff who everyone loved."

"Then why would someone kill him?"

"My grandfather's theory? He stumbled over evidence that pointed to the truth about what happened to you and your parents, and someone didn't want that truth to come out."

"Where did your grandfather's theory come from?"

"My dad spoke with my grandfather about the case back then, asked for some advice. My dad was struggling to make sense of what he discovered. And my grandfather was convinced—absolutely one hundred percent convinced—that my dad discovered something about the night you and your parents disappeared, and that's what got him killed. The timing was just too suspicious."

"What did he discover?"

"Good question. I'm hoping you'll help me answer it."

"Me? I was an infant when all of this happened. I have no idea what happened to my birth parents. Or your father."

"But you can help me figure it out. You're actually the *only* one who can help."

The waitress walked over and slid a large pepperoni pizza between them, along with plates and napkins.

"Can I get you anything else?"

"We're good, thanks," Eric said.

"You've lost me," Sloan said once the waitress was gone. "How am I supposed to help you figure out what happened to your dad?"

Eric lifted a piece of pizza and took a bite. "News is sure to break that Charlotte Margolis has resurfaced nearly thirty years after she went missing. I'm sure the FBI will inform the family. When they do, the Margolis family will want to meet you. It will be the perfect opportunity to go to Cedar Creek."

"To Nevada?"

"Yes."

"To do what?"

"To work with me, secretly. No one can know we're in contact with each other."

"Work with you to do what?"

Eric moved his plate to the side and placed his elbows on the table so his face was closer to Sloan's.

"You asked me why I can't just go to the state police, request all the files, and start poking around. The reason is because it would get back to the Margolis family. And if I overtly start asking questions, the family will know I'm looking into my father's death."

"And that's a bad thing? Why?"

"Someone inside the Margolis family knows what happened to my dad, and maybe even to you and your birth parents. According to my grandfather, my dad was convinced that another crime he was investigating was linked to your parents' disappearance."

"What other crime?"

"A hit-and-run accident that killed a local Cedar Creek resident."

Sloan paused a moment as her mind retreated back to the articles that chronicled her and her parents' disappearance. "I read something about that."

Eric nodded. "I've looked into it, too, and it's legit. My grandfather was old and suffering from dementia before he died. I wasn't sure how much of what he was telling me about my dad was true, or just the ramblings of a dying man with dementia. But he was on to something. I went back through old cases that were still archived at the Harrison County Sheriff's Office and learned that my dad *had* been investigating a hit-and-run accident that happened the summer you disappeared. According to my grandfather, my dad believed the case tied directly to the disappearance of you and your parents."

"Have you looked into it?"

"Yes. No one was ever formally charged, and the case is still cold today. But when Annabelle and Preston Margolis disappeared, Annabelle was the main suspect in the case. And the guy she mowed down? He was a partner at the Margolis law firm. The case went cold after you and your parents went missing."

Sloan sat back in her chair and tossed the piece of pizza she had been eating onto her plate.

"Someone inside the Margolis family knows what happened that summer," Eric said. "With that hit-and-run case. With you and your parents. And with my dad. We have to find that person and convince them to talk."

"Why don't you find them and question them, or subpoena them?"

"This many years later? I wouldn't know where to start. And even if I did, it wouldn't matter. The family has a code—as strong as the Kennedys, or maybe stronger. The family doesn't talk to outsiders."

Sloan raised her chin slightly, Eric's plan finally dawning on her and the reason he had come across the country to find her. "But I won't be an outsider."

"Nope. You're a Margolis pureblood. They'll welcome you with open arms."

Eric took a deep breath and Sloan knew this would be his final push.

"I'm asking you to go to Cedar Creek and reunite with the Margolis family. You're the perfect Trojan horse. You'll be able to infiltrate the family in ways no one else can."

Sloan picked up the pizza and took a bite as she considered Eric Stamos's plan.

"You looked into the hit-and-run case?" she finally asked.

"I did."

"Let's start there. Tell me about it."

THE PAST

Cedar Creek, Nevada

Saturday, June 24, 1995
10 Days Prior . . .

DALE PICKETT WAS A LONG-HAUL DRIVER WHO OWNED HIS OWN RIG and sold the hours of his life the way a prostitute sold their body. But driving his eighteen-wheeler across the country was all he knew, and for thirty years it had paid the bills. He parked his rig in his driveway each December and took the month off to spend the holidays with his family—his wife, three kids, and eight grandchildren. Then, starting January second, he damn near killed himself for the other eleven months hauling freight for long and lonely hours. His current gig had him on a round trip from Boise to Reno. He was working on little sleep by 1:00 a.m., fueled by Adderall and Jolt Cola, and didn't believe his eyes when he first saw the body in the road.

Positioned in the middle of the two-lane highway, he initially thought it was roadkill. He slowed down as he approached. The breakdown lanes on this stretch of highway were too narrow for his big rig, and due to the size of the heap in the road, he worried that speeding over it would cause a mess to the undercarriage. But as he got close enough for his headlights to fully brighten the highway, he saw that it wasn't an animal in the road, but a body.

The brakes squealed into the night as he pulled partially onto the shoulder and brought the truck to a stop. He pushed open his door and climbed down from the cab. His Maglite flashlight was close to as bright as the truck's headlights, and as he approached the body, he sprayed the beam of his flashlight around the dark expanse of brush and desert that flanked this empty stretch of road. He saw nothing and heard only the rumble of his truck's diesel engine. But down the road, perhaps a hundred yards from where he stood, a car was parked in the breakdown lane. He pointed his Maglite into the darkness and saw that the driver's side door was open.

He registered the car into an organized spot in his mind, then returned his attention to the body, bringing the glow of the flashlight in front of him. The body was crumpled upon itself, with the man's legs splayed at odd angles and a circle of blood on the pavement that haloed the man's head. Dale didn't bother to check for a pulse. This man was as dead as any roadkill he'd ever seen. He pulled his cell phone from his pocket and dialed.

"Nine-one-one, what's your emergency?" a female voice asked.

"Not *my* emergency, but you've got a dead body in the middle of Highway Sixty-seven just north of Cedar Creek."

"A body in the road?"

"Yes, ma'am, someone ran the poor son of a bitch over."

"Is he breathing?"

"I doubt it."

"Have you checked for a pulse?"

"Not a chance. Send the cops. I'll wait for them, and they can do all the checking they want."

With that, Dale ended the call and walked back to his rig. From the side compartment he removed flares and cones and blocked off the road. Then he climbed back into the cab, reached between the seats, and removed the SIG Sauer handgun he always kept there. He didn't need to check if it was loaded, he knew it was.

In a slow walk, he set off toward the car in the distance, the headlights of his truck casting his shadow in a long, thin form in front of him.

Cedar Creek, Nevada

Saturday, June 24, 1995
10 Days Prior . . .

SHERIFF SANDY STAMOS DROVE NORTH ON HIGHWAY 67 WITH HIS FLASH-ers on. He kept the sirens silent. There was no traffic at the ghostly hour of half past one in the morning, and little reason to wake the county. A couple miles north of town, he saw headlights from a semitruck off in the distance. The big rig had parked on the south-side shoulder. About a hundred yards from the truck, Sandy passed a car that was also parked on the south-side shoulder. He slowed to see the driver's side door was open and the car was empty.

Sandy continued north until he saw the red flares glowing in the night. He pulled his sheriff's cruiser onto the shoulder, placed the vehicle in park, but left the engine running. He grabbed the handle of the side-mounted floodlight and directed the beam at the man standing next to the truck. Thin and wiry, he looked to be somewhere in his sixties. He wore jeans and a flannel shirt and was leaning against the side of his rig with his legs crossed and hands in his pockets. The man had the sense to take his hands out of his pockets but didn't go so far as to raise them. Sandy redirected his light to the middle of the road and the body that lay there before he climbed from his car.

"You make the call about a hit-and-run?"

"Yes, sir. Name's Dale Pickett. I'm doing a run from Boise to Reno. Thought it was a deer 'til I got closer."

The sheriff walked across the highway.

"Sandy Stamos." He extended his hand. "Thanks for flaring the area off, Dale."

"Sure thing."

"Did you touch the body?"

"No, sir."

"Not even to check for a pulse?"

"Figured that was your job. And there's no doubt he's dead, so I didn't see the point."

Sandy nodded. "What can you tell me about the car down the road? I've got a good friend who hauls for a living. He's not the type to just hang out by his rig in this type of situation."

Dale smiled. "No, sir. Me either. Full disclosure, I've got a firearm in my cab. Registered and legal and I've got the papers to prove it. After I flared off the body, I noticed the car down the road and took my firearm to have a look. I didn't touch anything, didn't want to tamper with evidence. But I wanted to see if anyone was in the vehicle."

"And?"

"Empty. Driver's side door was open, engine was off, and interior lights were dark, so I'm guessing the battery ran down. Front bumper is dented, and the headlight is shattered to hell."

A *hit and* literal *run*, Sandy thought.

He took a moment to look up and down the road, then cocked his head toward the body.

"I'm gonna have a look at this poor guy."

The spotlight from his cruiser provided plenty of light but Sandy removed the flashlight from his belt anyway. The man was in a heap, lying on his back with legs splayed, one arm pinned and hidden underneath him, and the other straight out to the side. There was a lot of blood. A circular pool around the man's head as well as a streak on the pavement that ran for about ten yards from north to south, matching the direction the abandoned car would have been heading.

"What do you do in a case like this?" Dale asked. "Calling an ambulance seems pretty useless."

"I'll have to get the medical examiner up here to move the body.

And we're going to have to shut the highway down. I'll also call Highway Patrol. They'll want to get their accident investigation team on this. Give me a minute to make all those calls? Then I'll take a formal statement from you before you get back on the road."

"Sure thing."

Cedar Creek, Nevada

Saturday, June 24, 1995
10 Days Prior . . .

By 6:00 A.M., NEARLY FIVE HOURS AFTER THE ACCIDENT WAS CALLED in, investigators from the Nevada Highway Patrol had taken control of the scene, shutting down Highway 67 for a mile in either direction of the accident site. As they continued the tedious process of evidence collection—taking thousands of photos and hours of video that documented everything about the scene and the body—Sandy sat in his cruiser and waited for the plates to come back on the abandoned car.

"You there, boss?" the female dispatcher's voice squawked from his shoulder-mounted radio.

"Yeah, go ahead. You have an ID on those plates?"

"Yes, sir. Car is registered to Annabelle Margolis."

Sandy's pulse quickened. An ugly situation had just gotten messier. Annabelle was the newly minted wife of Preston Margolis. Sandy walked a fine line when dealing with the Margolis family. For the last century, the Margolis clan had acquired such a stranglehold on Harrison County that the family believed they were above the law. There was no problem that could not be solved with influence and money. And on the rare occasion when neither worked, the family resorted to good old-fashioned intimidation or worse. But Sandy Stamos today, and his father before him, had kept the Harrison County Sheriff's Department clear of the Margolis shadow. Having just won his fourth reelection campaign, Sandy assured that the last vestige of power in Harrison County would remain free from Margolis corruption for at least another few years. The rest of Harrison County was another story. From the state police to the prosecutor's office, most of the public sector was firmly under the control of the Margolis family.

"You still there, boss?" the dispatcher asked.

"Yeah, thanks. I'll head out to the house. Keep that info to yourself for now, will you?"

"Roger that, boss."

Sandy knew he'd have to be careful with the details of his investigation. All around him were members of law enforcement who could be manipulated and influenced by the Margolises, including the Highway Patrol and the accident investigation unit. He'd have to be selective with whom he shared details of his investigation, because as soon as word broke that Annabelle Margolis's car had been found near the scene of the hit-and-run, he'd feel pressure from every direction.

At just past six in the morning, as the sun was brightening the horizon, Sandy twisted his cruiser in a U-turn and headed into town to find Annabelle Margolis. He was about to go toe-to-toe with the Margolis mob.

Cedar Creek, Nevada

Saturday, June 24, 1995
10 Days Prior . . .

HE PULLED UP TO ANNABELLE AND PRESTON MARGOLIS'S HOUSE, A new-construction Victorian that overlooked Lake Harmony on the south end of Cedar Creek. So new, in fact, that the property was still under construction. Preston, the youngest son of Reid and Tilly Margolis, was fresh out of Stanford Law and an up-and-coming star at the Margolis & Margolis law firm. That he was building an obnoxious lake house was no surprise. As a junior associate at the firm, there was no way he made an income to support the home Sandy was looking at. But Sandy knew that family money financed the home's construction, not Preston's income.

The house itself looked shored up, but earth-moving equipment—bulldozers and backhoes—sat in the backyard. A pool, Sandy figured, was being installed. The four-car detached garage was still under construction. An extension ladder leaned against the side of the garage where a man stood perched on the upper rungs and painted the eaves.

It was still early, just after six in the morning, and Sandy was greeted by an oxymoronic stillness as he stood from his car. The early morning offered the calm chirp of bluebirds and cardinals, the still reflection of clouds on the lake's surface, and a gentle breeze of summer. But the calm, Sandy knew, was about to be shattered. He headed over to the garage.

"You start early," Sandy said to the man on the ladder.

The man looked down. "Promised Mrs. Margolis I'd have the garage painted by tomorrow."

"Sandy Stamos."

"Lester Strange."

He wore cargo pants and a T-shirt under an apron covered by a lifetime of paint. He couldn't have been older than twenty.

"The Margolises home?"

Lester shrugged. "Not sure. I just got started."

Sandy smiled. "Have a nice day."

Lester waved his brush and went back to work.

Sandy climbed the front steps and knocked loudly on the door. He waited a full minute, noticing Lester the painter glancing his way a few times, before he knocked again. Finally, Preston Margolis appeared, peeking through the glass to the side of the front door before opening it.

"Sheriff," Preston said. "Something the matter?"

"Unfortunately, yes. Is your wife home?"

"She's in bed."

"Could you let her know I need a word?"

Preston, ever the attorney, stepped onto the front porch as he pulled the door closed behind him.

"What's going on, Sandy?"

"I just need to speak with Annabelle. Will you tell her I'm here?"

"Not if you don't tell me why you need to speak with her."

Sandy had no intention of getting into a legal argument with Preston Margolis, who would prop himself up as Annabelle's attorney and deny Sandy access without taking her to the sheriff's department for formal questioning.

"Look, Preston. There was a situation overnight. A hit-and-run up on Highway Sixty-seven. Annabelle's car was found down the road from the body. There's obvious damage to the front headlight."

"A hit-and-run?"

Sandy nodded.

Preston shook his head as if trying to clear his mind. "When did this happen?"

"Early this morning. Call came in at about one in the morning.

I'm just coming from the scene. I've been there all night. Sixty-seven is shut down and state investigators are on the scene."

"Is the person . . . ?"

"Yeah, he's dead."

"She's been here, Sandy. Annabelle's been here the whole night."

Sandy nodded. "I still need to talk with her."

"You don't believe me?"

"It doesn't matter if I believe you, Preston. I still need to speak with Annabelle."

"Is she . . ." Preston took a step closer. "You don't think you're going to arrest my wife, do you, Sandy?"

The words came out as a challenge. Reid Margolis's sons had been raised to believe they were above the law. Sandy wasn't about to take the bait.

"I'm not here to arrest anyone, Preston. Just to ask a few questions. Her car was found at the scene of the crime. I need to figure out how it got there."

Sandy saw Preston look off into the distance, out at the lake, as he thought through his options. The man was either genuinely confused by the news Sandy had delivered, or he was one hell of an actor.

"Mind if I check the garage first?" Preston finally asked. "To see if Annabelle's car is there. Maybe there's been a mistake."

"Sure thing," Sandy said, following Preston down the front steps and over to the garage.

"Your crew always start this early on a weekend?"

"Lester?" Preston said. "He's the family's handyman, a sort of jack-of-all-trades. He's always around. Annabelle asked him to finish the garage, so he's been here at sunup every day this week."

"Morning, Mr. Margolis," Lester said as Preston and Sandy passed the base of the ladder.

Mr. Margolis was a snot-nosed twenty-five-year-old kid just out of law school, and Sandy found it odd that someone barely his junior would address him so formally. Welcome to the life of a Margolis.

"Morning, Lester," Preston said.

"Is there a problem, Mr. Margolis?"

"No problem."

Preston opened the side door of the garage and flipped a wall switch. Overhead fluorescents brought the garage to life. Of the four bays, only the first held a vehicle—Preston's BMW sedan. The second bay was empty, the third occupied by a 4x4 Gator tractor, and the fourth filled with a workbench and tools hanging neatly on the wall.

"What the hell?" Sandy heard Preston whisper to himself.

Finally, he turned to Sandy and nodded.

"I'll wake Annabelle and we can all talk in the kitchen."

"Thanks."

Ten minutes later, Sandy stood in the kitchen of Preston and Annabelle Margolis's lake house. When the couple came down, Sandy noted that Annabelle, much like Preston, looked to have just climbed from bed. Typically, this would not be surprising for a Saturday morning, but it added to Sandy's confusion about how this woman could have mowed down a man just hours earlier, abandoned her car on the side of the road, found her way home, and then slept soundly until Sandy's house call.

"Morning, Annabelle," Sandy said.

"Sheriff." Annabelle's voice was groggy. "Preston told me about a hit-and-run, or something?"

"Yeah. It happened on Highway Sixty-seven early this morning. A man was killed and his body was found in the middle of the road. Your car was found abandoned on the side of the road about a hundred yards from the body."

"*My* car?"

"Yes, ma'am."

"Are you . . ." Annabelle looked from Sandy to Preston, then back to Sandy. "Are you sure it was my car?"

"Silver Audi. Plates are registered to you."

Annabelle looked at Preston again.

"Garage is empty," Preston whispered to her. "Your car's not there."

"Were you driving on Highway Sixty-Seven last night?" Sandy asked.

"No. I was here. At home."

"Maybe you went out for something quickly?"

"No. I was with Charlotte all night. She's got the croup, and we were keeping a close eye on her."

"Charlotte?" Sandy asked.

"Our daughter," Preston said. "She's got a cough. We took turns checking on her all night."

Sandy nodded. He'd forgotten that the newlyweds had a baby together.

"So you were both up all night, or you took shifts?"

"A little bit of both," Preston said.

"Annabelle?" Sandy asked, trying to keep the conversation between the two of them.

"I don't remember every minute of the night, but Preston and I were both up at times. We also took turns checking on her and sleeping in her room."

Sandy nodded but didn't mention that their explanation allowed times during the night when Annabelle was awake while Preston slept, which made it possible that Annabelle could have gone out without Preston's knowledge. He'd save that theory for later, if things got that far.

"Does anybody have keys to your car other than you?"

"No. Actually," Annabelle said, and went to a bowl that sat in the corner of the kitchen counter. She grabbed a set of keys. "These are my keys."

"When was the last time you drove your car?"

Annabelle shrugged. "Charlotte's been sick for a few days, so I've been a homebody. It's been a couple of days since I was last out."

"A couple of days?"

Annabelle looked up at the ceiling while she thought. "Wednesday. The last time I left the house was Wednesday. I drove into town with Charlotte. I stopped at the pharmacy to pick up medicine for her nebulizer."

As Sandy listened to Annabelle Margolis, he noticed that something felt off about the whole scenario and, not for the first time since he'd knocked on the front door, he had doubts that Annabelle Margolis was driving the car found abandoned out on Highway 67.

"I need you to be available for the next few days as we try to get to the bottom of this. So if you have any travel plans, I need you to cancel them."

"We're not going anywhere," Preston said.

Sandy nodded. "I'll be in touch. Hope your daughter feels better."

"Thank you," Annabelle said.

Sitting in his cruiser a few moments later, Sandy looked back to the Margolis home. Preston and Annabelle stood on the front porch. Preston's arm was around Annabelle's shoulder. At the sight, a sinking feeling came to Sandy that Annabelle Margolis had nothing to do with the hit-and-run. The many enemies of the Margolis family blinked through his mind, and the chances of a simple open-and-shut case evaporated like a scent in the wind.

Cedar Creek, Nevada

Monday, June 26, 1995
8 Days Prior . . .

D R. RACHEL CRANE WAS THE CHIEF MEDICAL EXAMINER FOR WASHOE County. Her morgue was located in Reno and Sandy knew it well. Over the course of his tenure as Sheriff of neighboring Harrison County he'd visited her on a number of occasions. Dr. Crane handled the postmortem exams when Nevada State Highway Patrol was involved in a case. Baker Jauncey, the man found dead on Highway 67, had been transported to the Reno morgue after the scene was secured and all evidence had been collected. The revelation that Mr. Jauncey was a partner at the Margolis law firm further guided the collision course Sandy was on with the family, and he was happy to have an impartial player such as Rachel Crane handling the autopsy outside of Harrison County.

Sandy made the drive to Reno and now paced Dr. Crane's office while he waited, finally stopping to peer through the window. He thought back to his visit Saturday morning with Annabelle Margolis and how little sense it made that her car had been found at the scene of the accident if, in fact, she had not been driving it. A trickle of perspiration beaded on the base of his neck before rolling down his spine.

"Sandy," Dr. Crane said when she entered the office. "I didn't expect you so soon."

Pulled back from his thoughts, Sandy turned from the window. "Sorry. I drove straight down after you called. I'm feeling the pinch on this one and need answers before the Harrison County political machine starts churning."

Dr. Crane nodded. "I've tried to stay clear."

"Lucky you. I'm perpetually in the middle of it."

"I'm afraid my findings are not going to make your job any easier. I finished the autopsy this morning. I'm still putting my notes together, but I'll bring you up to speed."

"Something interesting?"

"Unfortunately, yes. Follow me, it'll be easier to understand if I show you what I found."

Sandy followed Dr. Crane out of her office and down a long hallway. The smell of formaldehyde filled his nostrils the closer they got to the double doors he knew led to the morgue. Dr. Crane pushed through the doors while Sandy stayed close behind. In the atrium outside the autopsy suite, they both donned surgical masks before entering. The six stainless steel tables were empty, and Sandy looked curiously at the contraptions that hung from the ceiling above each—a surgical light, an X-ray machine, and various hoses for spraying or washing or vacuuming or whatever other hellish things took place when bodies occupied the tables.

He walked with Dr. Crane to a row of coolers where the bodies were stored—first, before autopsy, and then again as they waited transport to the funeral home. She opened one of the doors and Sandy saw a pair of pale blue feet poking from under a white sheet, an ID tag hung from the big toe. Dr. Crane slid the shelf out and pulled back the sheet without ceremony or prompting. For Dr. Crane, staring at a dead body was a daily ritual to which she was as indifferent as Sandy was about strapping his firearm to his waist.

"Can't you just *tell* me what you found, Doc?"

"You didn't come all the way down to Reno for me to *tell* you what I found. You need to see it to understand it."

"Understand what?"

"The giant problem you have on your hands."

Sandy's head ached from the thought of going toe-to-toe with the Margolis family. "I've got too many problems to count. Are you going to add to my list?"

"Yes. And this will be your biggest," Dr. Crane said. "Because this guy wasn't hit by a car."

Cedar Creek, Nevada

Monday, June 26, 1995
8 Days Prior . . .

"I LITERALLY FOUND HIM IN THE ROAD," SANDY SAID. "A TRAIL OF blood was streaked on the pavement. It sure as hell *looked* like a car hit him. Plus, investigators found this guy's blood on the underside of the car that was abandoned down the road."

"Sorry," Dr. Crane said. "Let me rephrase. This guy was definitely *run over* by a motor vehicle. But that's not what killed him."

Sandy watched as Dr. Crane turned Baker Jauncey's body onto its side, a task she accomplished by pulling on the sheet under him with one hand while simultaneously pushing on the man's shoulder blade. The maneuver caused the man's right arm to flop onto the metal gurney before hanging limp off the edge. No matter how many times Sandy saw it, the lifeless slump of the dead surprised him, as if iron filled their insides and the world were a magnet.

"See this?" Dr. Crane asked, pointing to the back of Baker Jauncey's head.

"What?" Sandy said, half looking through squinted eyes. "The big, black hole in his head? Yeah, I see it."

"The wound broke the skin and cratered the skull."

Sandy looked at Dr. Crane. "I'm assuming skull fractures are common when people are hit by speeding cars?"

"No. They're possible, but not common. The most common injury is femoral fracture, assuming the victim was standing when the vehicle struck them. In this case, he was not—no fractures anywhere on his body other than the skull. But back to your question, depending on how the body reacts after being struck by the vehicle, many other injuries could follow. Usually, internal organ damage and bleeding. Head injuries can occur if the victim is thrown upwards, sort of somersaulted, and collides with the windshield. That wasn't the case here, since there was no damage to the vehicle's windshield."

Dr. Crane used her gloved hands to expose the injury to the back of Baker Jauncey's head by peeling away the scalp, which she had dissected during the autopsy, so that bare skull was visible. The squishing noise roiled Sandy's stomach.

"A skull fracture this extensive would certainly have caused the windshield to crack. But even if, miraculously, the glass didn't shatter, this wound is definitely not from impact against a smooth, flat surface like a windshield."

"What if he was struck by the car, sent into the air, and then landed on his head?"

"That's an acceptable observation, but the dynamics of the skull fracture disprove the theory. Again, this fracture was not caused by impact with a flat surface—whether it's argued to be a windshield or the pavement. And then," Dr. Crane said with a sympathetic shrug, "to follow your theory, the victim would have needed to be thrown upward, land on the pavement, sustain the head injury, and *then* get run over by the speeding car. Essentially, your theory requires the car to hit the victim twice, which is impossible by the laws of physics."

"Then what caused the head injury?"

"My best bet? A baseball bat."

Sandy blinked several times. "A baseball bat?"

"Based on the shape and depth of the fracture, as well as the discovery of wood fragments in the wound, some sort of rounded piece of wood moving at a high rate of speed created the fracture. A baseball bat is the most likely culprit."

"What are you telling me, Dr. Crane?"

"I'm telling you that this guy was struck in the back of the head, likely with a baseball bat, causing blunt force trauma that fractured his skull and caused a brain bleed that killed him. Then, *after* he was dead, he was run over by a car."

Sandy's mind returned to his visit with Preston and Annabelle

Margolis, remembering how the couple seemed genuinely surprised to hear that Annabelle's car had been involved in a hit-and-run.

Dr. Crane pointed again to Baker Jauncey's head. "My official opinion on cause of death will be blunt force trauma resulting in a fatal brain bleed. Manner of death, homicide."

Sandy ran his hand through his hair as he took in the news.

"All the other injuries I documented," Dr. Crane continued, "were caused postmortem."

"*After* he was dead?"

"Correct."

Sandy ran his tongue along the inside of his lower lip as he considered his next move, and the one after that.

"I need you to sit on the autopsy findings for a while," he finally said. "Don't share them with anyone. Can you do that?"

"I haven't even written up my report. I can stall for a few days. Maybe even a week or two. But the state police are involved, so I'll have some pressure on me."

"Stall for as long as you can. And don't talk to anyone else about this, okay? Especially anyone from Harrison County."

"What's going on, Sandy?"

Sandy exhaled a long breath.

"The car found at the scene belonged to a member of the Margolis family. And the vic was a partner at the Margolis law firm."

"For shit's sake," Dr. Crane whispered.

"Exactly. Once it becomes public knowledge that this is being called a homicide rather than a hit-and-run, the shit's going to hit the fan and I need to prepare for it. Give me a week?"

"I'll try."

Sandy nodded and hurried out of the morgue. He knew there was no rain suit or umbrella strong enough to protect him from the shitstorm that was coming.

Reno, Nevada

Tuesday, June 27, 1995
7 Days Prior . . .

Iт was just past midnight when the windowless van pulled down the alley and stopped outside the back door to the Washoe County morgue in Reno. Two men climbed from the van. They wore dark windbreakers that would hide their builds, and ball caps pulled low on their foreheads so that surveillance cameras would have no clear image of their faces. Although they had a master key set if needed, when the first man reached for the handle of the morgue door, it opened with a simple twist. They had an inside man who promised the morgue would be unlocked, and so far he was true to his word.

The men slipped inside, pulled out flashlights, and headed down the hall. They took the stairs to the underground level, their soft-soled tennis shoes making little noise. They found the autopsy suite and headed to a row of coolers on the back wall. They found the third door and opened it, the only one that was unlocked. They pulled the gurney and the body it held from the freezer as cold air billowed into the suite. One of the men pulled on the sheet to reveal the dead man's feet, found the tag hanging from his toe, and confirmed the name.

Baker Jauncey

To be sure, they pulled the sheet down to expose the man's face and checked it against a picture they had. Confirmed, they wheeled the body out of the suite and down the hall, this time opting for the elevator rather than the stairs. Back on the first level, they guided the body through the halls, to the unlocked door, and into the night. They opened the back doors of the van and slid Baker Jauncey's body in. A few minutes later they were on the highway and headed north.

An hour and a half later they arrived in Cedar Creek, where they pulled up to the back door of the town's morgue. Inside, they pushed the gurney containing Baker Jauncey's body through the dark hallways until they reached the autopsy suite, where they deposited the body in the cooler. They swapped the Washoe morgue tag that was attached to Baker's right big toe.

Just before 2 a.m., Baker Jauncey became the property of the Harrison County Medical Examiner's Office in Cedar Creek, Nevada. The ME promised his boss he would perform the autopsy first thing in the morning.

PART II

Undercover

CHAPTER 16

Raleigh, North Carolina
Friday, July 19, 2024

IT WAS 8:30 P.M. BY THE TIME SLOAN LEFT THE PIZZERIA. SHE HAD SAT with Eric for two hours discussing her still-missing biological parents, Sandy Stamos's mysterious death, and the old, forgotten hit-and-run case that Eric believed was at the heart of Sloan and her parents' disappearance in 1995. Sloan felt Eric's desperation as she sat across from him. The man truly believed, after taking on his grandfather's burden, that Sloan was his only hope of discovering what happened to his father.

Sloan promised Eric she would be in touch, but there were too many variables for her to commit to helping him. She apologized again for the Mace incident, and then watched Sheriff Stamos drive off in his Toyota SUV with Nevada plates. She ran up the steps of her apartment, locked the door behind her, and opened her laptop as soon as she sat at the kitchen table. Her fingers raced across the keyboard as she typed into the search engine:

Eric Stamos Cedar Creek, Nevada.

A slew of information popped onto her screen, and she clicked on the first link. It was an article from the *Harrison County Post.*

Stamos Wins Reelection in Landslide

CEDAR CREEK, NV, November 9, 2022—Eric Stamos was easily reelected sheriff of Harrison County last night, earning 72% of the

*vote. What was originally believed to be a tight race ended up a run-
away. The latest polls offered mixed results heading into Tuesday's
election. Most showed Stamos with a narrow lead, while others showed
Trent Dilbert as the frontrunner. Dilbert ran an aggressive campaign
fueled by massive donations from some of Harrison County's wealthi-
est residents. Dilbert was endorsed by several prominent political figures, as well as the District Attorney's Office. But Stamos and his
no-nonsense approach to law enforcement, as well as his family's long
lineage of peacekeepers in the county, resonated with voters more than
Dilbert's pricey campaign.*

    *This will be Stamos's second term as Harrison County Sheriff. He
succeeds his father and grandfather, both of whom served several con-
secutive terms as sheriff. Stamos's father, Sanford Stamos, died in
1995. Eric Stamos was just nine years old at the time.*

Sloan typed Eric's father's name into the search engine and
found pages of articles about the man. She clicked again on an article from the *Harrison County Post*.

Sheriff Stamos Found Dead, Overdose Suspected

    *CEDAR CREEK, NV, July 15, 1995—Sandy Stamos, the multi-
term sheriff of Harrison County, drowned when his car crashed into
Cedar Creek sometime late Thursday night. Preliminary toxicology reports from the coroner's office in Harrison County indicate that Stamos had heroin in his system. Sources close to the investigation tell the
Post that a syringe was found in Stamos's arm when the sheriff's body
was pulled from Cedar Creek.*

    *Stamos was on duty Thursday night and failed to respond to sev-
eral dispatch calls. A jogger spotted Stamos's squad car submerged in
Cedar Creek early Friday morning with just the rear taillights above
the water. Divers were eventually brought in to remove Stamos's body.
The cruiser was pulled from the creek late Friday morning.*

The article showed a photo of Sandy Stamos's squad car as a tow
truck hauled it from the water. Sloan clicked through several more
articles about Eric's father. Finally, she searched *hit-and-run accident
in Cedar Creek, Nevada 1995* and clicked on the first link that came up.

Hit-and-Run Leaves Local Man Dead

CEDAR CREEK, NV, June 26, 1995—Police were called to the scene of a hit-and-run accident on Highway 67, just north of Cedar Creek, in the early morning hours of June 24. The man, identified as Baker Jauncey, was discovered by an out-of-state truck driver making a haul from Boise to Reno.

"I just saw a heap in the middle of the road," Dale Pickett, the trucker who spotted Jauncey's body and called 9-1-1, said. "I thought it was a deer or some other large animal until I got closer. Then, I knew it was a body."

Harrison County Sheriff Sandy Stamos was the first law enforcement officer on the scene. The highway was shut down and the accident investigation unit from the Nevada State Highway Patrol was called in. Sources tell the Post *that a car was located close to Baker Jauncey's body, but neither the Sheriff's Office nor the Highway Patrol would offer details.*

"This is an ongoing investigation," Sandy Stamos said. "My department, as well as the state authorities, are working tirelessly to determine how this accident happened and the parties involved."

So far, however, no arrests have been made. Baker Jauncey was a partner at the law firm of Margolis & Margolis in Cedar Creek.

Sloan closed her laptop. She could spend all night running down the rabbit holes of Eric Stamos, his father, the mysterious hit-and-run accident, and speculating about what any of it had to do with her disappearance thirty years ago. But she didn't have time for that now. She still had to see her parents. She'd missed several calls from them while she was at dinner listening to Eric Stamos pitch his wild idea.

She pushed the brooding Cedar Creek sheriff from her thoughts, grabbed her keys, and headed out the door. In just a few short days since submitting her DNA, her world had been turned upside down.

"Where have you been?" her dad asked when Sloan walked through the front door.

"Long story. You first. What happened with the FBI today?"

"They're finished with the formal questioning," her dad said.

"We told them everything we know—starting with how we adopted you and who we adopted you from. We provided all the paperwork we had. They finished a very deep dive into our backgrounds and, after three days, we're cleared."

"Cleared?" Sloan said.

"The FBI is convinced we know nothing about the disappearance of your birth parents."

"So now what?" Sloan asked.

"They want to speak with you tomorrow morning."

"What do they need from me? I know less than you or Mom."

"They want to speak with you about their next moves," her mother said.

"The agent's name is John Michaels," her dad said. "Nice guy."

"Did they say how they would investigate this?"

"I think that's what they're going to discuss with you tomorrow morning. Are you going to tell us where you've been?"

Sloan considered telling her parents about her visit from Eric Stamos but thought better of it.

"A body turned up in the morgue," Sloan said. "I'm in the middle of dealing with it."

She didn't mention that it wasn't her morgue, or that the body was from 1995. Sloan considered the omission less deceitful than a full-blown lie. Back at her apartment, she spent the small hours of the night on her laptop, reading about Eric Stamos, his dead father, and the Margolis family of Cedar Creek.

CHAPTER 17

Raleigh, North Carolina
Saturday, July 20, 2024

T HE FOLLOWING MORNING SLOAN WAS AT HER PARENTS' HOUSE BRIGHT and early. Her mother had a pot of coffee brewing and they all waited anxiously for the FBI to arrive. At promptly 9:00 a.m. the doorbell rang, and Special Agent John Michaels stood on the front doorstep dressed in a crisp suit and tie.

"Good morning," Michaels said when Dolly Hastings answered the door.

"Please, come in."

They walked into the kitchen. "Sloan, this is Agent Michaels. This is our daughter, Sloan."

"Hi," Sloan said.

"Nice to meet you," Michaels said, shaking Sloan's hand.

"We can talk at the kitchen table here," Todd Hastings said. "Coffee?"

"That would be great, thank you."

Once all four were seated around the table, coffee mugs in front of each of them, Michaels got right to the point.

"I wanted to speak with you all this morning about where our investigation will go from here, some potential hazards we face, and ones that you'll want to be aware of."

"Hazards?" Sloan said.

"We believe the key, one of them, is to track down the woman who put you up for adoption. From the paperwork your parents provided, we have some leads. We'll see where they take us. The woman named in the documents is Wendy Downing. There are only two possible conclusions to draw about your adoption. The first is that your birth mother, Annabelle Margolis, posed as Wendy Downing. But your parents"—Agent Michaels gestured at Dolly and Todd—"emphatically deny that the woman who called herself Wendy Downing matched the photos we showed them of Annabelle Margolis. There's always the possibility that Annabelle used a disguise, but that's a stretch. Still, we'll pursue the possibility."

"And the second conclusion?" Sloan asked.

"Wendy Downing is in no way related to you or your birth parents."

"You think I was kidnapped?"

"It'll take some time to determine that. But, yes, that's our suspicion. There are lots of Wendy Downings in the world, and we suspect the name was an alias to begin with. The attorney listed in the adoption paperwork, and the man who brokered the deal, was someone named Guy Menendez. We also suspect, based on some early field work, that this was an alias."

Sloan registered both names. *Wendy Downing. Guy Menendez.*

"Adoption, unfortunately," agent Michaels continued, "has a very large and active black market. We believe you are a product of it."

"But for what reason?" Sloan asked.

"Your parents paid close to twenty-five thousand dollars for the private adoption, so there was a financial motive for such a crime."

"From everything I've researched about the Margolis family, they're wealthy. Preston Margolis was an attorney at his family's law firm. He went to Stanford Law. It makes no sense to think he and Annabelle fraudulently gave up their daughter to pocket some quick cash."

"We agree," Michaels said. "Which is why we suspect you were abducted."

The word pushed Sloan to the verge of tears.

"So . . ." Sloan looked quickly across the table at her parents as she blinked back the tears, then back to agent Michaels. "If that's true, if I was abducted . . . what happened to my birth parents?"

"We're going to try to figure that out."

Sloan glanced again at her parents and felt sorry for what they were learning, and for what she had accidentally dragged them into. She also, for the first time in her life, felt detached from them. Sloan was no longer just their adopted child whom they loved unconditionally. Now she was the product of fraud and deceit. Dolly and Todd Hastings had not plucked a child from the world to give her love and a wonderful life; they had unknowingly participated in a crime that stole a child from loving parents. The unspoken realization created a divide between them, as if a tornado had touched down and ripped a chasm between their worlds.

Sloan's thoughts drifted to Eric Stamos and the story he told about his father. Had Sandy Stamos stumbled over information that would have shed light on who took her and what had happened to her birth parents? Had that information gotten him killed? And could it be true that someone inside the Margolis family knew the truth? The thoughts brought with them a wave of urgency that crashed over her. The sensation drew her, somehow, to her *birth* parents—people she had scarcely thought of before this week, and with whom she had never before felt a connection. But this morning she felt not just tied to her birth parents, but a deep sense of obligation to figure out what happened to them. Eric Stamos's words echoed in her mind.

Someone inside the Margolis family knows what happened to you and your birth parents. You're the perfect Trojan horse.

"The other thing I wanted to speak with you about," Agent Michaels said, pulling Sloan from her thoughts, "is that we have notified the Margolis family about the developments in the case. Specifically, that DNA testing has confirmed that we've found Charlotte Margolis. We didn't share your personal information, but we were duty bound to provide the Margolis family with an update, as this investigation has never been formally closed. Annabelle Margolis's parents are deceased, and she was an only child. There's no one on her side to tell. You're under no obligation to speak with the Margolis family, but I wanted to let you know that they have been informed. Unless you ask us to do so, we'll provide the family no other personal details about you."

I want you to go to Cedar Creek. The family would welcome you back with open arms.

Sloan shook her head. "I'll need a day or two to think about whether I want to reach out to the Margolises or not. I need to talk with my parents about it."

"Of course," Agent Michaels said. "There's one last thing I need to caution you about. When you and your birth parents went missing in 1995, it was national news."

Sloan nodded. "I've seen the tabloid covers."

"If news breaks now that baby Charlotte has resurfaced, I'm sure there'll be a media storm. My office will do its best to keep things quiet, but just a warning that if the media discover this story, they'll likely track you down and hound you for interviews. The press can be relentless. They'll start with phone calls, but they'll also show up at your home, your place of employment, the health club. Anywhere they think *you'll* be, *they'll* be."

Sloan never thought of that possibility. She questioned whether the country would still be interested in her after three decades. But this was America, Sloan remembered. Of course the public would still be curious. Hers was a sensational true crime story the tabloids would be happy to salivate over a second time. Hell, true crime fanatics would flock to Raleigh to find her, and podcasters would race to produce a series around the story.

If Sloan wasn't careful, Agent Michaels warned, she could end up again on the cover of every tabloid in the nation.

CHAPTER 18

Raleigh, North Carolina
Sunday, July 21, 2024

SLEEP WAS ELUSIVE. HER CONVERSATION WITH AGENT MICHAELS RAN in a repetitive loop through her thoughts. Her mind stirred with terrors about being snatched from her birth parents and sold off to an unsuspecting couple so desperate for a child that they bypassed the mainstream channels for something shadier. Sloan held no ill will toward her parents. She loved them and always would. But she also felt a foreign pull toward Preston and Annabelle Margolis, and a blossoming need to find out what happened to them.

She finally pushed the covers to the side and climbed from bed. The alarm clock told her it was 2:30 in the morning. In the kitchen she grabbed her phone and wrote a short text to James the genealogist.

James,
Is there a way you can get me Nora Margolis's home address? She's the woman whose husband's DNA profile I matched to.
Just curious, Sloan

She opened her laptop, ready to spend another obnoxious chunk of time reading about the Margolis family, Sandy Stamos's death, and the mysterious hit-and-run case from 1995. But before she got the chance, her phone buzzed with a reply text from James.

Sloan,
As an admin of the site, I have access to users' personal informa-
tion. But I could lose my job if I shared it with you. Also, IMO showing
up on your aunt's doorstep and announcing that your DNA profile
matches that of her missing niece sounds like a really bad idea.

Sloan typed back.

Oh, James, that ship has sailed. If you can't give me her address, is
there another way for me to get in touch with her?

The reply was instant.

Yes, you can direct message her through the site.

Sloan stared at her phone and thought again about her birth
parents. She picked up one of the printed pages that rested on her
kitchen table. It was of Preston and Annabelle Margolis from the
cover of a tabloid. It was difficult to imagine them as her biological
parents since Annabelle Margolis was younger in the photo than
Sloan's present age. Still, the sight of that young couple touched
her heart. She felt sorry for Preston and Annabelle Margolis,
whose two-month-old daughter had been taken from them and
sold off through the adoption black market. God only knew what
had happened to them.

Sloan looked back at her phone and typed a short reply to
James.

Thanks.

With a new sense of resolve and responsibility, she turned back
to her laptop and pulled up her Your Lineage profile page. Before
she had the opportunity to access the family tree that James had
created and find Nora Margolis's profile, Sloan noticed a red circle
at the top right of the screen indicating that another user had mes-
saged her.

An eerie feeling sent her stomach into free fall. She looked around her dark apartment and took a moment to shake the sensation that she was not alone. Finally, she clicked on the message.

Dear Sloan,
My name is Nora Margolis and I'm taking a chance here . . .
I see that your profile matched to my husband, Ellis, indicating that you're his biological niece. Such a strange question, but in light of the news that law enforcement delivered to us just a couple of days ago . . . are you Charlotte?

—Nora

Sloan's DNA profile was public. It was the only way James could set up the account to see if she matched to other users. Nora Margolis would have been informed about the connection, as the website called it, when Sloan's DNA profile matched to the Margolis family. It was likely the only hit Nora Margolis had received in the last week. And after the FBI informed the family that Charlotte Margolis had been found, it wouldn't take a seasoned detective to figure out how it happened, just an aggressive user of online ancestry sites, which Nora Margolis was.

Sloan stared at the message for several minutes. Where this situation was headed, she had no idea. She only knew that a mounting sense of duty was bubbling up inside of her, one that called her to look into what happened to her birth parents all those years ago.

She dug Eric Stamos's card from her purse and fired off a quick text.

Eric, it's Sloan Hastings. I think I found a way into the Margolis family.

CHAPTER 19

Raleigh, North Carolina
Sunday July 21, 2024

SLOAN SPENT HER SUNDAY AT THE LIBRARY. SHE RESERVED A PRIVATE, glass-walled room tucked in the corner behind rows of books where no one would bother her. On the table in front of her was her research—pages and pages of archived newspaper articles, magazine pieces, and photographs she had pulled from the library's microfilm covering the 1995 disappearance of Preston and Annabelle Margolis, and their infant daughter, Charlotte. Every major newspaper in the country covered the story. Not just with one-and-done mentions, but ongoing features about the suspicious circumstances that shrouded the family's disappearance. As the investigation dragged on and no suspects were named, the news stories evolved from foul play to the theory that the Margolis family had disappeared of their own accord. Specifically, that Annabelle Margolis, because she was a person of interest in the hit-and-run death of a local Cedar Creek man at the time of her disappearance, had packed up her family and vanished to avoid prosecution.

Sloan had dug as deeply as she could on the hit-and-run, but there were scant details about the case. She'd need to rely on Eric Stamos on that front. She shifted her focus to the Margolis family. Her laptop sat in the middle of the paper stacks displaying several websites that detailed the history of Cedar Creek, the Margolis family, and their reign of power over Harrison County, Nevada, for the past century. When her DNA profile first came back, she had taken a shallow plunge into the details of the family with James the genealogist. Today, Sloan was diving deep.

Hours of digging had painted an elaborate picture of the Margolis empire. Family members occupied several seats on the county board, controlled the District Attorney's Office, and made up the largest personal injury law firm in the county, aptly named Margolis & Margolis. The biggest employer in Harrison County was Margolis Timber, a logging company that provided lumber to most of the West Coast. A review of county records told Sloan that much of the land and many of the town's buildings were owned by Margolis Realty, LLC. The family was the very definition of a monopoly. They had taken a sleepy town tucked in the foothills of the Sierra Nevada Mountains and made it their own. Hell, the family even owned and operated their own winery—Margolis Manor—located in Oregon, which produced wines that were distributed around the world. With a family as powerful, affluent, and well known as the Margolises, it was not surprising that the disappearance of family members had garnered so much national attention.

To the best of Sloan's research abilities, the disappearance of her and her birth parents hung around the news cycle for eighteen months before it finally faded. But every decade since the July 4, 1995, disappearance, some branch of the media revisited the crime. In off years it was a short article in the local paper or a feature in the *Reno Gazette.* For bigger anniversaries, like the twenty-fifth anniversary, the *New York Times* ran a feature. This past Fourth of July had marked the twenty-ninth year since Sloan and her parents had vanished.

Sloan pushed her laptop away and rubbed her eyes. She'd been at it for hours and needed a break. As she looked at the mounds of information in front of her, she wondered, not for the first time since she had texted Eric Stamos, whether she was insane for believing that she could go to Cedar Creek and find answers to a decades-old mystery that had eluded so many others who had looked.

Fried from her research into the Margolis family, she needed to give her mind a rest. She headed to the gym. Now, along with ten other CrossFitters, her heart raced as she stood in front of the bar that sported a single, round forty-five-pound bumper plate on each side. She clapped her hands together and a cloud of white chalk dust plumed into the air as Aerosmith blared from the gym's speakers. She bent over the bar, grasped it with her chalked-up hands, and hoisted it up to her shoulders as she dropped into a squat. Pausing for just a moment, she drove out of the squat, feeling her quads burn, before pushing the bar over her head as she hopped into a split step. She held the bar high in the air, locking her elbows to control the shake in her arms as she steadied her core, completing a single clean and jerk. She dropped the bar to the ground where it bounced until it came to rest. Then she repeated the process for a total of fourteen reps, barely securing her elbows on the last one. She dropped the bar a final time and bent over her knees, giving in to the exhaustion. Her quads were saturated with lactic acid and her shoulders were numb. Her heart pounded against her ribcage while sweat covered her body and dripped from her chin.

A few other CrossFitters applauded her effort, knowing Sloan had reached a PR—personal record—during the final rep of the night. She headed to the stationary bike to burn off any remaining anxiety. With her legs spinning and her arms in a continuous back-and-forth motion as she pushed and pulled the handles, Sloan contemplated the upcoming week. She was scheduled to fly to Reno on Friday afternoon and would arrive in Cedar Creek sometime in the evening. She had purchased a one-way ticket, not knowing when she would return to Raleigh. She'd have at least a month before she'd have to be back at the Office of the Chief Medical Examiner to satisfy August's required autopsy observations. To make up for her extended leave, Sloan was scheduled to scrub in with Hayden Cox every day this week, which would buy her some breathing room while she headed to Cedar Creek to meet the Margolis family and look for answers.

The timer on the bike sounded, but with so many thoughts running through her head, Sloan pressed the button for another twenty minutes. She melted on the bike, sweating until her breath was gone and her muscles fatigued. But even her hellish workout wasn't enough to curb the nervousness she felt about her upcoming trip to meet Nora Margolis.

CHAPTER 20

Cedar Creek, Nevada
Friday, July 26, 2024

SHE MANAGED THE FIVE-HOUR FLIGHT FROM RALEIGH TO RENO WITH-out incident, found her rental car, and headed out of Reno International Airport right on schedule. Cedar Creek was perched in the foothills of the Sierra Nevada Mountains an hour and a half to the north. The largest city in Harrison County, Cedar Creek was a mini metropolis flanked by the Great Basin to the east and the insurmountable peaks of the Sierra Nevada Mountains to the west. The creek for which the town was named originated from a large lake in Oregon, merged with tributaries that funneled down from the snow-capped Sierra Nevada peaks, and split the town in half before emptying into Lake Harmony on the south side of Cedar Creek.

As Sloan crested the bluff that overlooked the town, she took in the aerial view. The quaint town sprawled out below her revealing beautiful homes lining each side of the creek, and three arch bridges—one to the north, another to the south, and the third smack dab in the middle of town—that vaulted over the water to connect one side of town to the other. Had Sloan been visiting for reasons other than reuniting with the family she had been abducted from and trying to wiggle her way into their good graces to find answers to what happened to her birth parents nearly thirty years earlier, she might have considered the place beautiful. Instead, she took a scientific approach to the town of Cedar Creek, the same way she had to the five autopsies she assisted with during the past week. Like the bodies and the clues they offered, Cedar Creek held something deeper than its beauty. The town held secrets, and Sloan was on a mission to dissect them from wherever they hid.

For one hundred years, and three generations, the Margolis family had run this small splinter of the country, controlled the local government, and had managed to stretch their reach into state-run industries and offices. Sloan was unsure what sort of dangers lurked in Cedar Creek. She knew only that since discovering she was baby Charlotte, a girl who had disappeared when she was two months old and separated from parents who loved her, she had a burning desire to find answers. As Sloan drove down into the valley and toward Cedar Creek, she knew she was headed to the only place on earth where she might find them.

The two-lane road twisted for a mile until it skirted along the creek, which Sloan estimated to be two football fields wide. On the edge of town a sign welcomed her to Cedar Creek—A PLACE WHERE DREAMS COME TRUE. From what Sloan had learned so far about the things that had taken place here, she wasn't so sure about that.

She drove north with a perfect view across the water, where the setting sun lit the creek-side homes in the splendid glow of evening. When she entered the town center she took a few minutes to explore, navigating through a series of roundabouts until the last spun her into the heart of town, a place known locally as The Block. She took in the shops, galleries, and restaurants the quaint town had on display. On the north side she found the Louis-Bullat Bridge—named, Sloan knew from her research, for the structural engineers who had designed it—which stretched over Cedar Creek and took Sloan to the east side of town. She turned down a side street and found the Vrbo home she had rented until September. A month felt suddenly inadequate to figure out what had happened to her parents three decades earlier.

Sloan parked in the driveway and pulled her suitcase from the backseat. She looked at the mountains to the west, which cast long shadows over the town as the sun began its descent behind their peaks. At once she felt small and insignificant standing in this valley in northern Nevada, but also like she was meant to be there.

Like the universe had brought her to this exact place, at this exact time, to somehow right an injustice from decades earlier. To find answers for the Margolis family, Eric Stamos, and herself.

She heard the crow of a bird—a long squawk that echoed into the evening. When she turned, Sloan saw a Cooper's hawk balanced at the top of a lodgepole pine. It crowed again before taking flight, pumping its powerful wings and soaring high over Sloan's head. She followed the hawk's flight as it headed west into the setting sun, until it was just a small speck on the horizon before disappearing.

Her phone buzzed with a text message from Nora Margolis.

Did you make it?

Sloan stared at the phone and tried to calm her nerves. Her anxiety felt less like butterflies swarming in her stomach and more like luna moths ricocheting off the inside of her ribcage as they attempted to escape her chest.

Sloan typed back:

Just pulled up to my rental house.

NORA: I'm literally shaking with excitement. What time can we meet?

SLOAN: I need a minute to put myself together. Long travel day.

NORA: Take your time. I can come to you, or you can come here. I'm on the north side of town.

SLOAN: Address?

NORA: 378 Chestnut Circle.

SLOAN: See you soon.

NORA: Can't wait!

Sloan took a deep breath. There was no turning back now.

CHAPTER 21

Cedar Creek, Nevada
Friday, July 26, 2024

B<small>Y 8:00 P.M. SLOAN HAD UNPACKED HER SUITCASE AND FILLED THE</small> drawers of the bedroom armoire with a month's worth of clothes. She ditched her cross-country travel attire and slipped into a pair of jeans and a white halter top. She took a moment to comb her hair and freshen her makeup before she climbed into her rental car and, with the flutter still constant against her ribcage, headed to Nora Margolis's home. Sloan followed the creek north until she found Chestnut Circle and navigated the long, bending road canopied by the arching branches of bristlecone pines that lined each side until she arrived at Nora Margolis's home.

It was a beautiful, two-story Victorian with a wraparound porch and meticulously manicured lawn. A flood of adrenaline pumped through her veins as Sloan pulled into the driveway. She took another deep breath before she climbed from the car and smoothed the front of her jeans, a nervous tell she'd performed her entire life—before important tests, before her first day in the morgue, and now, before meeting a member of her biological family. Sloan walked up the front steps of the wraparound porch, potted plants hanging in rows on either side of the front door, and rang the bell.

The door opened a moment later and it took only a second before Nora Margolis began to cry.

"Oh my God," Nora said, standing in the doorway and staring at Sloan. "You look just like Annabelle."

The woman moved in for a hug, and Sloan felt obligated to not only accept the gesture, but return it. She couldn't quite understand why Nora's emotions were so contagious, but before Sloan knew it she was crying, too. She had no emotional connection to this family, but understood that for just a short while she had once been a part of it. And so Nora Margolis's reaction to laying eyes on her husband's biological niece was logical, and Sloan was not about to fight against it.

Nora broke free from the embrace and held Sloan at arm's length as she stared.

"It's uncanny," Nora said. "The resemblance."

Sloan had seen dozens of pictures of her biological mother over the last many days, and had also noted her haunting likeness to Annabelle Margolis from thirty years ago.

"And you have his eyes. You have Preston's eyes."

Nora teared up again and she wiped her cheeks with the backs of her hands.

"Oh, will you look at me?" Nora said. "I promised myself I'd hold it together, and here I am falling to pieces the moment I lay eyes on you."

Sloan wiped her own tears. "It's alright. I understand how shocking this must be."

Nora Margolis, Sloan guessed, was in her late fifties—about the same age Annabelle Margolis was today. Assuming, Sloan considered, her birth mother was still alive.

"Not just to us," Nora said. "For you as well."

Sloan smiled. "It's been an interesting couple of weeks. And I have to admit that I'm *really* nervous right now."

"Don't be. Not tonight, anyway. It's just you and me this evening. You'll meet everyone else tomorrow. Come in. Did you find the place alright?"

"Yes. You've got a beautiful home."

"Oh." Nora pulsed her eyebrows. "It's a Margolis Victorian."

Sloan followed Nora into the foyer.

"A *Margolis* Victorian?"

Nora plastered a fake smile onto her face. "We're not allowed anything else. Since the house was purchased through my husband's trust, it had to match all the other Margolis homes. All Victorians, all constructed by the same builder, and all designed by Tilly and Reid Margolis. My in-laws. God forbid we build our own home." Nora rolled her eyes. "Oh, listen to me. I'm already dishing family gossip and you've just walked through the door. Anyway, thank you. Ellis and I decorated it ourselves and we've always loved it. Can I get you something to drink? Wine?"

"Sure. Thank you."

Sloan followed Nora into the kitchen, where Nora poured two glasses of white wine.

"Judging by your body," Nora said, handing Sloan a glass, "I'm guessing you're a health junkie?"

"Oh." Sloan smiled. "CrossFit."

Nora raised her eyebrows in the way of a question.

"It's a type of exercise—weight lifting and cardio. High intensity stuff. It's a little sadistic, but it's also addictive. I discovered it in medical school and am quasi obsessed. It helps clear my head when my mind gets cluttered, which is often."

"Are you married?"

Sloan smiled. "No."

"Dating?"

"Negative on all fronts having to do with men."

"Are you gay?"

"No. Just not ready to hitch myself to anyone yet."

"Well, I guess that's the way these days. I married Ellis when I was young, but kids nowadays aren't getting married until later. Sometimes not at all."

"I don't really have a timetable. I just haven't met the right guy I guess."

"There're plenty of fish in the sea, and you're quite a catch so it'll happen when it happens. Plus, you're a doctor, right?"

Nora's words carried an aura of pride.

"Yes. A pathologist."

"I think that's a first. This family runs thick with lawyers and politicians, but you're the first doctor the family has produced."

Sloan had trouble getting her mind around the idea that Nora Margolis considered her part of the family. Nora asked questions about Sloan's life for an hour—about her childhood, her adoptive parents, medical school, and residency. There was something gentle and pleasing about Nora Margolis and her manner. She possessed a charisma that made Sloan feel like she'd known her much longer than an hour.

"Tell me about your interest in genealogy," Sloan said. "Since that's how this whole thing started."

"It's been a hobby of mine for years. It started when my son needed to create a family tree for one of his high school courses. I became so fascinated with the science and history of genealogy that I just kept going even after the project was turned in. I traced my own heritage back to Wales, several generations. The process was captivating. Then I thought it would be fun to surprise my husband by creating a family tree for his side—the Margolis side. I'm so far down a rabbit hole I'll never stop. For goodness sakes, look at what's happened from it."

"So let me see if I have my research straight," Sloan said. "Your maiden name is Davies, and you married into the Margolis family?"

"That's right. My husband is Ellis Margolis—Preston's brother. Here, I'll show you."

Nora pulled her laptop over and fired up the genealogy site. Over another glass of wine, Sloan listened to Nora Margolis explain her heritage. The woman was clearly a genealogy buff, and her quest to find the origins of her ancestry was something more than a hobby.

Nora pointed at the family tree displayed on the monitor.

"I married Ellis Margolis who, along with Preston—your biological father—were the only two descendants of Reid and Tilly Margolis. Ellis and I have two children, no grandchildren yet. Preston married Annabelle Akers and had one child . . . you obviously know that part. So my kids are at the bottom of the Margolis family tree, but I've traced our ancestors back over a hundred years. And I'm still going."

For thirty minutes Sloan listened to Nora dissect the Margolis family tree. Finally, somewhere in the seventeenth century, she stopped.

"Sorry, I'm probably boring you to death with all this."

"Not at all. It's part of why I came all the way to Cedar Creek. I wanted to see how a simple genealogy site brought us together after so many years."

"It really is amazing. But . . ." Nora said before she hesitated. "I suppose the genealogy can explain *how* we found you after so many years, but it will never be able to tell us what happened to you and your parents all those years ago. I have to admit that part of the reason I reached out to you was selfish. I'm hoping your story can help shine light on what happened to Preston and Annabelle."

Sloan smiled. "That's the thing, Nora. I don't know what happened to me. Until a couple of weeks ago, I thought I had a pretty normal childhood. I knew I was adopted, but that just became my normal existence. It was part of my identity. My parents loved me, and I loved them. They provided a great childhood for me. That's all I knew. But after what I've discovered, I'm hoping to learn about my birth parents and what happened to them. I'm hoping you can help me, probably as much as you're hoping I can help you."

"It's been a mystery for thirty years—what happened to you and your folks. Unfortunately, I don't know any more than you probably do."

"That can't be true. You knew my birth parents, so that alone gives you a leg up on me. Can we start there? Can you tell me about my birth parents?"

"Sure," Nora said. "Your mother was a dear friend of mine. I'll tell you anything you want to know."

Your mother.

Sloan's mind flashed to her mom, who was recovering in Raleigh from a week of interrogation by the FBI. It was hard to find room in her mind for another parent figure, but somehow Annabelle Margolis had taken root somewhere in her thoughts, morphing from a stranger Sloan had first seen on a tabloid cover to something else. What, exactly, Annabelle represented was unclear. But the woman was a stranger no more.

"You were the light of her life during that summer," Nora said. "Annabelle loved being a new mom, and she was absolutely smitten with you."

Sloan attempted to swallow but her esophagus constricted. She took a deep breath to collect her emotions, barely containing the tears that welled at the bottoms of her lids.

"You and my birth mom were close?"

"Ours was a short friendship, but a strong one. We only knew each other for about a year, but we became kindred spirits during that time. Mostly, I think, because we were both outsiders as far as the Margolis family was concerned. I mean, by the time Annabelle came into the scene I had established myself enough that I was accepted. Annabelle was a different story."

"The family didn't accept her?"

"Oh, Christ no. And I knew exactly what she was going through because I'd once been there myself when I first started dating Ellis. So Annabelle and I became close. I was the person she could lean on when things got heated in the family."

"When you say the family didn't accept her, who are you talking about?"

"Reid and Tilly."

"Why didn't they accept Annabelle?"

Nora raised her eyebrows. "Lots of reasons. But the biggest was that Preston started dating Annabelle while he was engaged to another woman."

CHAPTER 22

Cedar Creek, Nevada
Friday, July 26, 2024

"MY FATHER WAS ENGAGED WHEN HE MET MY MOTHER?"

Nora nodded. "To Stella Connelly. She was a perfect match for Preston. On paper, anyway. She came rubber-stamped and approved by Reid and Tilly. Stella, like Preston, was a young, up-and-coming attorney at another prominent Harrison County law firm. Because she came from a wealthy and powerful family, Reid and Tilly loved her immediately."

Sloan crossed her arms awkwardly. "Did my father cheat on her with my mother?"

"Stella Connelly certainly thought so."

"What do you think?"

"I think Preston and Annabelle were in love. A much deeper love than Preston ever experienced with Stella Connelly. I got close with Annabelle through everything—Preston's broken engagement, her pregnancy, and the general shunning Annabelle experienced from the rest of the family. I knew how that girl felt because I had once been there myself."

"They didn't approve of you, either?"

"Not at first. But I had an advantage Annabelle did not. I came from money. My folks, before they passed, owned a string of restaurant franchises. When Tilly and Reid first heard that my family was in the fast-food business, I was shunned. But when they heard my parents owned over a hundred franchises, and had made a fortune, I was welcomed with open arms."

"Just because your family had money?"

"Absolutely. Before they knew that my parents were wealthy, I was just a lowly photographer who sunk her fingers into their son so I could suck from the Margolis spigot for life."

"That's awful. They told you that?"

"Not in so many words. But it's what they thought. Reid especially. He's very protective of the Margolis family fortune, and always careful to fend off those he believes are after it. Ellis and I used to laugh about it because it was so absurd. Being a Margolis boy came with power and prestige, but also with an overbearing parental presence that festered into every part of life."

"Like what type of home they can own."

Nora opened her arms to display their lovely, cookie-cutter Victorian that every Margolis family member owned.

"Anyway, when Preston called off his engagement to Stella, it caused quite a stir. When he started bringing Annabelle around, the mood around here turned icy. And when they announced that Annabelle was pregnant with . . . you, well, let's just say the shit hit the fan. Cedar Creek is a small town, and it was even smaller thirty years ago. Preston and Annabelle were in the middle of lots of rumors before they disappeared. And after."

"What kinds of rumors?"

"Oh, the usual kind when something like that happens. When one relationship ends right about the time another begins. Annabelle was a home wrecker. Annabelle was a gold digger. Annabelle got pregnant to trap Preston. Those sorts of things. That poor girl walked straight into the flames of hell when she married into this family, and I felt terrible for her. Other than Preston, I was her only confidant when it came to family happenings. Like I said, that's why she and I became so close so fast."

"And then she disappeared."

Nora offered a sad smile. "And then she disappeared."

There was a pause in the conversation before Sloan continued.

"I've read a lot about my birth parents' disappearance. One of

the things that came up often in the articles was the mention that
Annabelle was a suspect in a hit-and-run investigation."

Nora nodded. "That was another big rumor around here. Still is,
really, because every few years the disappearance gets stirred up
and the town starts talking about it again. I own a photography studio in town. I talk with lots of people and hear all the theories
about Annabelle and Preston disappearing with baby Charlotte.
The biggest of those rumors is the hit-and-run."

"Can you tell me about it?"

"It's been decades, so I don't remember everything perfectly.
But in the summer of '95, just a couple of weeks before you and
your parents went missing, one of Reid Margolis's law partners was
hit and killed out on Highway Sixty-seven. Annabelle's car was
found at the scene, and was determined to be the car that hit the
guy. His name was Baker Jauncey. The sheriff was investigating the
hit-and-run. He questioned Annabelle a few times and rumors flew
through town that she was about to be arrested for manslaughter."

"And then she disappeared?"

"Yep. A picture of the car made it into all the papers, with the
headlight smashed and the front fender dented. One of the rumors, then *and* now, is that Annabelle went on the run to avoid
being arrested for Baker Jauncey's death, and she convinced Preston to go with her. I always doubted that theory, but now I know for
sure it's incorrect."

"How do you know?"

"Because you're sitting in front of me. The FBI told Reid and
Tilly that you were given up for adoption. And although I have no
idea *how* that happened, I know Annabelle and Preston were not
part of it. You were their entire world. They loved you to death and
would never have willingly given you up."

Another lump formed in Sloan's throat, a tumor made of guilt
and angst. In the course of just a couple of weeks, her birth parents
had morphed from mythical figures who crossed her mind only in
fleeting glitches of thought, to people she felt a deep connection
with. Her obligation to them was like a snowball rolling downhill,
picking up speed and girth as it went and becoming a relentless
force that only answers could stop.

"And if the theory about Annabelle and Preston going on the run is wrong," Nora said, "it means what I've feared all along is true."

"What's that?"

"That something very bad happened to them."

CHAPTER 23

Cedar Creek, Nevada
Friday, July 26, 2024

"W ERE THERE EVER ANY SUSPECTS?"

"Oh, sure," Nora said. "But none panned out. With as much news coverage as your disappearance generated, there were never many answers. The Harrison County sheriff who originally investigated the case provided updates every day or two. But once the state police took over, the updates ended."

"Why did the state police take over the case?"

"Probably for many reasons. It was a big case, and the sheriff's department here in Harrison County hadn't handled a lot of missing persons cases. Certainly none that were as high profile as yours. But also because the sheriff died shortly after he started investigating. Got doped up on heroin and drove his car into Cedar Creek."

Sloan remembered Eric Stamos's words.

The man never took a sip of alcohol in his life. I don't believe for a second that he overdosed on heroin.

"After the state police took over, the investigation got very formal and very distant. The town got its updates from the news outlets. I got some tidbits because the state police were speaking with Reid and Tilly, and by default a few details trickled down to me through Ellis."

"Was Stella Connelly ever questioned? Just off the top of my head, the woman had a hell of a motive to cause harm to both Preston and Annabelle."

"Of course, but she was protected by her parents' wealth and their law firm. Stella was never formally considered a suspect or person of interest."

"Did anyone else's name come up as being tied to the case?"

"Depends who you ask. There was a big divide in the town. Half the folks thought Annabelle and Preston went on the run to avoid being charged with Baker Jauncey's death. The other half suspected foul play. On that front, the only other name that came up was Lester Strange."

Sloan narrowed her eyes. In all the research she'd done, she'd never come across the name.

"Who was he?"

"The family's handyman. Back then he was a young guy who was doing work at Preston and Annabelle's house, which was under construction at the time you all disappeared. There were rumors that Lester was infatuated with Annabelle. They went as far as to suggest the two had some sort of torrid affair."

"What happened to this man?"

"Nothing. He was a kid back then—nineteen or twenty. He's fifty or so today and still works for the family. The Margolises are always building something—homes, buildings, fences, you name it. And good ole Lester Strange still runs every project. He also does a lot of work up at the winery, Margolis Manor. It's up in Oregon. We use the main home up there as a getaway sometimes. Lester maintains the property. It's a full-time job."

Sloan made a mental note about Stella Connelly and Lester Strange. Leads she would pursue with Eric Stamos.

"Well, listen," Sloan said, checking her watch. "It's getting late and I don't want to take up any more of your time tonight. And I'm exhausted from travelling all day. Thanks for all the background information on my birth parents, and sorry for asking so many questions."

"Please. It was my pleasure. And I'm so glad you decided to come out to Cedar Creek. Reid and Tilly know that I was meeting with you tonight. They don't want to put any pressure on you, but they wanted me to pass along a message that they'd love to meet you if you're comfortable with that."

"Of course. I'd love to meet them, too."

"Try not to judge them too harshly," Nora said. "I give them a lot of grief, but they're good people. And they're wonderful grand-parents to my children."

Sloan smiled. "I can't wait to meet them."

"Tomorrow? They were hoping."

Sloan nodded. "Sure, that would be great."

"How about this." Nora handed Sloan a business card. "That's my photography studio. It's in the heart of town, in the middle of The Block. Come by tomorrow afternoon. Annabelle was sort of my protégé. She and I bonded over our love of photography. I was teaching her everything I knew. Throughout her pregnancy, she dabbled in photography and took some great photos of you just after you were born. That whole summer, really. I'm sure I still have them somewhere, Annabelle's pictures. If you'd like to see them, I'll dig around my house and look for them. I know we stashed them somewhere."

"I'd love that."

Nora smiled. "I'll look tonight."

She pointed at the business card in Sloan's hand.

"The address of my studio is on the card. One o'clock tomor-row? I'll have Reid and Tilly meet us there."

Sloan smiled. "See you then."

"Sloan," Nora said before she was out the door. "I'm not sure we'll ever know what happened to you and your parents, but I'm sure glad I found you."

Sloan smiled. "Me too."

Sloan waved to Nora Margolis as she backed out of the driveway, and it occurred to her that, without too much effort, she had man-aged to get her foot in the door of the elusive Margolis family. Whether there was anything to find once she was inside was to be determined.

CHAPTER 24

Cedar Creek, Nevada
Saturday, July 27, 2024

THE FOLLOWING MORNING, BEFORE THE SUN WAS UP, SLOAN WENT ON a run and explored the town of Cedar Creek. She'd been at it for forty minutes when the sun crept from under the horizon. She made her way along the running trail that hugged the water, pausing as she crossed the Louis-Bullat Bridge that arced over Cedar Creek. Below her, the water's surface was peaceful and calm as it reflected the cotton-ball clouds bruised lavender by the rising sun. To the south she saw the other two bridges that curved over the creek and connected each half of the town. To the west, the Sierra Nevadas absorbed the glow of the rising sun. From her perched position atop the bridge, the white courthouse was visible in the center of town, and she resumed her jog in that direction.

She worked up a nice sweat and good burn in her lungs and legs as she approached the town center, picking up her pace and taking the two dozen courthouse steps in a staccato of high knee raises that drained the last bit of energy from her quads. When she reached the top, she placed her hands on her head and sucked in the morning air as she slowly walked along the courthouse promenade, which was made up of two giant, rounded doors flanked by four thick pillars on either side.

When she had her breathing under control, she examined a placard near the front door that listed the mayor of Cedar Creek, the district attorney of Harrison County, and several county board members. Of the twelve names, nine were Margolises. It dawned on her, as she stood in front of the courthouse in the center of the town that was owned and operated by the Margolis family, that her sudden reappearance had the potential to turn Cedar Creek upside down.

She took one more look around The Block, then skipped down the stairs and jogged back to her rental home. Showered and dressed an hour later, she drove out of Cedar Creek and into the foothills of the Sierra Nevada Mountains, following the GPS as she navigated to the address Eric Stamos had given her. It took thirty minutes to traverse the serpentine roads and navigate the switchbacks that snaked through the mountains. Eventually Sloan found the wooden bridge that crossed the gully below, the one Eric had told her marked the final leg of the journey to his cabin.

She turned right at the end of the bridge and a quarter mile later found the driveway's entrance. The mailbox was hidden, and the address was poorly marked. She turned and drove through the canopy of trees until she reached the cabin and found Eric sitting in a chair on the front porch. He raised his hand as Sloan parked and climbed out of the car. The A-frame cabin was surrounded on three sides by thick forest and butted up against the gully she had crossed in her rental car. The one-lane, wooden bridge was visible in the distance behind the cabin. It was the very definition of isolated.

"Find it okay?" Eric asked from the porch.

"Just barely. You like living out here so far from civilization?"

"It's my family's cabin. Come on in, I'll show you the place."

Sloan walked up the porch steps.

"Good to see you again," Eric said.

"You, too. And I promise I won't mace you this time."

They both shared a laugh. Eric had fully recovered from the pepper spray incident, and Sloan was able to see both his eyes today—still a light caramel brown that accented his dark olive complexion, evidence of a life spent outdoors. He wore a T-shirt that stretched under the tension of his broad shoulders and revealed the powerful cords in his forearms, suggesting that he found the gym as often as Sloan.

"My grandfather built this place in the fifties," Eric said as Sloan followed him inside. "He used it as a family getaway spot and a hunting cabin. It's only thirty minutes from town but feels like you're in another dimension."

"That's for sure."

"I inherited the place when my grandfather died last year. I've since turned it into ground zero for my research and investigation into what happened to my father."

Sloan followed Eric through the cabin. Everything was bold oak and leather. The ceiling of the A-frame peaked thirty feet above their heads and was lined by broad wooden beams. The dining room table—a heavy slab of polished oak with a long bench on one side and four chairs on the other—was covered with boxes and papers.

"This is everything I've collected on my father's case. It includes everything I could get my hands on pertaining to the disappearance of you and your parents, as well as the old hit-and-run case that was linked to your birth mother."

Sloan approached the table and the stacks of papers it contained.

"This is all from the Sheriff's Office?"

"No. Some was there, and I copied all of it before the FBI showed up to collect it the other day. Some of it came through freedom of information requests. Other parts came from contacts I have at the investigation unit of the Nevada State Police. And a lot of it is stuff my grandfather collected over the years as he searched for answers to what happened to my dad. It's kept me busy since he died. I've gone long stretches where all I do in my free time is work on the case and read through the files. Then, I take breaks and don't look at the stuff for weeks. But since the FBI told me that Charlotte Margolis had resurfaced, I've been neck deep in all of this."

As secretive as Eric had been about tracking Sloan down in Raleigh the week before, it was little wonder why he had turned his family's remote cabin into the hub of his investigation into his father's death.

Sloan checked her watch. "I'm ready to dive in. I've got to be back in town by one this afternoon. I'm meeting the Margolises."

Eric raised his eyebrows. "That was fast."

"I met with Nora Margolis last night. We had a good chat, and I learned some things. I'm meeting Reid and Tilly Margolis today. I don't think it'll be a problem to work my way into the family. Nora is just about the sweetest woman I've ever met, and she tells me Tilly and Reid are anxious to meet me. She also offered some information about my birth parents."

"Oh yeah?" Eric pointed to the table. "Like what?"

Sloan took a seat at the table. Eric sat across from her.

"My father had been engaged when he met my mother, and so there were rumors the summer they disappeared that his jilted ex-fiancée was upset. Naturally, I'm interested in looking into her."

Eric reached for a stack of papers and shuffled through them.

"Stella Connelly. I found something in my father's notes about her. He and his deputies had made some visits to Preston and Annabelle's home on domestic disturbance calls, and each time it was due to Stella Connelly showing up and raising hell."

He found the pages and handed them to Sloan. She read through handwritten incident reports dated the summer of 1995—four in total. Each described a 9-1-1 call made from Preston and Annabelle's home to report that Stella Connelly was trespassing, belligerent, and would not leave the property. Each incident ended with either Sandy Stamos or one of his deputies escorting Stella Connelly off the premises. There was never an arrest, but the final incident on June 30, 1995, was the closest the Harrison County Sheriff's Department came to hauling Stella Connelly to jail. Her father, a prominent Cedar Creek attorney, had been called to the scene to corral his daughter under the threat of arrest if he couldn't calm her down. Preston, Annabelle, and baby Charlotte disappeared four days later on July 4, 1995.

Sloan looked up from the police report. "Nora Margolis said Stella Connelly was never an official suspect in my parents' disappearance." She held up the report. "She'd be the first place I looked."

"She still lives in town. We should find a way to speak with her."

Sloan nodded. "Maybe I'll give her a call and ask to meet under the pretense of learning more about my birth father."

"That's probably the safest angle. What else did Nora Margolis mention?"

"She told me about a handyman who worked for the Margolises that summer. They still employ him, from what Nora said."

"Lester Strange. My dad had a file on him but never made any progress. He'll be tougher to approach because he's tied so closely to the family. But that's where you come in, depending on how deep you get into the Margolis machine."

"Nora said the guy was quasi obsessed with Annabelle that summer. He's worth talking to. Or at least looking into."

"I'll add him to the list. What else?"

"From Nora? Not much, other than that Reid and Tilly Margolis didn't like Annabelle."

"Why was that?"

"She was from the wrong side of the tracks, according to Nora. Her family wasn't wealthy, and Reid Margolis was suspicious that she was trapping Preston to gain access to family money. That she got pregnant with me, out of wedlock, sort of reinforced the theory. Again, all of this is according to Nora Margolis, who was and technically still is an outsider with a bitter taste in her mouth from how Reid and Tilly treated her when she started dating Ellis. I believe everything she told me, but it's only one person's perspective."

Eric nodded. "You mentioned that you met with the FBI."

"Yeah. Before I left Raleigh, I met with the agent who is heading up the investigation."

"And?"

"They cleared my parents, for one. It took three days, but they came to the conclusion that my parents were victims of adoption fraud."

"Adoption fraud?"

"My parents have legit, or what appears to be legit, adoption papers written up by an attorney hired by my supposed birth mother. Only problem is that the lady who claimed to be my mother wasn't Annabelle Margolis."

Eric raised his eyebrows. "Who was she?"

"Wendy Downing. They're trying to track her down, but they don't have much beyond the name, and they're sure it was an alias.

The FBI is working off the theory that I was abducted from my birth parents and sold into the black-market adoption world. The attorney who brokered the deal and created the paperwork was named Guy Menendez."

Eric grabbed a legal pad and scribbled the names.

"My department here has some resources, but we can't match the power of the FBI. We could spend a lot of time on these two and get nowhere. Let's leave Wendy Downing and Guy Menendez to the feds, and you and I will concentrate on leads here in Cedar Creek."

"Agreed. Last night Nora also mentioned the hit-and-run investigation Annabelle was involved in."

"Yeah. I found something strange when I went through the files on that."

Eric fingered through the pages on the table once more until he found the stack he was looking for.

"Look at this."

Sloan took the page. It was letterhead from the chief medical examiner's office in Washoe County.

"Because Baker Jauncey's body had been discovered on a state highway," Eric said, "and since Nevada Highway Patrol was involved, the body was transported to the ME's office in Reno. But after a couple of days it was transferred to Harrison County for the autopsy."

"If the body was taken to Reno out of formality, because Nevada Highway Patrol was involved in the investigation, why transfer it for autopsy two days later to a morgue a hundred miles away?"

"Good question. My first thought was that Baker Jauncey was a partner at the Margolis law firm, and someone wanted the autopsy performed by a doctor they could control. The Harrison County coroner would certainly fit the bill. I haven't been able to find any paperwork on the transfer—why it was made or who requested it."

"Sounds suspicious."

"Par for the course around here. If the Margolises wanted to control the narrative, they'd want their doctor performing the autopsy."

"Control what narrative?" Sloan asked.

"One of their bigwig partners had been killed. They wanted to control how that looked and how it reflected on the family and the law firm. It's just how they do things around here. Bringing the body to Cedar Creek allowed the family to make sure the autopsy said anything the Margolises wanted it to say."

"What did the autopsy say?"

"That Baker Jauncey died from head trauma caused by Annabelle Margolis's car. Cause of death, traumatic brain bleed. Manner of death, involuntary manslaughter."

"If that was concluded by the autopsy, why didn't your father immediately arrest Annabelle?"

"Another good question, and one I have no idea how to answer. But you see now why I think this hit-and-run case is linked to your parents' disappearance?"

Sloan thought for a moment before she spoke.

"But if Preston was worried that Annabelle would be charged with Baker Jauncey's death, he would have used the Margolis family influence to pressure the coroner to find a way to explain Baker's death as something *other* than Annabelle's car having killed him."

"Exactly," Eric said. "That's what I can't figure out. If the Margolises were behind the unauthorized transfer of Baker Jauncey's body so that only their doctor could perform the autopsy and determine the formal cause and manner of death, then why did the autopsy so clearly state that Annabelle Margolis's car killed him? The only answer I can come up with is that someone wanted Annabelle to take the fall for Baker Jauncey's death. And we need to figure out who that was."

Sloan lifted the file from the Harrison County coroner. It contained the formal autopsy report on Baker Jauncey, as well as photos taken during the exam and those shot by scene investigators before the body was transferred to the morgue.

"Let me make a call," Sloan said. "I know someone who could dive into this report and pick it apart to let us know how accurate it is."

"Who?"

"My department chair back in Raleigh. Dr. Livia Cutty."

Eric wrinkled his brow. "Isn't she the lady I see on TV all the time on *American Events?*"

"That's her. She's an expert in forensic pathology and will be able to tell us if anything is off about the postmortem exam."

Eric reached for another file that was mixed in with the stacks on the table.

"Can you have her look at this, too? It's my dad's autopsy report."

A few minutes later Sloan was driving back over the arched wooden bridge that connected Eric's secluded cabin to the rest of the world. On the passenger's seat were the autopsy reports on Baker Jauncey and Sandy Stamos.

CHAPTER 25

Charlotte, North Carolina
Saturday, July 27, 2024

SPECIAL AGENT JOHN MICHAELS SAT AT HIS DESK AT FBI HEADQUARTERS and finished the brief he was writing about the Charlotte Margolis case. His supervisor had asked for a full summary of developments, including Agent Michaels's plan for the first phase of the investigation. Michaels dedicated a good portion of the brief to Wendy Downing and Guy Menendez—the duo whose names were on the adoption paperwork the Hastings had provided.

Michaels spent the week reviewing the original investigation into the missing family, conducted initially by the Harrison County Sheriff's Office and then taken over by the Nevada State Police and detectives from the investigation unit. Eventually, Michaels read, agents from the FBI stationed in Reno had gotten involved. The resurfacing of Charlotte Margolis was the first movement in the case in decades, and the information Dolly and Todd Hastings provided about the adoption was the biggest lead the case had ever seen. The original investigation centered around two theories: The first was that Annabelle Margolis had disappeared with her family to avoid being charged with the hit-and-run death of Baker Jauncey. The second was foul play.

The surfacing of Sloan Hastings, and the new development that baby Charlotte had been adopted by an unsuspecting couple, made the second theory much more likely: Annabelle and Preston Margolis had been killed, and baby Charlotte abducted by a woman

using the name of Wendy Downing and an accomplice going by the
name of Guy Menendez. Michaels was convinced that his best chance
at figuring out what happened to baby Charlotte Margolis and her
parents was to find these two individuals.

He finished the brief and printed it off. He grabbed the pages
from the printer and brought them to his assistant's desk.

"You finished for the day, boss?" Zoë Simpson asked.

"All finished. And thanks again for coming in on a Saturday.
This new case has me swamped, and I appreciate the extra time
you've put in the last couple of weeks."

Zoë Simpson was his new assistant, assigned to him after his
longtime aide retired earlier in the year. Nancy had been with him
long enough to be called a *secretary* when she started, and never
much liked being an *executive assistant*. Michaels loved Nancy and
was still getting used to her replacement.

"It's no problem," Zoë said.

"I'll let you get out of here and enjoy the weekend, but I need
one more thing."

Michaels handed Zoë his brief.

"Would you mind proofing it for me? I'll make corrections on
Monday before I send it off."

Nancy used to read every brief Michaels wrote and was a master
proofreader. Writing had never been his forte, but somehow he
had chosen a profession where nearly every thought that ran
through his mind was required to be summarized in writing. He
felt strange asking this twenty-something-year-old girl to correct his
errors. Nancy was twenty years his senior, and any corrections or
suggestions she made to his briefs came from a place of wisdom
and experience.

"I'll take care of it," Zoë said. "Have a good weekend."

"Thanks," Michaels said. "See you on Monday."

He left FBI headquarters and decided to take Sunday off. His
first day of rest since baby Charlotte Margolis had resurfaced.

Zoë Simpson finished the email she was working on, checked her
watch, and figured she would stay for an extra fifteen minutes to
make sure Agent Michaels was out of the building before she left.

She was supposed to stay at her desk until 5:00 p.m., which she did most days. But when her boss left early, or was called out of headquarters with no chance of returning for the day, she always cut out early. And working Saturdays was a drag. Had she known John Michaels was such a workaholic, she'd have thought twice about taking the job.

She grabbed the three-page brief he'd given her to proof. She thought about stashing it in her drawer until next week, but that would require her to get up earlier on Monday. She decided she'd spend the final fifteen minutes of her Saturday reading it. A few sentences in, she was glad she had. Baby Charlotte Margolis, missing since 1995, had resurfaced, and Agent Michaels was heading up the investigation. Zoë knew the case well. She was a true crime fanatic and had taken a job at FBI headquarters—and endured the long series of rigorous interviews and background checks—specifically for the thrill of being so close to criminal investigations. Now, after three months on the job, she was getting a look at her first salacious case.

Zoë was active on many true crime websites and was a regular listener of the podcast *Unsolved* with Ryder Hillier. Ryder had covered the Westmont Prep killings in Indiana a couple of years earlier, and had since taken on rock star status in the true crime universe. Ryder depended on her listeners to provide clues and tips about the cases she covered on her podcast. Baby Charlotte and the missing Margolis family from 1995 had been featured on *Unsolved*. Ryder Hillier promised to keep the case high in her stack of stuff, and to revisit it for the thirtieth anniversary next year. Ryder had also encouraged her army of loyal listeners to drop her a line if they stumbled over any new leads or tidbits about the case. Zoë had stumbled over more than a tidbit. Baby Charlotte Margolis had resurfaced in Raleigh, and her boss was working the case. It was pure gold.

Not only was Zoë in a position to break a new lead for Ryder Hillier and *Unsolved*, if she played her cards right she could continue to follow the case secretly from behind her desk and without her boss knowing about it. In her excitement, she considered ripping off an email to Ryder Hillier, but reconsidered. The FBI did not tolerate leaks, so she'd have to be careful. She shouldn't use her work computer to reach out to a well-known journalist. She'd wait until she was at home. Or better yet, she'd go to a coffee shop and log in through their free Wi-Fi using a secure VPN. Then, she'd break the story about baby Charlotte's miraculous return.

THE PAST

Cedar Creek, Nevada

Wednesday, June 28, 1995
6 Days Prior . . .

FOUR DAYS AFTER BAKER JAUNCEY'S BODY WAS SNATCHED FROM THE Reno morgue in the dead of night, the *Harrison County Post* ran a story on the death of the prominent attorney. Since Sandy had called in Nevada Highway Patrol, he'd been relegated to the bench like a second-string quarterback on Friday nights. He was still running his end of the investigation from the sheriff's office in Cedar Creek, but ascertaining details about the state's investigation had become increasingly difficult. He had no reliable sources inside the Nevada State Police force, and all the people he knew from the Highway Patrol had gone quiet about the case.

Something odd was happening and Sandy was working hard to figure out what it was. He'd placed several calls to Dr. Rubenstein's office, the coroner in Harrison County, asking for an update and an explanation of his autopsy findings. Sandy wanted to know how the coroner—who was a family doctor by training, but elected coroner of Harrison County by the Margolis political machine—could even perform an autopsy on a body that had already undergone a postmortem exam in Reno. And Sandy was curious to hear how Dr. Rubenstein had come to a conclusion about the cause and manner of death that was in direct contradiction to Rachel Crane's analysis.

None of his calls were being answered, so Sandy had to get his information from the newspaper. He opened the *Post* and read the article:

Hit-and-Run Death Turns Up New Details

CEDAR CREEK—The investigation into the hit-and-run death of Baker Jauncey, a local Cedar Creek resident, has been taken over by the Nevada State Police. Baker Jauncey, a partner at the Margolis & Margolis law firm, was found deceased on Highway 67 in the early morning hours of June 24. Accident investigators from the Nevada Highway Patrol located a car near the scene of the accident that is believed to have struck the victim. The car was registered to Annabelle Margolis, the wife of Preston Margolis, an attorney at Margolis & Margolis, and the daughter-in-law of Reid and Tilly Margolis.

An autopsy performed by Dr. Barry Rubenstein, the Harrison County coroner, confirmed that Baker Jauncey's death was consistent with being struck by a vehicle at high speed.

"We are looking at every and all possibilities in this case," said Nevada State Police Chief Patrick O'Day.

When asked if he had reservations about the case involving the prominent Margolis family, Chief O'Day said, "My office will follow the evidence, wherever it leads. Annabelle Margolis is a person of interest in the investigation, but that's all I'm willing to share at this time."

He folded the paper and picked up his desk phone. Rachel Crane answered on the first ring.

"You see the *Post* this morning?" Sandy asked.

"I did."

"Rubenstein is claiming his autopsy showed that Jauncey's death is consistent with a hit-and-run."

"Which means he's either totally incompetent, which is possible—he's a goddamn family physician who's never trained a day in forensic pathology—or, he's a bold-faced liar."

"I suspect a little of both."

"I reported the transfer to my boss," Dr. Crane said. "He told me the order came from the higher-ups and that I should leave it alone."

"Don't touch it, Doc. This is my fight and I'll take it on. Stay clear of the nonsense up here, you don't need the headache."

"Sorry I wasn't able to keep the cat in the bag, Sandy."

"Not your fault. But now that the feline is loose and roaming, I'm curious what it plans to devour next."

Cedar Creek, Nevada

Wednesday, June 28, 1995
6 Days Prior . . .

M ARVIN MANN HAD BEEN A LEGAL INVESTIGATOR FOR MARGOLIS & Margolis for over a decade. As was the firm's policy, after five years investigators were assigned to one of the partners. Marvin had been assigned to Baker Jauncey, and the two had developed not just a great working relationship, but a friendship as well. There was a socioeconomic gap between the two that could not be denied. Baker Jauncey was a white, fifty-two-year-old partner at one of Nevada's largest personal injury firms and made close to a million dollars a year. Marvin was a black, thirty-four-year-old investigator who cleared $36,000 a year. But as different as they were, his boss gave off a vibe of decorum that drew Marvin in.

Baker Jauncey was not presumptuous or condescending, as Marvin often experienced with other partners at the firm. To the contrary, Baker treated Marvin as an equal, and had never made the man feel inadequate. Baker had invited Marvin and his wife to dinner at his home—a palatial estate in the foothills three times the size of Marvin's house in town. A few weeks later, Marvin returned the invitation. It was nothing fancy—burgers on the grill and beers on the back patio—but they all had a grand time and ended the night playing cards until the early hours.

A friendship had blossomed, and Marvin found that he had never been happier than the years he worked for Baker Jauncey. Margolis & Margolis was a cutthroat environment. Especially before investigators were assigned to partners. Early hires worked for two years as independent contractors and freelance investigators, taking any job Margolis & Margolis dished out and doing anything necessary to stand out and make a name for themselves. For investigators that made it past the two-year initiation, a three-year apprenticeship followed that required junior investigators to work under senior investigators. Those that hung in and made it that far earned the privilege of being assigned as the sole investigator for one of the partners.

Marvin had made the rounds and served his time. But now he was an orphan. Baker Jauncey's death had shaken the staff at Margolis & Margolis. Baker's longtime paralegal had not been back to work since the news broke, and Marvin saw Baker's secretary crying as she packed up her desk after she was assigned to another partner. Marvin sat at his desk—a cubicle on the first floor where investigators spent their time when not out in the field. He wasn't sure what his future at Margolis & Margolis looked like. The death of a partner had never happened before and so there was no precedent for his situation.

Partners had retired, of course, but by that time the attorney had typically slowed down enough that their investigator was reassigned. Marvin suspected a reassignment was in his future. But if, instead, the partners indicated that there was no room for him at Margolis & Margolis, he would not be disappointed. He'd accept his severance package, pack up his pregnant wife, and run far away from Cedar Creek. And he'd take his secrets with him and hope no one ever came looking for him.

Marvin lifted the manila envelope from his desk and held it in his hands. The way he figured things, he had two options. He could burn the envelope and the documents it contained, go to Baker's funeral, and pretend he knew nothing. That was the safest option. The other was to give the documents to the one honest man in town who would do the right thing with them.

Cedar Creek, Nevada

Wednesday, June 28, 1995
6 Days Prior . . .

His YEARS AS AN INVESTIGATOR HAD SHARPENED HIS SURVEILLANCE skills. Although his work frequently sent him out of Harrison County, there had been plenty of times when Marvin Mann had to tail a Cedar Creek resident through town. It took a herculean effort, and some serious skill, to stay anonymous when tailing a subject through a small town. Over the years Marvin had become a master. Although following Sheriff Sandy Stamos out of town and into the foothills was dangerous, it was not difficult. He knew Stamos's family owned a remote cabin out in the mountains. Details about the location, however, had never been made public.

Marvin wasn't going to get to choose where he cornered Sandy Stamos; he only knew it couldn't happen in Cedar Creek. Sheriff Stamos was investigating Baker Jauncey's death, and Marvin was sure there were people keeping close tabs on the sheriff. And calling him was not an option. Marvin had tapped too many phones to believe the sheriff's department was clean. Plus, Marvin couldn't predict how Sandy Stamos would react if he told him what he knew over the phone. The sheriff might show up on Marvin's doorstep asking questions, which would put Marvin in as much danger as Baker Jauncey had been before his death. Speaking to Stamos at his family's remote cabin was his only option.

As the sun set and painted the horizon in a purple glow that backlit the Sierra Nevadas, Marvin saw Sheriff Stamos's headlights come on. Marvin kept his own lights off, stayed at a safe distance, and continued to follow.

Cedar Creek, Nevada

Wednesday, June 28, 1995
6 Days Prior . . .

STAMOS'S CABIN WAS TUCKED INTO A CLEARING IN THE FOOTHILLS ON the far side of a gully, access to which came from a single-lane wooden bridge that jumped the gorge. Marvin kept his headlights off and pulled to the shoulder as he watched Stamos's Suburban cross the bridge. Marvin was frozen with indecision. He wanted to speed across the bridge but feared being spotted now that they were off the highway. He watched the Suburban turn right at the end of the bridge, waited another thirty seconds, and then pulled forward.

Dusk cloaked the sky and as Marvin exited the bridge he saw Stamos's taillights. He stopped in the middle of the road and pulled out a pair of binoculars. The sheriff climbed from his Suburban and walked to a mailbox on the other side of the street. Stamos retrieved the mail, climbed back into his vehicle, and turned into a driveway before disappearing into the foliage that canopied it. Marvin pulled to the shoulder and waited twenty minutes. Then, he crept forward and found the long driveway that led to Stamos's cabin.

Dark now, with only a faint lilac painting the sky, soft amber spilled through the windows of the cabin. Marvin was about to turn into the long driveway when he heard three loud bangs on the trunk of the car. When Marvin looked in the rearview mirror he saw Sandy Stamos pointing his gun through the back window.

The sheriff quickly came around to the driver's side, keeping his gun trained on Marvin.

"Put your hands on the steering wheel!" Stamos yelled.

Marvin did not hesitate. Both hands went to the wheel. The sheriff opened Marvin's door.

"Out," he said. "On your knees."

Marvin followed the directions and climbed from the car, quickly getting to his knees.

"This isn't what you think, Sheriff."

"On your stomach, now!"

Marvin lowered himself onto the pavement. He felt the sheriff quickly place a knee in the middle of his back and then pull his hands behind him. Marvin was in cuffs a moment later.

"Why are you following me?" Stamos asked.

Marvin closed his eyes. Maybe he wasn't as good as he thought.

The sheriff pushed the revolver into the back of his head.

"Why!"

"Because I need to talk with you, and I couldn't chance doing it in Cedar Creek."

"Talk about what?"

"Baker Jauncey. That hit-and-run was no accident."

Cedar Creek, Nevada

Wednesday, June 28, 1995
6 Days Prior . . .

S ANDY STAMOS SAT AT THE KITCHEN TABLE OF HIS FAMILY'S CABIN. Marvin Mann was across from him. Bottles of Sierra Nevada Pale Ale sweated beads of condensation onto the table in front of each of them. Sandy had noticed the tail just north of town and decided he had two options. The first was to try to lose whoever was following him. The second was to lure them out to the cabin where Sandy knew the terrain and would have a tactical advantage. Because he was certain, some way or another, that whoever was following him was involved with the Baker Jauncey case—on which he was stuck in a stalemate with the Nevada state investigators—Sandy decided to bait the tail into the foothills.

When he arrived at the cabin, he turned on the lights, ducked out the back door, and backtracked through the woods—the trails of which Sandy had hiked hundreds of times. He found the car parked on the frontage road just outside his driveway. Now, he sat across the table from the man who was following him.

"Tell me what you know," Sandy said.

"Baker Jauncey's death was not an accident."

Sandy took a sip of beer. "Tell me something I *don't* know."

Marvin's lips separated. "You know he was killed?"

"Yes. But that's about as far as I've gotten."

"Yeah, well, whoever ran him over did it on purpose."

"I take that back," Sandy said. "I know a little more than what the newspapers reported. Baker Jauncey wasn't killed during a hit-and-run accident. Someone cracked him in the head with a baseball bat first. Only *after* he was dead did they run him over with a car."

"What? Everything I've read about the case said he was killed in a hit-and-run."

"Everything you've read is wrong. I met with the medical examiner in Reno and her unofficial opinion is that Baker died from a brain bleed caused by blunt force trauma to the back of the head. All the injuries from being run over by a vehicle happened *after* he was dead."

"Christ on the cross. It's worse than I thought."

"The state boys very much want this to be a simple hit-and-run, nothing more. I can't figure out why that is, which is why you're sitting in my house drinking a beer and not bleeding to death on the street. I'm hoping you can fill in some holes for me."

Marvin shook his head. "Here's what I know. I work for . . . *worked* for Baker Jauncey. He was a partner at Margolis and Margolis. I was his investigator. A few days ago, the night before he died, he told me he'd discovered financial malfeasance at the law firm and was looking into it."

Sandy sat forward in his chair and put his elbows on the table. This was news. "What sort of malfeasance?"

"Someone at the firm was stealing client settlement money—and a shit ton of it."

"How?"

"Skimming it. I don't know exactly how it was being done. Neither did Baker, but he asked me to help him figure it out. The next day he was dead."

A web of thoughts congested Sandy's mind. If someone inside Margolis & Margolis had learned that Baker Jauncey was about to uncover financial fraud at the firm, and killed him before he could do it, how the hell did Annabelle Margolis's car end up on Highway 67?

"Start from the beginning," Sandy said.

"I just did. That's the beginning, the middle, and the end. That's all I know."

"What did Baker do about it?"

"Took a deep dive into the financials at the firm. He was a partner, so he had access. Once he sniffed out the con and found the paper trail, he started collecting evidence. Printed out every sordid detail of the fraud and created one big-ass file. Problem was, Baker couldn't figure out which attorney or attorneys were involved, or how, exactly, they were doing it. He could tell there was money missing, but couldn't figure out how it was stolen or who was behind the theft. There were shell companies and shadow entities and numbered bank accounts, but no names attached to the fraud. At least not that he could find. So he asked me for help. He wanted to put my investigative skills to work and asked me to find proof that one or more of the firm's attorneys were living beyond their means. He had the dollar amounts that were stolen. It was my job to figure out where that money went and what it had been spent on. I was supposed to look into the private lives of every attorney at the firm, starting with the partners, and look for anyone who had purchased boats, second homes, elaborate vacations. If I could spot someone living exorbitantly, Baker would add it to the evidence he'd already collected, backtrack through the firm's files, and see if he could pin down who, exactly, was skimming the money."

"What did you find?"

"Nothing. I never got the chance to look. Baker told me what he needed one day, and was dead the next. That's why I'm here, Sheriff. Baker gave me all the paper evidence he'd extracted from the firm and told me to keep it in a safe place. He was dead the next day, and I was left with the evidence that killed him."

"Damn."

"See why I didn't want to talk with you in town?"

Sandy cocked his head. "Now I feel like crap for putting a gun to your head."

"Hell, I'd have done the same thing if someone followed me to my home."

"Do you have the files Baker gave you?"

"In my car."

"Have you looked at them?"

"Yeah, but I'm a legal investigator not a forensic accountant. I can't make heads or tails out of any of it. But if the right people look at the files, they'd be able to figure out who was skimming the money. And whoever was stealing the money killed Baker and made it look like a hit-and-run."

"And you're willing to hand the files over to me?"

"Sheriff, I can't wait to get rid of them."

Cedar Creek, Nevada

Thursday, June 29, 1995
5 Days Prior . . .

SANDY SPENT ALL NIGHT MAKING A LIST OF EVERY ATTORNEY THAT worked at Margolis & Margolis. Reid Margolis, along with his brother Jameson, were the senior partners. There were twenty-two other partners now that Baker Jauncey was dead, and nearly one hundred associates. Attempting to pick through the files Marvin Mann had delivered to determine who was involved was a monumental task.

Sandy clipped the list of names to the papers Marvin Mann had delivered to him the night before. Someone on the list, Sandy believed, had killed Baker Jauncey. He needed help figuring out who it was and didn't dare ask anyone inside the Nevada State Police for assistance. He was hesitant to mention the lead to anyone in his own department for fear that somehow it would leak to a Margolis family member. His plan was to stash the files in a safe place until he could recruit some trusted help. He had an old college friend who had worked for the IRS for twenty years before moving to the private sector. Now he managed other people's money and was a financial genius. If anyone could decipher the pages of evidence Baker Jauncey had extracted from Margolis & Margolis, it was his friend.

Sandy pulled up to the Reno National Bank at just past nine in the morning. He parked the car and turned to Marvin Mann, who sat in the passenger seat.

"Ready?"

Marvin nodded. "The sooner I get these files off my hands, the safer I'll feel."

They walked into the bank and told the receptionist they wanted to open a safe deposit box. She guided them to the elevators where they descended into the basement level and filled out paperwork. For safety, Sandy asked that Marvin be the primary name on the safe deposit box and for Sandy to be added as the only other person granted access.

A polite woman collected the paperwork and distributed two keys before showing them into the vault where the boxes were located. Theirs was number 311. The bank employee inserted her master key into the top slot, and Sandy inserted his personal key into the lower one. Once the box slid out of place, the bank employee smiled and left them alone in the vault. Marvin Mann took the files and placed them in the box. A few minutes later, they were headed back to Cedar Creek.

PART III

Reunion

CHAPTER 26

Cedar Creek, Nevada
Saturday, July 27, 2024

S LOAN MADE IT DOWN FROM THE FOOTHILLS, WHERE SHE HAD SPENT thE morning combing through the files Eric had obtained on his father's death, the hit-and-run accident that killed Baker Jauncey, and the disappearance of baby Charlotte and her birth parents. She was due to meet Nora at her studio at one o'clock, and had thirty minutes to freshen up. She pulled across the Louis-Bullat Bridge, found her quiet cul-de-sac, and parked in the driveway. The autopsy reports for Baker Jauncey and Sandy Stamos were on the passenger seat. She grabbed them and hurried inside.

She popped open a Diet Dr. Pepper, pulled out her phone, and sent a text message.

Hi Dr. Cutty,

Would you have time to review a couple of autopsy reports for me? They have to do with my research into forensic genealogy. Let me know. Thanks!

Sloan took ten minutes to run a brush through her hair and touch up her makeup. As she applied a fresh coat of lipstick she noticed the tremor in her hand. She had no idea what was waiting for her at Nora's studio in Reid and Tilly Margolis, but she'd travelled all the way across the country to find out. She finished her Dr. Pepper on her way into town, found Nora Margolis Photography on the corner, and parked.

A quick glance into the rearview mirror was meant to settle her nerves. She'd spent twenty-nine years as Sloan Hastings, never once thinking of herself any other way. Yet now, in just the last couple of weeks, her identity had morphed. She'd become a part—small or large, she wasn't sure—of another family. Acceptance was not what she was after. She was looking for answers. But some part of her understood that to the grandparents she was about to meet, Sloan was something more than a stranger. They had once known her, if for just a short moment in time, as Charlotte Margolis. They had held her and fed her, and then that child was gone. Now, nearly three decades later, she was returning as someone else. For as nervous as Sloan felt, she could only imagine what Tilly and Reid Margolis were going through. She decided answers could wait. This afternoon she'd simply be present.

She finally stood from her car and walked to the front of Nora's studio. As soon as she opened the door, a crowd of people yelled "Surprise!"

Sloan froze in the doorway. In front of her were fifty strangers, all smiling and cheering. Nora emerged from the crowd and embraced Sloan in a hug.

"Not my idea," Nora whispered into her ear. "But Tilly and Reid were just too excited. They invited the whole family. I've got a bottle of rosé chilling for after this is over."

"God bless you. Stay close."

"I won't leave your side."

Nora disengaged from her hug and took Sloan's hand as the room quieted. Sloan felt every set of eyes fall onto her.

"Everyone," Nora said loud enough to be heard over the whispers that filled the studio. "This is Sloan. Sloan, this is the Margolis family."

"*Your* family," a woman yelled from the back of the studio.

"Hear, hear!" a man yelled, and the family cheered again.

That same man walked from the crowd with a woman by his side. Sloan knew without introduction that she was looking at Reid and Tilly Margolis. She was not sure what she had expected her biological grandparents to look like, but the couple in front of her was not it. Sloan had done the math and knew Reid and Tilly were in their eighties, but money, privilege, and what appeared to be a hell of a lot of Botox, kept them looking younger. Reid Margolis wore a crisp, white button-down under a navy sport coat. Tall with broad shoulders, his hair was snow white and contrasted against his tanned skin. Khaki pants and docksiders gave the appearance of a man who had just stepped off a yacht in the Caribbean.

Tilly was slighter in stature and sweeter in presence. Less intimidating, for certain. Tall and thin, she, too, sported a head of white hair perfectly styled in a pixie cut. Her lips were plumped by filler and her face tight but softening from a long-ago lift. Despite the surgical augmentations, there was something sincere about the woman's presence. Unlike her husband's smile, which was plastic-banana fake and the same one he'd likely plastered across his face during countless business deals over the years, Tilly's was kind and genuine.

Tilly approached and, without hesitation, lifted a hand to Sloan's cheek.

"My sweet Charlotte," Tilly managed before her eyes filled with tears.

Caught off guard by both the outpouring of emotion, and from being called Charlotte, Sloan took Tilly's hand, feeling the soft redundancy of skin that betrayed the woman's true age, and hugged her.

"Don't cry," Sloan said. "Because I'll cry if you cry."

The embrace lasted a full minute as the family applauded the reunion. Tilly finally relinquished her grip and looked from Sloan to her husband.

"Her eyes, Reid. I see him in her eyes."

"It's crazy, isn't it?" Nora said. "That's the first thing I noticed. You have Preston's eyes."

"And Annabelle's smile," Reid said. "It's beautiful."

Sloan shrugged. "I've only seen pictures from the tabloids."

"We're going to fix that," Nora said. "My husband dug Annabelle's photos out of the attic. I'll show them to you. They're much better than the stock photos the media used."

"I'd love that."

"I suppose introductions are not necessary. But Sloan, this is Tilly and Reid Margolis."

"Hi," Sloan said.

"I just can't believe it," Tilly said, still staring into the eyes Sloan knew reminded her of her son.

"I'd love to tell you everything," Sloan said. "How I found you and how Nora helped and, well, you know, the whole story."

"We'd love that," Reid said. "We're so very curious, as you can imagine."

There was an awkward pause as Sloan looked at Tilly and Reid. Behind them she sensed the rest of the family staring.

"Okay," Nora said to the room. "Let's not gawk at the poor woman like she's on display at a museum. I'll introduce Sloan to each of you. Remember, you all know each other and for the last few days you've all known about Sloan. Sloan, however, knows no one. So let's not make this more overwhelming for her than it already is."

For the first time, Sloan noticed the nametags—sticky white squares scrawled with blue Sharpie ink and attached to everyone's chest.

"Let me bring Sloan around to everyone," Nora said to Tilly and Reid. "Then we'll circle back so you all can chat."

Tilly reached out again and placed her hand on Sloan's cheek.

"She's not going anywhere, Tilly."

Sloan smiled and allowed Nora to whisk her away. For a hectic two hours she met the Margolis family—aunts and uncles, cousins and second cousins. Each of them playing some role in the family empire, whether it be the real estate holdings, the timber company, or the law firm aptly titled Margolis & Margolis. Sloan heard, as the parade of people came to speak with her, every family member's memory of Preston and Annabelle—from short quips to long stories. About Sloan, too, as an infant, and what they recalled about her short two months in Cedar Creek before the family up and vanished.

Food had been catered, and they ate lunch at tables that had been erected around Nora's studio as if they were all at a baby shower. By three o'clock the crowd began to thin. By four o'clock the studio was empty but for Sloan and Nora sitting with Reid and Tilly.

Sloan retold the story of the last month of her life, from first submitting her DNA to the online website, to discovering she was Charlotte Margolis, to learning that her birth parents were still missing, to the FBI questioning her adoptive parents, and finally to Nora reaching out and inviting her to Cedar Creek. Left unmentioned was the part about Eric Stamos tracking her down in Raleigh and convincing her that wriggling into the Margolis family was the only way for Sloan to figure out what happened to her and her birth parents nearly thirty years ago.

Tilly asked a hundred questions. Reid listened but added little to the conversation. Instead, he sat back and observed, guiding Tilly's inquiries every now and then as if he were her attorney at a deposition, present only to make sure she didn't say the wrong thing. The man's unrelenting stare set Sloan on edge, and only when Nora's husband arrived did Reid Margolis loosen up.

"Finally," Nora said when her husband walked into the studio.

"The boy will be late to his own funeral," Reid said.

Ellis Margolis walked into the studio pulling a dolly on which several cardboard cartons were stacked.

"Sorry I'm so late. I got caught at the office, and then Nora asked me to dig through our attic for these old photos."

Sloan stood up and Nora immediately took her hand. "Honey, this is Sloan. Sloan, this is my husband, Ellis."

"Nice to meet you," Sloan said.

Ellis, like nearly every other Margolis Sloan had met that day, looked at her with a quizzical expression. He put a hand to his mouth and fought back his emotions.

"Damn." Ellis offered an awkward smile. "You look like Preston."

"So I've heard."

"Sloan just made it through two hours of folks gawking at her," Nora said. "Are you going to do the same?"

Ellis laughed. "Sorry. I'm sure it was overwhelming."

"No, it was . . . special. I can't remember everyone's name, but I was touched they all came to meet me."

"You know, I've given Nora a hard time about the genealogy stuff over the years. How many great-great-great uncles and their farmland do I need to hear about? But I guess the joke was on me, because she's the one who made this possible."

Sloan smiled at Nora. "She did, indeed."

Nora pointed to the boxes stacked on the dolly. "You found them?"

Ellis shrugged. "I think. I didn't go through every box, but the couple I looked at had the pictures."

Nora turned to Sloan. "Annabelle's pictures."

"Here," Ellis said. "Look at these."

He opened the lid from the top box and pulled out an envelope filled with photos.

"This first box has a bunch of Preston. Look."

Ellis pulled out a photo and handed it to Sloan.

"Look at my brother's eyes."

Sloan took the photo. She saw it now as she looked at Preston Margolis. Her birth father's eyes were haunting as they stared back from the photo, as if Sloan's eyes had been Photoshopped into the image. They spent an hour perusing through the first box and passing photos back and forth, reminiscing about the images they found. Sloan listened to stories about Preston and Annabelle.

Finally, Ellis looked at his watch. "It's just past six. Why don't we go for a sail? It's a gorgeous evening."

"Yeah," Nora said, collecting the photos and returning them to the box. "I think Sloan needs a break." She looked at Sloan. "Are you up for a little cruise on our boat? We can look through the rest of Annabelle's photos tomorrow."

"We'll show you the town from the creek," Tilly said. "It's the best way to see it, and Ellis is a wonderful tour guide."

"I'll bring that bottle of rosé," Nora said.

Sloan smiled. "I'd love that."

CHAPTER 27

Indianapolis, Indiana
Sunday, July 28, 2024

RYDER HILLIER SAT IN THE TERMINAL OF THE INDIANAPOLIS INTER-national Airport. She was the host of *Unsolved*, the most popular true crime podcast in the country. She dropped one new episode each week that was downloaded millions of times and listened to by hoards of adoring fans. Ryder mostly covered obscure cold cases whose victims her listeners had never before heard of. But she occasionally tackled well-known stories like the JonBenét Ramsey murder and the tragic death of Julian Crist, the American medical student who fell to his death under suspicious circumstances in St. Lucia. Her biggest story to date had been breaking, covering, and then playing a crucial role in solving the Westmont Prep killings in 2020. The murder of two prep school students in Peppermill, Indiana, had taken the country by storm. The solving of the case, due to evidence Ryder uncovered through her podcast, captivated the nation and made Ryder Hillier a household name. Soon after, and riding a once-in-a-lifetime wave of popularity, Ryder signed a lucrative deal with the world's biggest streaming service for the exclusive rights to *Unsolved*. Since then, she'd become one of the biggest podcasters in the country, and *Unsolved* showed no sign of slowing down.

Along with the big contract came a big promise: Ryder would deliver edge-of-your-seat content and would continue to solve unsolvable cases. She'd come a long way since writing puff pieces for the

Indianapolis Star. But her success did not come without effort. She poured her heart and soul into her work, which was why she was sitting in an airport terminal on a Sunday, working on no sleep, and on her umpteenth Red Bull.

What made *Unsolved* so wildly popular, and a big part of its allure, was that Ryder enlisted the help of her listeners to solve the cold cases she featured on the podcast. She recruited her army of fans, termed *Unsolved* Junkies, to help her find answers to crimes that had long been written off by police and detectives. She relied on her audience of armchair detectives to provide tips about unsolved cases, and one hell of a tip had come in the previous afternoon. A woman named Zoë Simpson had slipped into her DMs to tell a fantastic story about the missing Margolis family from the '90s. So fantastic, in fact, that Ryder hadn't believed it. But thirty-six hours of fact-checking changed her mind.

Zoë Simpson *did* work for the FBI field office in Charlotte, North Carolina. And Special Agent John Michaels *was*, in fact, her boss. Ryder had confirmed these details, and more, about Zoë Simpson, and then closely read the FBI brief the girl had sent her. If it was true—and so far, despite Ryder's best efforts to prove otherwise, it appeared to be—baby Charlotte Margolis, who up and vanished with her parents nearly thirty years ago and set off one of the biggest media storms in history, had resurfaced in Raleigh as a woman named Sloan Hastings.

Ryder received her contract, and the millions of dollars that came with it, because she promised to break huge stories like this one. But a story this big would not stay quiet for long, and Ryder was determined to be the journalist who broke it. She was headed to Raleigh to find Sloan Hastings, aka baby Charlotte, and convince her to appear on the podcast.

An airline employee's voice came over the gate's speakers. First-class passengers were invited to board. Ryder stood from her seat and walked toward the jetway, prepared to break the biggest story of her career.

CHAPTER 28

Cedar Creek, Nevada
Sunday, July 28, 2024

ON SUNDAY MORNING SLOAN HEADED BACK TO NORA'S PHOTOGRAPHY studio. Despite the overwhelming reception she had received the day before, and the emotions it brought up, she had managed to refocus her energy once she arrived back to her rental house. Working from the list she and Eric had made, Sloan did an online search for Stella Connelly, Preston Margolis's previous fiancée, and found on the woman's law firm's website a message to clients that Stella had recently taken a leave of absence. A list of other attorneys who were taking over her active cases was offered. Sloan had managed to find Stella Connelly's cell phone number, but when she called it went straight to voicemail. The timing was strange and Sloan planned to speak with Eric about it next time they met.

She stopped at a coffeehouse in town and purchased two Americanos and a bag of bagels. As she approached Nora's studio her mind flashed back to the previous afternoon when she'd opened the door to a chorus of cheers from the Margolis family. Sloan was relieved this morning to see the studio empty but for Nora leaning against the counter and scrolling through her phone.

"I grabbed coffee and bagels," Sloan said when she walked in.

Nora looked up from her phone. "Ah, you're a godsend. Let's sit."

Nora pointed to a table in the corner of the studio where the cardboard boxes were stacked. Nora had unloaded them from the dolly Ellis had wheeled in the previous afternoon.

"I'm excited to look through the rest of the photos," Nora said. "I haven't been through these boxes since that summer."

"All the photos were taken by Annabelle?"

"Yes."

"The summer . . ."

"She disappeared, yes."

They sat at the table and forgot about the bagels.

"I told you Annabelle and I became good friends in the short time we knew each other. And that she became fascinated with photography."

Nora pulled the top off the first box.

"Back then, when I met Annabelle, I had just started my photography business and was trying to make a name for myself."

Sloan looked around the massive studio that appeared to have every modern photography gadget that existed.

"I'd say you've done pretty well."

"Thanks. But it took years. And much to the chagrin of Tilly and Reid, I never allowed Ellis to bankroll my business. Everything you see is mine, built organically from the ground up."

"After I got home last night from our sail, I looked you up and did some stalking. You're pretty much the only gig in town. If people want photos or portraits, they call Nora Margolis Photography."

"I love the people of this town, the families. I've taken photos of some of my clients' kids when they were born, when they graduated high school and college, when they got married, and then when those kids had kids of their own."

"It must be special to be a part of their lives like that."

"It's my passion."

Nora placed the lid to the side and pulled the box to the middle of the table.

"I thought you'd like to see these, because in just the few months that Annabelle and I were friends, photography became her passion as well. She was eager for me to teach her everything about the craft. Not for professional purposes. Annabelle was never interested in the business of photography, only the art. And she was good."

Nora lifted an envelope of pictures from the box and handed it to Sloan. The envelope was thick with glossy 4X6s.

"I gave her one of my cameras as a birthday gift that summer, and she took hundreds of photos with it. Pictures of the town. Pictures of the creek. Pictures of sailboats. Pictures of her and Preston. Pictures of their home being built. And, of course, pictures of you."

Sloan smiled and felt that same lump forming in her throat at the thought of her birth mother snapping photos of her as an infant.

"You're obviously too young, but back in the nineties photography started making the transition from film to digital. But the early digital cameras were expensive, and the switch was slow. In '95 I was still doing most everything on thirty-five-millimeter film. Are you familiar?"

"With film photography? Not really. I'm an iPhone kid."

Nora smiled. "Back in the day, a roll of film had twenty-four exposures, sometimes more depending on the make and model of the camera and film. There were no smartphones back then. The world didn't walk around with a camera in their pocket prepared to photograph every event of every day. Back then, you'd use an actual camera, take a bunch of shots, and hope you captured something interesting."

"Hope?"

Nora smiled. "God, you *are* young. Yes, *hope*. You wouldn't know if you got a good picture until you developed the film, which was what Annabelle loved most about the process. The darkroom."

"The darkroom? Where you develop photos?"

"Yes. Where negatives on a roll of film are turned into the glossy pictures you're holding. The film can't be exposed to ambient light, or the images it holds will be ruined. So you have to go into a 'dark room,'" Nora said, using air quotes, "to develop them. All the pictures you're holding now, and all the ones filling these boxes, were developed in a darkroom. *My* darkroom, actually, right here in the studio."

Nora pointed behind her.

"I still use it every now and then, mostly for nostalgia. I enjoy the process. But Annabelle adored it and couldn't get enough."

"Explain it to me."

Nora smiled, and as she explained the nuances of photography, Sloan got the impression that she missed her old friend.

"You take a photo today with your phone's camera and get instant feedback. You can tell immediately whether the picture is good or bad. Same thing with modern digital cameras. They have a display screen that will show the photographer if the image is clear or blurry, overexposed or just right, and a hundred other factors that enable the user to decide to save or delete the photo. But back in the day you had to press and pray. You'd look through the viewfinder of the camera, frame the image, press the shutter button, and pray everything turned out perfectly. You wouldn't know, however, until the film was developed. Most folks used to drop their film off at photo studios or drugstores to be developed. A few days later, their pictures came back, and they'd shuffle through an envelope just like the one you're holding to see how their photos turned out."

"Sounds archaic."

"Compared to today's technology, it was. But it was also thrilling. For the general consumer, it was exciting to get photos back and see how they turned out. For me, and for Annabelle when she went into the darkroom, it was an obsession. In the darkroom, the images captured on film were projected onto photo paper and only became visible when the paper was submerged in a bath of chemicals. Then, the image slowly came to life, gradually appearing like a living, breathing thing being born. And when the photo was of something special or magnificent, the process was electrifying. Like I said, Annabelle had a passion for the darkroom."

Nora smiled and shook her head.

"Will you listen to me? I'm boring you to death."

"Not at all," Sloan said. "I'm intrigued to hear what my birth mother was so passionate about."

Nora raised her eyebrows.

"I could show you, if you're interested."

"How to develop film?"

Nora nodded. "Yes. In the darkroom."

"I'd love that."

"Hold on," Nora said.

She hurried over to the counter and grabbed a camera.

"Stand up," Nora said as she walked back to Sloan.

Sloan stood and Nora peered through the viewfinder of the camera and pointed it at Sloan.

"Smile."

Sloan offered the camera a huge grin and heard the shutter rattle as Nora snapped a photo.

"Come on," Nora said. "I'll show you how we used to do it."

CHAPTER 29

Raleigh, North Carolina
Sunday, July 28, 2024

RYDER HILLIER DROVE THE RENTAL CAR OUT OF THE RALEIGH
International Airport. She'd done her research, tapped her sources,
and had the address to Sloan Hastings's apartment on her GPS. A
twenty-minute drive led her to the tree-lined street and into the
parking lot of the three-story complex. She took a minute to get
herself settled by attaching the microphone to her collar and setting up the video display on her smartphone before she exited the
vehicle and climbed the stairs to Sloan Hastings's apartment.

After three rounds of knocking, Ryder cupped her hands and
peered through the window next to the door. The blinds were
open, and she could see into the small apartment. The lights were
off with no activity inside. She headed back to her car to wait. As
the hours passed without a baby Charlotte sighting, Ryder knew
she needed to move to Plan B.

CHAPTER 30

Cedar Creek, Nevada
Sunday, July 28, 2024

A RED LIGHT AT THE CORNER OF THE WORKSTATION CAST THE DARK-room into a shade of crimson.

"Ambient light will ruin the photo paper and destroy the images captured on the film," Nora said. "Red light is safe, so that's what we work by in here."

Sloan stood next to Nora. In front of them was a long work-bench stacked with photography and developing equipment.

"This is the enlarger," Nora said, adjusting the machine in front of her. "The film from the camera gets fed into the negative carrier here."

Sloan watched as Nora placed the roll of film into the machine.

"Then, the enlarger projects the image captured on the film onto a piece of photo paper that we place here."

Nora secured a sheet of glossy photo paper into the easel below the enlarger, then used the focusing scope to check the sharpness of the projected image.

"After the image goes through several seconds of exposure, which invisibly imprints it onto the photo paper, we move the paper through a series of chemicals."

The exposure process took nearly a minute before Nora unfas-tened the still blank piece of photo paper from the easel and used a pair of tongs to submerge it into a tray of liquid.

"This first tray is developing solution. We leave it here for about sixty seconds."

Sloan moved closer and watched over Nora's shoulder.

"Then," Nora said, using a different set of tongs, "we move it to the stop bath. It stays here for just a few seconds before we transfer it to the final tray here, the fixer."

"I still don't see anything," Sloan said as she stared at the photo paper that rested below the surface of the liquid.

"It takes a couple minutes. Keep looking."

Eventually, after three minutes in the tray, an image began to take shape on the paper. Faint at first, and then more vivid, Sloan watched the image of herself smiling into the camera come to life, slowly developing into a vibrant photo.

Nora used the tongs to remove the photo, which she clipped to a clothesline to dry. As the photo dripped, Sloan's face came fully into focus.

"There you have it. Nice picture of a beautiful young woman. It takes a long time, and it's a lot of work compared to today's world of instant gratification."

"Yeah," Sloan said. "But I can see why you love it so much. I knew what was on the film, and I was still excited to see how it turned out."

Nora smiled. Her face glowed in the red light of the darkroom.

"Your mom loved it, too."

Back in the studio, Sloan and Nora made it through the first box. They spent the morning poring through the photos Annabelle had taken the summer she disappeared. Nora gave a tutorial of every part of town captured in the pictures, and explained the techniques Annabelle had used so expertly. Annabelle was, Nora told her, becoming quite a photographer. After a couple of hours they decided to save the other two boxes for next time.

"This has really been a special morning for me," Sloan said. "Thanks for showing me Annabelle's photos. In some small way, I feel like these pictures have helped me connect with my birth mother."

Nora smiled. "And there're still two more boxes. We can go through them this week."

"I can't wait."

"I'm busy the next couple of days with photo shoots, but then I'm wide open."

"Tilly and Reid wanted to see me again this week. I'll call you Wednesday or Thursday?"

"Perfect."

A minute later Sloan sat in her rental car. Before she pulled away from the studio, she took out her phone and found *Nora Margolis* in her contacts. She clicked the edit button and changed the information to read *Aunt Nora*.

CHAPTER 31

Raleigh, North Carolina
Monday, July 29, 2024

RYDER HILLIER'S REPUTATION AS A TRUE CRIME REPORTER AND breaking-news podcaster had been partially built on her ability to give her fans new details about some of the country's coldest cases. But Ryder Hillier did not just *break* news. She found answers. And soon, after she broke the baby Charlotte Margolis story wide open, the mainstream media outlets would jump on the bandwagon and Ryder would be up against the bigwigs like Dante Campbell and Avery Mason and the lot of network reporters who had unlimited budgets and massive teams to chase the story. Ryder had spent the night in her car in the parking lot of Sloan's apartment complex. The apartment had stayed dark all night. If Ryder wanted to find Sloan Hastings, she needed to get creative.

In a strange twist to the story, Ryder had learned that Sloan Hastings was studying under Dr. Livia Cutty, who was a medical consultant for NBC, HAP News, and a number of other networks, which meant those outlets would have an inside scoop that Ryder did not. The pressure was on. Getting the first interview with Sloan Hastings, even if it was just an ambush video on her cell phone, would be huge for *Unsolved* and would generate millions of views on her YouTube channel. If Ryder could capture the first baby Charlotte sighting, it would have her ravenous audience salivating. The stakes were high to make something happen, and make it happen soon, which was what brought Ryder to Hastings Family Dental & Orthodontics Center under the ruse of a molar gone rotten.

She lay in the chair now with a bright light in her eyes and her mouth wide open as Dr. Dolly Hastings examined Ryder's upper right molar #2.

"Turn toward me please," Dr. Hastings said, her voice muffled by a surgical mask as she examined Ryder's teeth through loupes. "Your X-rays are clear, and the tooth is in good shape. I don't see a cavity, recession, or foreign body. No abscess either."

Dr. Hastings pushed away from the chair, placed the mirror and probe onto the tray, and removed her loupes. Dr. Hastings stepped on a foot pedal and raised the chair upright as Ryder rinsed her mouth.

"The pain is not coming from your tooth. It may be a sinus issue, and if it doesn't clear with antihistamines and decongestants, then you'll need a CT scan to more closely look at the maxillary sinus."

"I can do that," Ryder said. "I'll get a hold of my primary care doctor if I'm still feeling the pain in a few days."

"I'm happy to send a report if your doctor needs it."

"Thanks."

As Dr. Hastings was readying to leave, Ryder handed over her *Unsolved* podcast card.

"Dr. Hastings, one more thing. I'm the host of a true crime podcast, and I'd like to make you an offer."

Ryder saw the confusion on Dr. Hastings's face and knew she only had a few seconds to make her pitch.

"I'm sure you know that your daughter's story is about to go mainstream. When it does, reporters will approach you from all the major networks. I'd like to offer you an opportunity to bypass all the nonsense that's coming. I'd like to interview you on my podcast. The interview will be free from all the fluff and hype the major networks will attempt to place around you, your husband, and Sloan. This will be a sit-down interview where you can tell your story without corporate influence and without the mainstream media shaping the narrative."

"I'm not interested," Dr. Hastings said, handing Ryder's card back to her.

Ryder refused to take the card back.

"I understand if you're not ready to give an interview," Ryder said in a hurried voice, "but I'd love to speak with Sloan and give her the chance to tell her story. Again, once the story breaks, the mainstream media will put tons of pressure on her to secure the first interview. I'm here to help, Dr. Hastings. I'm here to take the pressure off your family. If you can tell me where Sloan is, or put me in touch with her, I promise that I'll be able to get the hardcore reporters off your case by coming out wide with Sloan's first interview on my podcast."

Dr. Hastings put Ryder's business card on the armrest of the dental chair. "I think it's best if you left my office."

"Sloan can either tell her story in her own words, or she can allow the media to tell it for her. One will be accurate. The other will be filled with rumors and salacious details. Your daughter is in the unique position to decide which way she wants things to go. And trust me, you won't get the same offer from the big networks. They'll shape the narrative to whatever brings them more viewers and more advertisers, and if that narrative is that you and your husband played some nefarious role in Sloan's disappearance, they'll run with it."

When Dr. Hastings didn't leave, Ryder knew she was getting to her.

"My number is on the card. It's my cell, not my assistant's and not my executive producer's—mine. Tell Sloan to call me. I'll talk with her directly and make sure she tells the story she wants told, and nothing else."

"My staff will check you out," Dr. Hastings said as she stood and walked out of the exam room.

Ryder noticed that she had taken the business card off the armrest before she left.

CHAPTER 32

Raleigh, North Carolina
Tuesday, July 30, 2024

RYDER HILLIER HAD SPENT MONDAY NIGHT PARKED AGAIN OUTSIDE Sloan's apartment. The apartment stayed dark through the evening and night, and Ryder knew the woman was not staying there. Now she was at the Raleigh Medical Examiner's Office with a different plan. Ryder's research told her that Sloan was assigned to a second-year fellow named Hayden Cox. She pulled a photo of Dr. Cox from the OCME website and was staring at the man as he walked from the building and toward his car. Ryder hustled across the parking lot.

"Dr. Cox?"

Hayden Cox paused as he was opening his car door. He looked at Ryder with a curious expression.

"Yes?"

"Hi. I'm friends with Sloan Hastings and in from out of town. I was hoping to see her before I left, but I can't seem to find her."

Dr. Cox smiled but kept the curious look on his face—or was it suspicious? The squinted eyes and half smile made it hard to tell.

"Why don't you call her?"

Ryder smiled. "I'm trying to surprise her. We went to college together."

"At Chapel Hill?"

Sloan Hastings had gone to Duke. Dr. Cox was testing her.

"Sloan said you were her second-year fellow. That she was studying under you."

"She is."

"So why don't you know what college she went to?" Ryder offered a faux nervous laugh.

Dr. Cox shook his head.

"Sorry, I got mixed up for a second," he said. "Duke. Of course. Uh, Sloan had to go out of town. I know this because last week she crammed all her scrub-ins into one week so she could be away for a while."

"Scrub-ins?"

"When she assists me with an autopsy. She's required to scrub in on a certain amount of cases each month. She did them all in a week because something came up and she had to go out of town, wasn't sure when she'd be back. I didn't get the whole story."

"Dang. I really wanted to see her. Well, I guess I'll call her now and tell her I missed her. Thanks."

"Sure thing."

Dr. Cox climbed into his car and Ryder watched him drive off. She wasted no time. Sloan Hastings wasn't staying at her parents' house or anywhere else in Raleigh. As soon as Ryder sat in her rental car, she pulled up the American Airlines app and booked a ticket to Reno for the next day. According to the app she consulted, Cedar Creek, Nevada, was an hour and a half north of Reno International Airport.

Late Tuesday night, Ryder Hillier sat in her hotel room and stared at the video camera set on a tripod. She was headed to Cedar Creek the next morning under the strong suspicion that Sloan Hastings had gone there to reunite with the Margolis family. She couldn't be certain, however, but was desperate to beat the networks to the story. To make sure it happened, it was time to enlist the help of her millions of listeners and recruit them in her search for baby Charlotte.

She picked up the remote, pressed RECORD, and spoke into the camera.

"Good evening *Unsolved* Junkies. This is Ryder Hillier coming to you from a hotel room in Raleigh, North Carolina, with breaking news and an urgent request for help."

CHAPTER 33

Cedar Creek, Nevada
Wednesday, July 31, 2024

THE SECOND TIME TO ERIC'S CABIN PROVED EASIER THAN THE FIRST. She crossed the long wooden bridge, turned right at the end, and found the driveway. She parked next to Eric's silver Toyota 4Runner. It seemed like a lifetime ago that she had sprayed him with pepper spray outside her apartment in Raleigh. Since then, she had agreed to work with him secretly to see if together they could uncover secrets about the summer her birth parents went missing and his father died. And she'd met Nora, who was growing into both a friend and confidant, as well as a conduit through which Sloan was getting to know Annabelle Margolis.

Since Sunday, when Sloan and Nora perused the photos Annabelle took the summer she disappeared, Sloan had spent Monday and Tuesday with Tilly and Reid. She'd spent the afternoon at their home, having lunch and swapping stories. Although Reid remained standoffish, Sloan found Tilly Margolis to be nothing like what Nora had described. Perhaps the years had softened the woman. Tilly and Reid had asked about Sloan's childhood, and dug softly, but deliberately into how her adoptive parents had gone about finding her in 1995. The two days she spent with Tilly and Reid were emotional and exhausting, and Sloan was happy to take a break from the Margolis family and head to the foothills to see Eric.

As she shut off the engine, the front door opened, and Eric hurried down the steps.

"Is something wrong?" Sloan asked as she opened the car door.

"I found something in the files," Eric said. "It has to do with what the state police discovered at Annabelle and Preston's house."

Sloan followed Eric inside and sat across from him at the large oak slab table covered with boxes containing the details of her and her parents' disappearance. Eric opened a file folder and turned a few pages.

"After the state police were brought in to investigate your parents' disappearance, according to what my grandfather told me, they became very tight-lipped about the investigation and stopped sharing details with the press and public. As I was digging through the case file, I found this."

Eric slid a piece of paper across the table for Sloan to read.

"What am I looking at?" she asked.

"A summary of what crime scene technicians discovered at Annabelle and Preston's home. Look at the last paragraph."

Sloan skimmed the page while Eric spoke.

"Crime scene investigators performed a luminol test of Annabelle and Preston's home."

"To look for blood evidence?"

"Yes. Crime scene investigators use luminol spray to look for diluted blood. It's sensitive enough to detect blood even if someone attempts to clean it up and hide its presence. Technicians spray a surface, wait a minute, and then shine blue light on the area. If the area lights up under the blue light, the techs know blood had been there and was cleaned up."

Sloan continued to read.

"They found blood in the kitchen of Annabelle and Preston's home?"

"Not just blood," Eric said. "A *lot* of blood. Here, check out the photos."

Eric slid another sheet of paper in front of her.

"My guy at the Nevada State Police Department couldn't get me the original photos, but he copied these for me. And they're in color, so you can appreciate how spectacular this finding was."

Sloan pulled the sheet in front of her, where Eric's source had photocopied six images onto a single page. The images were of

Annabelle and Preston's kitchen. On the floor was a large circle that glowed brightly under the blue light, signifying where someone had cleaned up blood that pooled there. Sloan estimated the circumference of the area glowing in the photo was five feet around.

"This was all blood?" she asked.

"That's what the techs believed, yes. Blood that someone tried to clean up and hide."

"Whose blood was it?"

Eric pointed to the bottom of the page and Sloan's gaze moved there. The blood belonged to Annabelle Margolis.

CHAPTER 34

Cedar Creek, Nevada
Wednesday, July 31, 2024

Iᴛ ᴛᴏᴏᴋ Sʟᴏᴀɴ ᴀ ᴍɪɴᴜᴛᴇ ᴛᴏ ɢᴀɪɴ ʜᴇʀ ᴄᴏᴍᴘᴏsᴜʀᴇ ᴀɴᴅ ꜰᴏʀ ʜᴇʀ ᴍɪɴᴅ to process what Eric was telling her. She knew her birth mother only through the tabloid articles she had read, the stories she'd heard during the short time spent with the Margolis family, and from the single box of photos Sloan had dug through at Nora's studio. But during those limited engagements, Sloan had learned that Annabelle was an aspiring photographer, a devoted wife, and a doting mother who loved her newborn child. It was enough for a connection, however frail, to develop. And now, to learn that Annabelle's blood had been detected in her home, and had been cleaned up, was heartbreaking news.

"Did the police ever do anything with this evidence?"

"I'm not sure how they pursued it. I only have what's here in front of us, and I haven't been able to track down anyone who worked the case back then. But I can imagine the riff this discovery caused."

"How so?"

"I have to assume that the state police, no matter how influenced they might have been by the Margolis family, suspected that Preston had something to do with this."

"Preston?"

"It's the most logical, and usually the first, conclusion we come to anytime a wife goes missing or is found dead. The husband is the first suspect. In this case, with all this blood having been discovered and then cleaned up, the detectives investigating the case had to believe the worst—that Annabelle was dead. And with her husband and child missing, they likely suspected that Preston killed Annabelle and disappeared with their infant daughter."

"Why? What was the motive? From everything I've learned about my birth parents, they were madly in love."

"I don't know. And this is just speculation, but from what I know about that summer, everything happened very fast between Preston and Annabelle. You know this from your conversation with Nora Margolis. Maybe he *did* feel trapped. Maybe he had buyer's remorse and wanted to be back with Stella Connelly, his old fiancée. Look, Sloan, I don't know the investigator's mindset back then, but if I can pluck a couple of potential motives out of thin air thirty years after the fact, rest assured they found a few back then."

"But now," Sloan said, "in retrospect, we have new information. I'm alive, and we know I was put up for adoption. My adoptive parents told me they only met the woman posing as my birth mother—Wendy Downing. They said my father was out of the picture."

"The FBI told you that an attorney going by the name of Guy Menendez helped Wendy Downing broker the adoption. For all we know, Preston Margolis was that attorney."

"No," Sloan said. "I don't believe that. I *can't* believe that."

Eric shook his head. "Then we have to keep digging. Let's get through the rest of the file and see what else we find. Specifically, we need to figure out how your disappearance is linked to Baker Jauncey's death. The theory that Annabelle and Preston disappeared to avoid Annabelle being prosecuted for Baker's death is supported by the fact that their house had been packed up and cleared out."

Eric slid another sheet of paper across the table. On it were photocopies of images of Preston and Annabelle's closets. The spaces were empty but for a few empty hangers and random items—a lone shoe, a sweatshirt in a heap, a makeup bag on the floor.

"Their closets were empty," Eric said. "As if they'd packed all their clothes to hit the road."

"But Annabelle's blood . . . if Preston killed her, why would he pack Annabelle's things, too?"

"Subterfuge? To make it look like they all disappeared together?"

Eric pointed at the boxes on the table. "There has to be more in the files that will help us understand what happened."

Sloan nodded. "Let's get busy."

But before they could begin digging, her phone rang. When she looked at the caller ID, she saw that it was Dr. Cutty. She held up a finger to Eric and answered.

"Hello?"

"Sloan? It's Livia Cutty. I was able to look at those two autopsy reports you sent. Do you have time to review them?"

"Yes, thanks for getting back to me. Did you come across anything interesting?"

"Much more than interesting. In my humble opinion, both reports are terribly inaccurate."

"How so?"

"Baker Jauncey didn't die from a motor vehicle accident, and Sandy Stamos didn't drown."

CHAPTER 35

Cedar Creek, Nevada
Wednesday, July 31, 2024

SLOAN SET DR. CUTTY UP ON A VIDEO CONFERENCE CALL AND SET THE phone at the head of the oak table so that she and Eric were in the frame. Introductions were made and Sloan and Eric explained why they needed Dr. Cutty's expertise on the two autopsy files Sloan had sent her.

"I see," Dr. Cutty said. "So it's likely the coroner who performed these autopsies was politically compromised, or at least motivated to come up with exam findings that fit a specific narrative?"

"That's entirely possible in this town, yes," Eric said.

Dr. Cutty nodded. "Then that, and the fact that he is a coroner and not a trained pathologist, could explain the discrepancies."

"What did you find?" Sloan asked.

"Let's start with Baker Jauncey. It's clear from the documented exam findings that this man was not killed by a motor vehicle, but rather from a blow to the head that caused a brain bleed."

"But the official cause of death was listed as a brain bleed from trauma suffered during the hit-and-run incident," Eric said.

"Yes. The official cause and manner of death were listed along with a brief summary of the exam findings. To a layperson, the truth would be difficult to find. It was only after I dug through the actual postmortem notes and reviewed the exam photos that I determined the cause of death was incorrect."

"Couldn't the head wound Baker Jauncey suffered have been caused by the car that hit him?" Eric asked.

"*A* head wound? Sure. This *particular* head wound? Not a chance. There are many factors that disprove the theory that a vehicle caused the head injury, but the biggest is that the wounds the vehicle produced to this man's body were caused postmortem."

Eric leaned his elbows onto the oak slab to get closer to Sloan's phone. "He was dead *before* the car hit him?"

"That's what the autopsy findings indicate, yes. Besides the wound to the head, all other injuries were caused after he was dead. And the head injury is inconsistent with a motor vehicle accident. From what I could see on the photos and in the coroner's notes, it was impossible for a car to have caused the head wound."

Dr. Cutty spent several minutes on the intricacies of person to vehicle encounters and the autopsy findings that are yielded in such circumstances.

"If Baker Jauncey wasn't killed by the car that ran him over, how did he die?" Sloan asked.

"I closely examined the photos of the skull fracture, along with the measurements that were taken, and my best guess would be that a rounded, wooden object was used to strike Baker Jauncey in the back of the head. The blow caused a brain bleed that killed him."

Sloan and Eric looked at each other. They didn't need to speak what they both were thinking: *Somehow, Sandy Stamos had learned that Annabelle Margolis was not responsible for Baker Jauncey's death, which explained why Sandy had never arrested her. And if Sandy knew that someone had killed Baker by striking him in the head and then staging the hit-and-run, that knowledge had likely gotten him killed. Had the same person who killed Baker Jauncey also killed Annabelle Margolis?*

"Thanks, Dr. Cutty," Sloan said, forcing her mind back to the present. "Did you look at the other report?"

"I did," Dr. Cutty said. "This was your father, Sheriff?"

"It was, yes."

"And the official line was that your dad drowned when his car went into a body of water?"

"The official report stated that my father was under the influence of heroin, lost control of his car, drove into Cedar Creek, and drowned."

"Your father didn't drown, Sheriff. That much is certain."

Sloan saw Eric squint his eyes and swallow hard at the revelation. She reached over and put her hand on his forearm.

"How do you know that?" Eric finally asked.

"Because there was no water in his lungs. If his body was found submerged in water, and he was still breathing at the time, there would be water in his lungs. The sad reality of drowning deaths is that victims hold their breaths for as long as possible. Eventually, however, they inhale. And when they do, water is ingested into their lungs. The lack of water in your father's lungs means he never inhaled after he was under the water."

"There was a theory," Eric said, "that he had been breathing from an air pocket that was trapped in the car. Isn't that possible?"

"I'm afraid not," Dr. Cutty said. "If he had been trapped in a vehicle that was submerged under water and breathing from an air pocket, there would have been evidence of carbon dioxide intoxication and subsequent suffocation. It's called confined space hypoxic syndrome. Sloan will know all about that."

Sloan looked at Eric and spoke.

"If your dad had taken his last breaths while trapped in his submerged squad car and breathing from an air pocket, eventually the air pocket would have filled with the carbon dioxide he exhaled. Once all the oxygen in the air pocket was depleted, he would have suffocated. And when this happens, there are clear signs of it on autopsy, including hypercapnia and respiratory acidosis. Basically, his bloodstream would have been saturated with carbon dioxide, and his lungs would have filled with frothy blood that's classic in carbon dioxide poisoning."

Sloan looked back to Dr. Cutty. "I'm assuming the lungs were clean?"

"Correct," Dr. Cutty said. "And there was no exaggerated amount of carbon dioxide in the bloodstream."

Sloan saw that Eric was struggling with the information and she kept her hand on his forearm.

"So what does it mean?" he finally asked.

"It means the last breath your father took was a regular one, from air filled with a normal mixture of oxygen. It means your father was already dead when his car went into the water. At least, he had died before the water submerged him."

"What killed him? How did he die?"

"A massive amount of heroin," Dr. Cutty said. "So massive, in fact, that it's impossible he injected it himself."

Dr. Cutty shuffled a few papers as she looked through her notes.

"Based on the metabolized heroin in his system, it appears the drug was administered in two doses. The problem is that the first dose was so large it would have rendered your father comatose. Unconscious, at least. The second dose killed him. So my question, Sheriff, is this: If the first dose rendered your father unconscious, how did the second dose get into his bloodstream? Because he certainly didn't inject it himself."

CHAPTER 36

Cedar Creek, Nevada
Wednesday, July 31, 2024

SLOAN STOOD IN THE BACKYARD OF ERIC'S CABIN WITH THE PEAKS OF the Sierra Nevada Mountains staring down at her. The revelation that Annabelle's blood had been discovered in her home, and what it meant for her birth mother's fate, had rattled her. The information Dr. Cutty had delivered about Sandy Stamos's cause of death had turned Eric's world upside down. There was some part of him, Sloan now understood, that had been skeptical of the stories his ailing grandfather told before he passed. They were tales of corruption and cover-ups that involved his father having discovered something sinister enough during his investigation into Baker Jauncey and the missing Margolis family that it led to his death. Eric had been chasing answers to satisfy the wishes of his dead grandfather. But now, with Dr. Cutty's interpretation of Sandy Stamos's autopsy, it was clear that Eric's grandfather's decades-long search into his son's death had not been a dying man chasing a conspiracy theory.

They both needed to clear their minds and settle their nerves. When Sloan mentioned a workout—the usual way she recharged her brain—Eric showed her his backyard. He had erected a Cross-Fit course complete with a torque sled, battle ropes, pull-up bar, kettlebells, and free weights. Just the sight of the equipment allowed Sloan's mind to drift from Annabelle Margolis's likely fate.

Wearing shorts and a tank top she had in her car, Sloan approached the giant tractor tire that rested in the middle of Eric's backyard. The sun was high in the cloudless sky and on a westward pitch that cast the Sierra Nevada Mountains in a bright amber glow. She crouched into a squat, reached her hands under the edge of the tire, and engaged her quads and glutes as she flipped the tire over. It landed a few feet away and Sloan jogged back to it, squatted again, and repeated the process—lift, pull, push, lift, pull, push—until she completed twenty-five reps. Once she finished, Eric attacked the tire. Sloan jumped rope to keep her heart rate up while Eric completed his reps. Her watch beeped just as Eric finished the last rotation. Sloan hustled over to the tire, and they swapped spots.

After fifteen minutes they were both breathing heavily and unable to talk. Eric pointed to the battle ropes—two thick cords, each twenty feet long and secured to eyelets screwed into the ground. Sloan grabbed the free end of each rope and began swinging in an up-and-down motion—right arm up, left arm down, zigzagging the ropes for two straight minutes until her shoulders burned and her chest heaved. Eric took over as Sloan recovered. They took turns, back and forth on the battle ropes in two-minute rounds until they completed ten reps and collapsed onto the ground.

They gulped from water bottles before heading to the kettlebells to complete a killer circuit of snatches and cleans. When they finished, they walked around the yard with hands on their heads and heaving for breath.

"I see you handle stress about as well as I do," Sloan said.

"It's either this or the bottle," Eric said. "And this is a lot healthier."

Eric had sweated through his shirt so that the fabric stuck to his skin, revealing the sculptured physique of his shoulders and chest.

"I take it you're not a drinker either?" Eric asked.

"Only Diet Dr. Pepper and the occasional glass of wine. Otherwise, I burn off my anxiety at the gym. Thanks for letting me crash what I assume is usually a one-man show."

"Are you kidding? This was great. You pushed me harder than I would have pushed myself. And it got my mind off of what your boss told me about my dad."

Sloan took a sip of water.

"So if the same coroner who performed Baker Jauncey's autopsy also did your father's, and both reports were blatantly inaccurate, the guy was either a hack or . . ."

"Or someone was in his ear telling him what they needed the reports to say."

Sloan took another swig from her water bottle. Sweat poured from her body, causing her shoulders and arms to glisten in the sun.

"So we have confirmation that someone killed Baker Jauncey and then tried to make it look like a hit-and-run. The fact that Annabelle's car was planted at the scene indicates that whoever killed Baker wanted Annabelle to take the fall. The discovery of Annabelle's blood at her home, and the attempted clean up, proves foul play was involved."

"And," Eric continued, "someone injected my father—the man investigating both crimes—with enough heroin to place him in a coma, or close to it. A second dose killed him. Then, if I'm figuring things correctly, they pushed his car into Cedar Creek so that it would look like an accident."

"Which it did to everyone except your grandfather."

"And your boss."

Sloan nodded. "So we've got three murders—Baker Jauncey, Annabelle Margolis, and your father. Someone wanted Baker Jauncey's death to look like a hit-and-run, and your father's to look like an overdose. And since your father was investigating the disappearance of my birth parents and me at the time, it's logical to conclude that all three crimes are linked. The question is how."

A bird crooned loudly and both Eric and Sloan looked up to see a black-tailed Cooper's hawk perched on the roof of the cabin. As soon as they spotted it, the hawk took flight, soaring overhead before diving down into the gorge behind the cabin.

After the workout they each showered and got back to work at the long oak table. For hours they pored through the case files looking for any hints the pages might hold to help them piece together the mystery. They worked until midnight without a break, reading page after page of detective's notes, reviewing interview transcripts, and combing through the list of evidence collected from Annabelle and Preston's home. They looked through crime scene photos of the house, images of Sandy Stamos's squad car dripping water after being freshly pulled from Cedar Creek, and snapshots of Annabelle's car and Baker Jauncey's body taken by accident investigators with the Nevada State Highway Patrol. Despite their efforts, when midnight came they were no closer to finding answers than when they had started.

Sloan looked up from the report she was reading.

"Anything?"

Eric shook his head. "No. And I think I've hit a wall. I'm not even sure what I'm reading is making it into my brain at this point."

"Yeah, I'm pretty spent myself."

Sloan looked at her phone.

"Oh my God, is it midnight already?"

Eric checked his watch. "Damn. Time flies when you're trying to solve three thirty-year-old crimes."

Sloan smiled. "This is not the most pleasant of topics, but I can think of worse ways to spend the day. It's been eye-opening."

"To say the least."

She stood and stretched.

Eric stood as well. "Thanks again for getting your boss's help on my dad's autopsy."

"Sorry it confirmed what you feared."

"It's better to know than to live in doubt."

Sloan nodded and offered a dejected smile. "I guess that's true. I better get going."

"There's no way I'm letting you drive those mountain roads this late at night. None of them are lighted and it gets dicey in the dark."

Sloan looked out the window and imagined herself attempting to navigate the steep, winding roads this late at night.

"I can drive you back to town," Eric said, "but you'd have to leave your car here and grab it tomorrow. Or . . ." he paused. "You can stay the night. The extra bedroom's all set—sheets are clean, and you already know I've got clean towels in the bathroom."

Sloan looked back from the window. "Are you sure?"

"Of course."

They cleaned up the table and stacked the boxes full of the notes they had spent all night reading. Eric walked her up the stairs and showed her the guest room. He grabbed two extra pillows from the top shelf in the closet and stuffed them into pillowcases. He fluffed them on the bed.

He pointed at the bathroom. "Bathroom's there, obviously. There's water in the fridge downstairs. And I'm across the hall if you need anything."

Sloan smiled. "Thanks. And thanks for letting me crash."

"Sure thing."

"I'm sorry again," Sloan said, walking over to him. "About your dad. I know it was a long time ago, and you were a kid, but I'm sure it's not easy to hear those things."

Eric nodded. "Not easy, but that's why I'm looking for answers. My grandfather would be proud I got this far."

"I'm looking with you."

"I know. And I appreciate it." Eric leaned in and kissed her cheek. "And I'm going to keep looking until we both have answers about what happened that summer."

Sloan put her hand on his chest. In a different moment in time, one where they had not spent the night looking through case files that dealt with the death of Eric's father and the disappearance of Sloan's birth parents, something more might have happened between them. But on this night, they were partners with a common goal. Nothing more.

"Good night," she finally said.

"See you in the morning."

THE PAST

Lake Tahoe, Nevada

Saturday, July 1, 1995
3 Days Prior . . .

Sandy steered his old-model Suburban down the long drive of the Stamos family's cabin, turned left, and crossed the bridge that curved over the gorge behind the property. He wound his way through the circuitous mountain roads until he found Highway 67, where he headed south and bypassed the exit for Cedar Creek. He was headed to Lake Tahoe.

The Fourth of July holiday made traffic nightmarish, and it took over two hours for him to reach Incline Village on the north side of Tahoe. He found an offshoot road named Beverdale Trail and slowed at each house he passed. The address he was looking for was scrawled on a scrap of paper and taped to the dashboard. When he spotted the numbers on the mailbox, he pulled into the driveway.

"Sandy Stamos!"

Sandy heard the voice of his old friend just as he was opening the driver's side door.

"Tom Quinn," Sandy said with a smile. "It's good to see you."

Sandy had grown up with Tom Quinn. Unlike Sandy, Tom had hightailed it out of Cedar Creek and Harrison County as soon as he could. He attended college in Los Angeles and now made his home in the small, East Bay town of Danville. He had a vacation home in Lake Tahoe and had agreed to meet Sandy there for an urgent matter.

The two men embraced in a hug before Tom pushed Sandy away by the shoulders.

"Damn, Cedar Creek must be treating you well. You look good, old friend." Tom wrapped an arm around Sandy's bicep. "You're built like a brick shithouse."

"Working hard," Sandy said. "You look good, too. And this house! It's gorgeous."

"Thanks. Elaine and I love it out here."

"Thanks for having me out, and for doing this on a holiday weekend. I'm in a pinch or I wouldn't have asked."

"Not a problem. Come on inside. We'll sit on the back deck. It's got a great view of the lake."

A few minutes later Sandy was sitting with his childhood friend and staring down at Lake Tahoe over towering pines that lined the mountainside. They each drank cold Sierra Nevada Pale Ale.

"You weren't kidding," Sandy said, taking in the view. "I'm impressed."

"Thanks, buddy."

Tom Quinn had studied finance and accounting at USC, and spent ten years on the government's dole running audits for the IRS before entering the private sector to open his own financial planning firm. Tom Quinn had the sharpest financial mind Sandy knew, and Sandy needed his help.

"So what's going on in Cedar Creek that's got the sheriff asking for favors from a finance guy?"

Sandy smiled. "People come and go but Cedar Creek never changes."

Tom nodded. "That means you're bumping heads with the Margolis clan."

"Trying not to, but can't seem to avoid it in this particular case."

"What's going on?"

"Earlier this summer, one of the partners at Margolis and Margolis was killed in what appeared to be a hit-and-run accident on Highway Sixty-seven."

"Appeared to be?"

"This stays between you and me, but it looks like someone actually hit the guy in the back of the head with a baseball bat and killed him first, then put him in the road and ran him over with a car."

"Damn. What has that hellhole turned into?"

Sandy pulsed his eyebrows. "It gets better. The car that ran the already-dead Margolis and Margolis partner over was registered to Preston Margolis's new wife."

Tom Quinn whistled. "You've got yourself a shit show."

"Don't I know it. But, wait, there's more."

"You sound like an infomercial."

"Yeah, well, this last bit is why I called you. The Margolis and Margolis partner who was killed was named Baker Jauncey. A couple of days ago his legal investigator paid me a visit. A guy named Marvin Mann. He told me Baker had sniffed out financial fraud at the Margolis law firm and recruited Marvin to look into it. The next day, Baker was dead."

"And his investigator thinks he was killed because he was looking into the Margolis firm?"

Sandy nodded. "And here's the kicker. The night before he was killed, Baker gave Marvin a thick file of documents he had extracted from Margolis and Margolis, detailing the financial fraud. Jauncey was a partner, so he had all the access he needed if he was looking in the right places. He gave the files to Marvin for safekeeping and was dead the next day. Marvin shared the files with me. I've looked through them but I'm not a finance guy. I can't make heads or tails out of them. I need you to take a look and explain to me what's going on at Margolis and Margolis."

"I sniffed out a lot of scams during my years at the IRS. Let me have a look."

"I've got the full file stashed in a safe deposit box because I'm not taking any chances with it. But I made photocopies of what I believe are the relevant parts. I've got everything in my car."

Lake Tahoe, Nevada

Saturday, July 1, 1995
3 Days Prior . . .

S ANDY SAT ON HIS FRIEND'S DECK AND SIPPED BEER WHILE HE STARED down at Lake Tahoe. Tom Quinn had moved into the den as he pored over the documents Sandy brought him. Sandy was admiring two sailboats cutting through the center of the lake when Tom reappeared through the sliding doors that led from the kitchen. He had two fresh beers gripped between the fingers of his left hand, the files in his right, and his laptop tucked under his arm.

"Here," he said, handing Sandy the beers.

"Figure any of it out?"

Tom nodded. "Most of it. And it's on a huge scale, Sandy. Lots of money and lots of laws being broken. It's no wonder these files got that guy killed."

Tom placed the files on the patio table. A yellow legal pad that contained his notes rested on top. He set his laptop computer next to the files and went back inside, emerging a moment later with a long cable and extension cord for power. He sat down and fired up the laptop.

"So here's what's going on," Tom said, tapping on the keyboard. "They're stealing client money, in a nutshell, but they're very clever about it. They're taking settlement checks from cases the firm has either won or successfully negotiated, depositing the full amount into a dummy account—essentially a shell company attached to the Margolis law group—and then issuing a formal settlement check to

Margolis and Margolis, which gets deposited into an escrow account. The key is that this formal payment into the escrow is less than the actual settlement.

"Let's say a five-million-dollar settlement comes in. This guy deposits the five million into the dummy account, then transfers four point nine million into the firm's escrow account. It's easy to miss a hundred grand when you're dealing with these huge sums, and from what I can tell Margolis and Margolis frequently does. The client then gets paid from the escrow account. The math gets complicated because the firm keeps thirty-three percent, plus expenses. The client gets the balance. And it's in the expenses where the firm is burying the skimming. In this example of a five-million-dollar settlement, the hundred grand skimmed off the top was explained away through a long list of bogus expenses and no client ever picked up on it. Until this guy, Baker Jauncey, sniffed out the fraud. Only once, according to what's in these files, had a client argued about the amount they received. And in that case, the inconsistency was blamed on an accounting error and was corrected. No other clients said a word. The scam's been going on for years according to the dates listed on the files."

Tom pulled one of the documents over so that Sandy could see.

"Here's an obvious one. The Margolis law group filed a suit on behalf of Janet Romo in 1993 against a grocery store chain where she slipped and fell, injuring her hip and back. The case was settled out of court for a hundred fifty grand."

Tom pointed at the page.

"See? It clearly states the settlement amount of one fifty right here, and that matches the amount deposited into the dummy account here."

Sandy followed Tom's index finger as it slid between the two matching numbers.

"But here"—Tom turned the page and pointed at a new number—"it shows that a settlement check was issued to Margolis and Margolis in the amount of one hundred *twenty-five* thousand."

"Twenty-five K off the top?"

"Exactly. The one twenty-five goes into the escrow account, the twenty-five grand is written off in expenses, and a check is issued to the client. And that's just the beginning. There are dozens of other examples in the files, and the amounts range from ten grand to a hundred."

"All stolen funds?"

Tom nodded. "Yeah. I haven't made it through all the files, but the total is just over five million dollars so far. Enough to kill for, had someone discovered this and threatened to expose those involved."

Sandy slowly nodded his head. "Who were the attorneys involved?"

"That's the problem. In order to pull off this level of fraud, shell companies and numbered accounts were created. One main company where the original settlement checks were deposited, and several others that the stolen funds were laundered through. I put a list together of every LLC, S corporation, and sole proprietorship listed. Other than those companies, there are only two other entities referenced in these files. The first is the Margolis firm. The second is the guy signing the checks that were eventually issued to the firm after a percentage was skimmed off the top."

"Who was it?" Sandy asked.

"He's listed in all the documents as Guy Menendez."

"Guy Menendez?"

"Doesn't ring a bell?"

"No."

"I'm not surprised." Tom opened his laptop. "Are you familiar with the Internet?"

"A little. The sheriff's office has a website but it was all set up by IT guys from the county."

"Margolis and Margolis has a site," Tom said, tapping his keyboard. "And on their website is a list of every attorney at the firm. One hundred sixteen in all." Tom turned the laptop to Sandy. "Not one of them is named Guy Menendez."

"So who the hell is he?" Sandy asked.

"An alias, I'm guessing. But if you figure out who this guy is, I'm pretty sure you'll know who killed Baker Jauncey."

PART IV

From the Shadows

CHAPTER 37

Reno, Nevada
Thursday, August 1, 2024

Margot Gray grabbed two breakfast entrees off the bar and hurried them over to table number eight. It was eleven o'clock in the morning and as soon as the two truckers finished their meal, her shift would mercifully end. She'd pulled a double and was going on fourteen hours straight—minus bathroom and cigarette breaks, and a half hour sometime in the middle of the night to eat a bagel with cream cheese and slurp down an energy drink to keep her going. Her knees ached and her ankles were swollen from so many hours on her feet.

She slid the plates in front of her last two customers with a pleasant smile she was no longer aware she even offered. She'd plastered it on her face for so many years that it came without conscious thought.

"Can I get you anything else?"

"Coffee, please," one of the truckers said.

Margot hustled over to the coffee station, grabbed the pot, and refilled the coffee mugs in front of each man.

"And then just the check," the trucker said. "We've gotta hit the road so we're gonna eat fast."

Margot smiled, pulled the check from the front pocket of her apron, and placed it on the table. She spent twenty minutes balancing out the tabs from her shift and taking out her tips—$113. There was always the temptation to calculate the number of hours of her life she gave up for the money she made, but she'd been down that road before and it led to dark places she cared not to visit again. She was a fifty-two-year-old waitress with no other skills. It wasn't enough in this world to *want* something different. She needed talent if she wanted her life to change, and Margot Gray had decided the only talent she possessed was a fake smile and the ability to spend hours on her feet hustling from table to table.

By the time she finished cashing out, the truckers were gone. After fourteen hours, there was no one left to serve. The diner was in a rare mode of calm—that peaceful time between the breakfast and lunch crowds. She said good-bye to a couple of the other waitresses, none of whom were anything more than acquaintances. They were younger than Margot and all had the same thought running through their minds—that there was no way in hell they'd be working at this diner, or any other place like it, when they were in their fifties. Margot knew the twenty-something waitresses thought this because Margot had once been one of them. When she was twenty-five she had also been convinced that running tables at a diner was just a temporary gig. She had convinced herself that things would get better, that other opportunities would come along, and that when she was "older" things would be better. A decade later, when she was in her thirties, she told herself the same story. But her conviction in the story weakened, as too did her belief in it. By the time she reached her forties, that little voice in her head had grown faint and quiet. It still whispered every so often that there was more to life than swapping hours for dollars, that things could still change, and that at some point she'd start living life rather than surviving it. But she hadn't heard that voice since she turned fifty. Mostly because she was as certain about the permanency of this life now that she was in her fifties as she had been about its temporary nature when she was in her twenties. But another reason was because it hurt too much to listen to it.

In the parking lot she climbed into her ancient Mazda, felt the pull of the hundred bucks of tip money in her pocket, and thought briefly about stopping at the liquor store and feeding the slot machine. She'd doubled her money doing that once, and the single victory helped her forget all the other times she'd worked ten straight hours only for the slots to steal everything in less time than it took truckers to drain a pot of coffee.

Resisting the urge, she decided she needed sleep more than anything else. She pulled into her mobile home complex, parked in
front of her trailer, and headed inside. She grabbed a Coke from
the fridge and pulled up her laptop—an aging Dell that miraculously booted up every time she opened it. She had no television,
and couldn't afford cable if she did. Her conduit to the world was
the Internet, and if her antique laptop ever crapped out on her,
she'd be disconnected from the world other than listening to CNN
and FOX squawk from televisions in the corners of the diner.

Margot pulled up the YouTube app and clicked on the *Unsolved*
channel—her favorite true crime fix featuring Ryder Hillier. Margot had been an *Unsolved* Junkie for as long as she could remember, and loved the way Ryder Hillier approached the stories she
told on her podcast. The woman presented the facts of a crime,
and then called on her audience to help solve the cold cases she
covered. The reason her podcast was so popular was because
Ryder's process worked. Over the years, Margot had seen Ryder
Hillier solve a number of cases that detectives had either given up
on or had deemed too cold to crack. And she'd done it by enlisting
the help of her audience. *Strength in numbers* Ryder always said.

Margot took a sip of Coke and clicked the play button to watch
the latest *Unsolved* video. Ryder Hillier's face filled the computer
screen.

> *"Good evening* Unsolved *Junkies. This is Ryder Hillier coming to
> you from a hotel room in Raleigh, North Carolina, with breaking
> news and an urgent request for help.*
>
> *"Today, I've got a story that all you* Unsolved *Junkies are going to
> go nuts for. I'm sure everyone at home is familiar with the case of the
> missing Margolis family from 1995."*

Margot curled down into her chair and pulled the laptop close
to her. She was familiar with the case.

> *"I've covered the missing Margolis family on the podcast in the
> past,"* Ryder continued, *"and have done a number of follow-ups.
> However, to those unfamiliar with the story, I'll offer a brief history.*
>
> *"Preston and Annabelle Margolis, along with their two-month-old*

*daughter—a beautiful infant the country knew as baby Charlotte—
disappeared from Cedar Creek, Nevada, on July Fourth, 1995. Preston
was the son of prominent attorney Reid Margolis, and an up-and-
coming legal eagle at the Margolis law firm. The Margolis family is
wealthy and established in Harrison County, where Cedar Creek is located. Despite a large-scale investigation and months of broad media
coverage, there were never any suspects in the family's disappearance,
and the case has been cold for decades.*

"But here's the kicker, Unsolved *Junkies. My sources tell me that
baby Charlotte Margolis has just turned up nearly thirty years after
she went missing. You heard me correctly, Junkies. Charlotte Margolis
has been living as a woman named Sloan Hastings in Raleigh, North
Carolina. According to my sources, baby Charlotte was adopted in November of 1995, a mere four months after she went missing. The adoptive parents—Todd and Dolly Hastings—named the baby Sloan, and
she has lived a quiet life for nearly thirty years. There is no indication
from my sources that Preston or Annabelle Margolis have surfaced,
but certainly this is the biggest break anyone has seen for decades.*

*"Authorities are looking into the method by which baby Charlotte
was put up for adoption, and I'm told that the couple who adopted
Charlotte Margolis are not, I repeat to all my* Unsolved *Junkies out
there, are not suspected in baby Charlotte's disappearance. Please re-
spect the privacy of this adoptive couple, as I'm certain their lives have
been turned upside down by the news.*

*"But, I do have an assignment for you. My sources tell me that the
main focus of the FBI's investigation is the woman who posed as baby
Charlotte's birth mother during the fraudulent adoption. A woman,
I've learned, named Wendy Downing. She was aided by an attorney
named Guy Menendez.*

"This is where we shine! I'm paging all Unsolved *Junkies! I need
your help. I need you to flood my inbox with any and all information
you find about these two people, Wendy Downing and Guy Menendez.
This is a breaking story, and we need to move quickly, Junkies!*

*"I will be heading to Cedar Creek, Nevada, this week to find and
interview Sloan Hastings, aka baby Charlotte Margolis. If Sloan is
listening, or if any* Unsolved *Junkies know where I might find her,
drop me a line. I hope to have more information for you soon.*

"That's all for now, but be sure to check back daily. I'll be making updates on this story here, and I'll be recording the first of a multipart podcast soon. Until next time . . . stay safe, Junkies."

Ryder Hillier's face faded, and the *Unsolved* logo came onto the screen. Margot slowly sat up and closed her laptop. She could hardly believe what she'd heard. Cedar Creek was just an hour or so from Reno. It took only a moment of contemplation before she pushed her chair over to the refrigerator and climbed up on it. In the cabinet above the fridge was her "someday" stash. Hidden in an old coffee container was fifteen hundred dollars that she'd managed to squirrel away over the years. Someday she'd use it to take a vacation. Someday she'd use it to buy a new computer. Someday she'd use it to put a down payment on a new car. There were so many things to do someday that Margot lost track of them all. But there had always been one thing she knew she would do someday, and that day had arrived.

She grabbed the roll of cash from the coffee pot and climbed off the chair. Over the last few years she had started to believe that fate was a fictional thing made up by people who had it good. Fate, Margot noticed, was never discussed by people with dead-end jobs and crappy lives. Fate only came into the picture when good things happened to lucky folks on the rise. Her life had never been touched by the mythical thing called fate. She'd been on a steady, downhill spiral since birth.

For her entire adult life Margot had bounced around the country chasing waitressing jobs and the fantasy of a better life. Somehow she ended up in Reno, serving truckers at a crummy diner. The last decade had provided little in the way of stability and had siphoned away any hope for a brighter future. But despite decades of proof that it did not exist, fate was the only way to explain why she was planning to drive to Cedar Creek with hopes of righting a wrong that had been a lifetime in the making.

CHAPTER 38

Cedar Creek, Nevada
Thursday, August 1, 2024

Whenn Sloan opened her eyes Thursday morning, it took a moment to remember that she'd slept at Eric's cabin. The scent of fresh-brewed coffee pulled her from bed. She walked down the stairs just as Eric was pouring a cup.

"Morning," she said, running a hand self-consciously through her hair.

"Morning. Coffee?"

"Yes, please. Smells wonderful."

They sat at the kitchen table. Sloan was never happier to have resisted temptation the night before. Had she given in to her urges, her and Eric's relationship would be something different this morning. She would be distracted and confused. Instead, she was laser focused on the task at hand. She had a vivid dream about her birth mother during the night. Annabelle was snapping photos of her infant daughter and then moving to the darkroom to develop them. When Annabelle emerged from the darkroom, photo in hand, baby Charlotte was gone. In the fog of the dream, Annabelle looked at Sloan and asked where her daughter had gone. Sloan woke with a startle. When she finally fell back to sleep an hour later, she did so with a fierce determination to find answers when she woke.

"Sorry to keep you up so late last night," Eric said.

"I just wish we'd have found something useful in the files. I feel like we've got more questions than answers at this point."

"I've got a call in to one of my contacts at the Nevada State Police. I'm trying to track down one of the detectives who worked your case and see if he can give me any more details about the crime scene and the blood they found. What's your plan for the rest of the week?"

"I'm meeting with Nora Margolis today to go through boxes of photos Annabelle took the summer she disappeared."

"What kind of photos?"

"Annabelle was an amateur photographer. Nora Margolis's protégé, you could say. Annabelle spent the summer, and the early part of motherhood, taking photos."

"Of what?"

"Of everything. Of the town, of me as an infant, of the house she and Preston were building. I got the impression from the photos I saw that Annabelle was lonely. She had Preston and me, her newborn daughter, but otherwise she was alone. Other than Nora, the Margolis family wasn't so warm and fuzzy toward her. The photos she took are . . . I don't know, fascinating because they provide a window into her life, but also haunting and sad."

Sloan took a sip of coffee.

"Anyway, I have plans with Nora to go through the rest of Annabelle's photos."

"I'll let you know if I'm able to track down the detective who ran the case. It was thirty years ago, so he might not be able to offer anything new or useful."

"It's worth a shot. Mind if I shower before I take off?"

"Be my guest. I'll make some breakfast."

Fifteen minutes later Sloan walked from the extra bedroom with wet hair to find Eric sitting at the kitchen table. He held up a copy of the *Harrison County Post*. Sloan saw her image on the front page.

"What the hell?"

She hurried over and took the paper, skimming the article.

"The FBI said they were keeping a lid on the story," Sloan said.

"Well, it leaked. And you're all over the Internet."

Eric turned his laptop. Another image of Sloan stared back.

"For Christ's sake."

"Sounds like Ryder Hillier broke the story on her *Unsolved* podcast."

"Awesome."

Sloan's phone rang and she saw it was Dr. Cutty calling. She closed her eyes before answering.

"Hello?"

"Sloan, it's Livia Cutty. You know you're in every paper across the country?"

"I'm just learning that now, and seeing it for the first time."

"Are the—"

Dr. Cutty's voice cut out and Sloan looked at her phone.

"Hello?"

"Sorry," Eric said. "Service out here is sketchy at times. It's spotty at best. Usually the front porch is the safest place."

Sloan hurried to the front door and stepped outside.

"Sloan?"

"Yes. Sorry, I'm in the mountains and cell service is bad."

"Are the stories true?"

"Yes. I found out when I did an online DNA search of myself for the forensic genealogy project."

"Wow," Dr. Cutty said. "Sorry the project has spun into all of this."

"For what it's worth, this will make for a great dissertation if I can get that far."

"Do you need anything?"

"You've already helped by offering your opinions on those autopsy reports. They're linked to my story."

"How?"

"I'm working on figuring that out."

"I hope I get to hear about it soon."

"Absolutely."

"Listen, Sloan, just a heads up. This morning there were news vans parked outside the office. I'm sure they're hoping to catch you entering the building. I've received calls from NBC and HAP News. Word has leaked that you're studying under me."

"Sorry to cause so much trouble."

"Please. None of this is your fault. I'll deal with the commotion here, you just take care of yourself. I told my networks that I have no comment on the story, and I won't be touching it unless you need my help."

"Thank you. I'm not sure what I need yet, but I'll call you when I figure it out."

"I have contacts, Sloan. So when you *do* want to tell your story, I can put you in touch with the right people. This story consumed the public back when it happened, and people will be interested in it until they have answers. You could consider beating them to the punch and giving an interview to the right person. Avery Mason or Dante Campbell. I could arrange it, and it would stop the stampede."

"Thanks. And I'll definitely consider it, once I have some answers to give them."

"Understood. One other thing," Dr. Cutty said. "Hayden Cox told me that a woman approached him in the parking lot the other day asking about you. She claimed to be an old high school friend who was trying to track you down. Hayden told her you were out of town. He now thinks the woman was Ryder Hillier. Have to suspect that she'll be the first journalist to Cedar Creek to find you."

"Damn," Sloan said.

She hadn't planned on having to dodge the press while she looked for answers to what happened to her birth parents.

"Thanks Dr. Cutty."

"Keep me posted, and let me know if you need anything."

"Will do."

As soon as Sloan ended the call, her phone rang again. It was her mother. She looked at Eric through the screen door and held up the phone.

"Sorry, I've got to take this."

She turned and walked down the steps of the front porch.

"Hello?"

"Have you seen the papers?" her mother asked.

"Just now, yes."

"It's in the *New York Times*."

"Delightful."

"Listen, Sloan. On Monday morning, I had something strange happen at the office."

Silence followed until Sloan realized the call had dropped.

"Dammit!"

She quickly redialed and listened through the static until her mother answered.

"Sorry. Cell service is terrible up here. What happened on Monday?"

"I had a patient ask about you," her mom said.

"A patient?"

"She pretended to have a toothache and came in as an emergency. Once I was alone in the exam room with her, she said she was a journalist and wanted to speak with you. She gave me her card, and now I see that she's the lady with the podcast."

"Ryder Hillier?"

"That's her, yes."

"Christ Almighty! Mom, why are you just telling me this now?"

"I didn't want to worry you. I thought she was a local reporter who was just fishing for information. I didn't know who she was. So you've heard of her?"

"Yes, Mom. She has the biggest true crime podcast in the country, with millions of listeners. She's the one who broke the story."

"How? Agent Michaels said they were keeping the investigation quiet."

"No idea. Did you tell her anything?"

"No. But now there are news vans parked outside the house."

"Oh my God," Sloan said. "This is spiraling out of control. I'm sorry, Mom. This is such a mess I've caused."

"We're just worried about you. Are you okay?"

"Yes. No one's found me here—I mean, no press or reporters. But it looks like it's only a matter of time."

"Just be careful, honey. And if you need us to come out there, we will."

"No, just do your normal life, Mom. Go to work. Tell the reporters that you've got no comment for now. I'll figure this out today and call you later."

"Okay, sweetie. We love you."

"Thanks, Mom. Love you, too."

Sloan walked back into the cabin. "News vans are parked outside my parents' house in Raleigh, and waiting for me outside the medical examiner's building."

"How long do you think it'll take for them to come to Cedar Creek?" Eric asked.

"Not long. Even if they haven't figured out that I'm here yet, they'll want to track down Tilly and Reid Margolis to get sound bites from them. I'd better warn them, and Nora."

"You're welcome to stay here," Eric said. "No one will find you out here."

Sloan thought about the offer and agreed that there was no better place to hide from the press than Eric's isolated cabin.

"Thanks. Let me go see Nora and tell her what's going on. Then I'll talk with Tilly and Reid. We'll make a plan, and I'll call you."

"Okay. I'll wait to hear from you."

A minute later Sloan was pulling down the long driveway and heading back to Cedar Creek. She worried that Ryder Hillier was lurking out there somewhere, but was wholly unprepared for what was actually waiting at her rental house.

CHAPTER 39

Cedar Creek, Nevada
Thursday, August 1, 2024

MARGOT GRAY SAT IN THE CEDAR CREEK COFFEEHOUSE WITH A COPY of the *Harrison County Post* opened in front of her. She'd made the drive from Reno early that morning. Since Ryder Hillier had dropped her video detailing the breaking news about baby Charlotte's return, pictures of Sloan Hastings had leaked. Of course, in typical Ryder Hillier fashion, she had created a "baby Charlotte" page on the *Unsolved* website and had pictures of Sloan there, comparing them to the age progression images that had popped up over the years guessing what Charlotte Margolis might look like as a child, teenager, and adult. But now they had the real thing, and pictures of Sloan were everywhere. The networks had gotten wind of the scoop and Sloan Hastings had gone mainstream. Overnight, newspapers across the country had picked up on baby Charlotte's return and Sloan was front-page news.

Margot looked at the black and white photo of Sloan Hastings in the *Harrison County Post* and read the story. Sloan Hastings was a medical doctor—a pathologist—who was completing a forensic pathology fellowship in Raleigh, North Carolina, on her way to becoming a medical examiner. Despite the shitty cards she'd been dealt, Margot thought, the girl had done well for herself.

Margot took a sip of coffee and opened her laptop. She typed *Sloan Hastings* into the search engine and watched her screen fill with links. She clicked on an article from the *New York Times*, skimming the details until she came to another image of Sloan Hastings. She studied it for several minutes, and then looked at the other photos that had trickled onto the Internet—Sloan Hastings from her senior prom; Sloan Hastings from her college sorority; Sloan Hastings from her medical school graduation; and, the most recent, Sloan Hastings as a fellow at the Office of the Chief Medical Examiner in North Carolina.

By the time Margot finished her coffee, she was confident that she'd looked at enough photos of Sloan Hastings to recognize the woman if she saw her, which was the plan. Margot's phone rang and she answered.

"Anything?"

"She's renting a house in Cedar Creek."

"Are you serious?"

Margot's waitressing job had put her in front of an interesting cast of characters over the years. One of them, a regular at the diner, was Wiley Wagner, a middle-aged IT guy who knew more about computers than anyone Margot had ever met. They'd become friends over the years, and even more than friends every so often. Margot had asked Wiley for a favor—to use his computer skills to find Sloan Hastings.

"Yep," Wiley said. "A Vrbo in Cedar Creek under Sloan Hastings. The rental agreement started on July twenty-sixth and goes all the way to August thirty-first."

"You got an address?"

"Of course."

Wiley ripped off the address and Margot scribbled it onto the edge of the newspaper.

"She's all over the news," Wiley said.

"No kidding. I'm reading an article about her as we speak."

"Why are you so interested in her? Is it because of that podcast you're obsessed with?"

"I owe you one, Wiley," Margot said in lieu of an answer. "I'll give you a coffee on the house when I'm back in Reno."

"Gee, thanks. I was hoping for dinner and a movie."

"I'll think about it."

Margot ended the call, packed up her laptop, and tore Sloan

Hastings's address off the corner of the *Harrison County Post* before tossing the paper in the garbage on her way out of the coffeehouse. She climbed into her ancient Mazda and twisted the key. The engine protested, turning over several times before finally roaring to life. She dropped the Mazda into gear and headed off to find the rental home where Sloan Hastings was staying.

CHAPTER 40

Cedar Creek, Nevada
Thursday, August 1, 2024

Sloan passed the welcome to cedar creek sign on the north side of town, and followed the roundabouts until she crossed the Louis-Bullat Bridge. She turned down the side street, cautiously watching for reporters or news vans. She saw none. But as she made the final turn to her rental house, she saw an old Mazda parked in the driveway. As she approached the house she noticed a woman sitting on the front porch smoking a cigarette.

Sloan considered turning around, but there was something about the woman that piqued her interest. She pulled her rental car into the driveway and parked next to the Mazda. When she did, the woman stood up. Sloan climbed from her car but did not shut the door. She kept the engine running in case she needed to make a fast retreat.

"Can I help you?" Sloan asked from the driveway.

"You Sloan Hastings?"

"Who's asking?"

"My name's Margot Gray."

The woman stepped down from the front porch and walked to the driveway. She spoke to Sloan over the roof of the Mazda, which sat between the two women.

"I'm Sloan Hastings. What do you need?"

Sloan saw what she thought were tears well in the woman's eyes.

"I need to talk with you and tell you a few things."

The woman's southern accent reminded Sloan of home. It wasn't Carolina twang, more Alabama drawl. But definitely different from the unrounded "awe's" of Northern California and Nevada.

"Talk with me about what?"

"About what happened to you when you were a baby."

A chill found Sloan's shoulder blades and quickly funneled down her back.

"Are you one of those true crime junkies?"

The woman rocked her head back and forth, and then shrugged. "Yeah, but that ain't why I'm here."

"What do you know about what happened to me when I was a baby?"

"Probably not as much as I should, considering. But definitely somethin'."

Sloan remained standing in the crook of the open car door, ready to drop back into the driver's seat and tear out of the driveway if need be.

"How do you know *anything* about what happened to me?"

The tears that had been building on the woman's lower lids finally spilled over and streamed down her cheeks.

"'Cause I was the woman who gave you up for adoption."

CHAPTER 41

Cedar Creek, Nevada
Thursday, August 1, 2024

Sloan's heart fluttered and a wave of heat coursed through her body, bringing with it a spell of dizziness. She held onto the car door for support.

"You . . ." Her eyes squinted to slivers. "*You* gave me up for adoption?"

"I ain't proud of it," the woman said, still standing on the other side of the Mazda. "I tried to hide from the guilt by telling myself that all's I did was help a baby find loving parents. But part of me knew something was wrong with the whole thing. Over the years I told that part of myself that even if the baby had been taken, you know, from her actual parents, that she wouldn't know no difference—she'd still be loved. I never had parents who loved me when I was growing up. So I convinced myself I wasn't really hurting you none. You were still gonna be loved by that couple who wanted a baby so bad. I seen 'em on the news this morning—Dolly and Todd. Still remember their names."

The woman wiped her cheeks with the backs of her hands.

"Anyway, I tried real hard to believe the lie I told myself. That I hadn't done nothin' wrong. I needed the money so bad back then. Hell, I'd have believed anything I told myself."

"How did you find me?"

"Back then?"

"No—well that, too. But start with today. How did you find me here, in Cedar Creek?"

"Story's all over the news. Plus, I follow the *Unsolved* podcast and Ryder Hillier was the one who first broke the story 'bout baby Charlotte turning up after nearly thirty years. I'd heard the story before. I mean, everybody knew about it when it happened. But I never put it together 'til I heard the lady's name who put you up for adoption."

"Wendy Downing."

"Yeah. That's the name the lawyer told me to use."

Sloan blinked and worked to understand what this woman was telling her. "You're Wendy Downing?"

"No, I'm Margot Gray. But in 1995 a lawyer named Guy Menendez paid me ten grand to pretend my name was Wendy Downing so that he could, what he told me at the time, make sure a little girl was adopted by a couple who deserved her."

Sloan looked around the quiet cul-de-sac and finally shut off her engine and closed her car door.

"How did you track me down here in Cedar Creek?"

"Got a friend who's good with computers. He hacked into the system or, I don't know, whatever he did, and figured out that you rented this house. He knew the dates and everything. So, I figured I'd sit on your porch 'til you showed up."

If this woman could find her, Sloan knew it wouldn't be long before Ryder Hillier and the rest of the press corps showed up. She hoped she had at least enough time to hear Margot Gray's story.

"Let's talk inside."

A few minutes later Sloan and Margot sat in the kitchen nook.

"Start from the beginning," Sloan said. "How did you meet Guy Menendez?"

"I was twenty-three years old in 1995 and working at a diner in Mobile."

"Alabama?"

"Yeah. I started seeing this guy come into the restaurant every morning. He always sat in my area. He was real nice and polite and always left big tips. I thought he was maybe gonna ask me out or something, but he never did. Instead, he asked if I'd do him a favor."

Sloan listened intently. "What was the favor?"

"He told me he was a lawyer. Gave me a business card and everything. Said he worked for an adoption agency and that there was a problem with one of the adoptions he was overseeing. He was having trouble cutting through red tape to get this one baby to a couple that wanted her. He told me he needed me to watch the baby for a couple of months until he could organize the adoption. Offered me fifteen grand to do it. And another ten if I'd pose as the baby's mother when the adoption went through. Back then . . . I mean, hell, even today, that was a lot of money. And I needed it real bad. So I told him I'd do it."

"So you took care of me?"

"Yeah, for 'bout four months 'til he could get the adoption finalized."

"What happened after four months?"

"To make the adoption legit, he needed to take some pictures of me and show them to the couple who wanted to adopt the baby. So he snapped some pictures while I stood in front of a white background. Couple of weeks later we met again, and he showed me a driver's license and passport with my picture on it. But not my name. The name on the IDs was Wendy Downing. He told me that for my protection I had to hide my real identity during the adoption process. 'Course, this got me nervous. And suspicious. Like, maybe the whole thing wasn't as legit as I thought. But when he gave me the passport and driver's license with that fake lady's name on 'em, he also gave me another five grand. He'd get me the rest after we were finished."

Sloan saw Margot Gray look up at the ceiling. Tears welled in her eyes again.

"I knew I was doing something wrong, but I felt trapped. After I took the first half of the money, I felt . . . I don't know, obligated or something, to go through with it. After I met the couple who wanted to adopt you, I told myself there were worse things in the world than helping a nice couple find a baby to love. I just sort of blocked out thoughts about where Mr. Menendez had gotten you from. Blocked out the idea that you might have already belonged to loving parents."

"When was this?" Sloan asked. "When you first met the attorney?"

"July of '95. I remember the date 'cause it was my birthday the first time we talked. It wasn't until November that we actually went through with the adoption. In September and October of that year, I met the couple who was gonna adopt you. We met twice for lunch, and I asked them a bunch of questions that Mr. Menendez wrote out for me, sort of like I was interviewing them."

Sloan slowly cocked her head. "I was . . . with you? When you met that couple?"

"Yeah," Margot said with a shrug. "I was supposed to be your mom, so 'course you were with me."

Sloan swallowed hard. She urged herself to think clearly, like she was back in the cadaver lab in medical school following the route a cranial nerve took through the brain. She forced herself to focus and get past the flood of adrenaline that came with somehow stumbling over what was certainly the biggest break in the case in decades.

"And you had no idea how Mr. Menendez originally gained custody of me?"

"No. Other than that he said he worked for an adoption agency."

"So how did you figure it out? That I was baby Charlotte Margolis?"

"I didn't back then. I never put two and two together. I remember that family going missing. Their story was all over the tabloids. But the way the news media told it, the entire family disappeared. I never thought what I was doing for Mr. Menendez was related to the missing Margolis family. After it was over, I took the money and got far away from Mobile. Tried to forget about the whole thing. But I couldn't. At first it really bothered me, and I became depressed about what I'd done. Even thought about going to the cops. Couple years went by and the guilt sort of faded. For a while I even thought it was gone. But that type of guilt never goes away. It just sort of becomes part of you. Then, the other day, I turned on my podcast lady, Ryder Hillier, and she broke this story about baby Charlotte from the nineties who had just resurfaced after being missing for nearly thirty years. Then I heard the name of the woman who had put baby Charlotte up for adoption—Wendy Downing."

Margot shrugged.

"That's when I put it all together and knew I needed to find you. I needed to tell you the truth 'bout what I'd done."

"This man, Guy Menendez. The attorney. Do you know any more about him?"

"A little. He's kept in touch over the years. Every couple of years I hear from him. Even if I move to a different state, and I've done that a lot, he somehow finds me."

"Finds you how?"

"Sometimes it's just a phone call. Sometimes he shows up in person to ask how I'm doing. He's helped me out with money a few times."

Sloan noticed that her fingers and hands were cold, as if all her blood had redirected to her cerebral cortex as she tried to understand what was happening. Guy Menendez, she suddenly knew, was the missing piece of the puzzle she'd been looking for. And Margot Gray was the link to him.

"When was the last time you spoke with him?"

"'Bout a year ago. He gave me his cell number in case I ever needed anything."

"Would you share his number with me?"

Margot shrugged. "Sure, I guess."

She dug in her purse until she found her phone, then swiped the screen to pull up the number. She pushed the phone over to Sloan. Sloan glanced at the screen and saw that it was a 530 area code. The same area code as Aunt Nora.

Guy Menendez was in Harrison County. Guy Menendez was probably in Cedar Creek.

CHAPTER 42

Cedar Creek, Nevada
Thursday, August 1, 2024

"LISTEN," SLOAN SAID, STANDING FROM THE KITCHEN TABLE WITH a brimming urgency to tell Eric what she'd learned from Margot Gray. Hell, she considered calling John Michaels at the FBI. She had a phone number belonging to Guy Menendez. Surely one of them could track the number and find the man.

"We can't stay here much longer. I mean, you found me through a records search of my Vrbo reservation, so it won't be long before the press shows up. I'm not ready to talk with them yet."

"Yeah," Margot said. "Makes sense. Ryder Hillier said she was coming to Cedar Creek to investigate."

"I have a friend who's a police officer. His name is Eric Stamos. He's the sheriff here in Cedar Creek. And I also know the FBI agent who's been investigating my case ever since I figured out that I was Charlotte Margolis. Would you be willing to talk to them?"

Sloan saw a change come over Margot's eyes.

"I . . . I'm not sure about that. The FBI? Would I get in trouble? I mean, I'm probably in some kinda trouble for what I did, right?"

"I don't know," Sloan said, and knew immediately by Margot's expression that it was the wrong answer. "Look, let's forget about the FBI. We'll just talk to my friend. He's local."

"The sheriff?"

"Yeah."

"I guess I didn't really think this through. I just wanted to tell you what I did so I could, I don't know, get it off my chest. I never planned to tell the cops 'bout none of it."

"I understand. And I'm grateful you tracked me down, Margot. I'm so, *so* grateful. But the authorities are going to want to talk with you. You're probably the biggest break this case has ever seen. Trust me, though, they're not after *you*. If you tell them everything you just told me, I'm sure they'll work with you."

Margot offered a nervous smile. "Work with me how?"

"I don't know, Margot. I'm not a cop. But trust me, the police and the FBI will be interested in what you can tell them."

"I don't wanna go to prison."

"You're not going to prison," Sloan said. "There's probably a statute of limitations on what you did. At this point, you're useful to the FBI for the information you can provide, that's it."

"The FBI scares me."

Sloan nodded. "Me, too. So let's start with my friend. He'll be able to help us figure out what to do next."

Margot slowly nodded. "Okay. I guess I'll talk to him."

"Perfect. Where are you staying?"

"Nowhere. I just drove up from Reno."

Sloan thought quickly of the best way to keep Margot Gray calm and close. "Let's do this. Let's get you a hotel room in town—"

"A hotel? I gotta be back in Reno for my shift tomorrow night."

"Fair enough. But you're available tonight, right?"

"I guess, yeah."

"Perfect. I'll put you up in a hotel tonight. We can go there now and I'll bring my friend over so you can talk with him. It'll be private."

Margot looked around and finally nodded. "Okay, yeah. I'll do that."

Sloan swiped through her phone and booked a room at the Cedar Creek Inn, then led the way through town with Margot following in her Mazda. They checked in at the front desk and accepted two keycards to room number 303. The elevator deposited them on the third floor and Sloan swiped her keycard to open the door.

"Just stay put," Sloan said, standing in the doorway as Margot carried her overnight bag into the room and sat on the bed. "I'll be back in about an hour."

"Promise me your friend ain't gonna arrest me or nothing."

Margot kneaded her hands together as she rocked on the edge of the bed.

"I promise," Sloan said, although she didn't know if she was telling the truth or boldly lying to this woman. Her college years, which had been spent studying criminology, told her that there was no way for Margot Gray to come out of this ordeal unscathed. But in that moment Sloan would have said anything to this woman, because Sloan knew that Margot Gray was a conduit to her past, through which all the answers about her birth parents' disappearance might be answered.

A few minutes later Sloan was in her rental car, driving toward the foothills and Eric's cabin. She tried his cell phone again, as she had on her way to the Cedar Creek Inn, but the call went straight to voicemail. No service. In a perfect world Sloan would have convinced Margot Gray to drive with her to Eric's cabin. But Sloan knew the woman, as jumpy as she was, would never go for that. Leaving her was a risk. But even if Margot ran, she wouldn't get far. Still, Sloan hoped she'd been convincing enough for Margot to stay put, safe and sound at the Cedar Creek Inn.

CHAPTER 43

Cedar Creek, Nevada
Thursday, August 1, 2024

MARGOT GRAY CONTINUED TO ROCK AT THE FOOT OF THE BED AFTER Sloan Hastings was gone. She searched for feelings that should be coursing through her body right about now. She waited for the relief she thought she'd feel after finally getting her secret off her chest. She tried to sense the weight of a thirty-year burden being lifted from her shoulders. She anticipated the joy of having finally done the right thing. She looked for the pride she should be feeling for having pieced together what had happened all those years ago, and the righteousness for tracking Sloan Hastings down to tell her the truth. She looked for the inner peace that should have been on the other side of three decades of lies. But none of those emotions were there with her. The only thing present in that hotel room was fear.

She didn't know much about the law, but it was hard to imagine that she wouldn't be in some kind of trouble for what she had done all those years ago. Even if the cops believed her story—that she didn't know the baby had been kidnapped at the time she went through with the adoption—she had still fraudulently posed as the baby's mother. That, alone, was probably some sort of crime.

She bit her thumbnail down to the cuticle, until she tasted the iron bitterness of blood. A thought occurred to her to run. To get in her car and drive far away from Cedar Creek. But where would she go? And how far would she get? She'd told Sloan Hastings her real name, and it wouldn't be hard for police to find her no matter where she went. Plus, all the money she had in the world was in her pocket, and it might last a week.

She stood from the bed and pulled her phone from her back pocket. Mr. Menendez's number was still displayed on the screen from when Margot had shared it with Sloan. A thought occurred to her, and it made sense. At some point in this process she would need a lawyer.

She looked at Mr. Menendez's number and pressed *send.* It rang three times before the man answered.

"It's Margot. I need your help."

CHAPTER 44

Cedar Creek, Nevada
Thursday, August 1, 2024

SLOAN TOOK THE LOUIS-BULLAT BRIDGE OVER CEDAR CREEK, FOLlowed the roundabout until she was heading north on Harmony, and tried not to speed as she merged onto Highway 67. She dialed Eric's number again and listened as the call went straight to voicemail. She kept trying with no luck and gave up when she exited the highway and entered the winding roads that twisted into the foothills. She'd already left two messages and sent several texts asking for a callback.

Somewhere in the back of her mind she felt the anxiety of a ticking clock that told her Margot Gray would not stay at the Cedar Creek Inn for long. After thirty minutes, she finally crossed the wooden bridge that jumped the gorge to Eric's cabin and turned down his long drive. Eric was packing his bag in the back of the 4Runner and turned when he heard Sloan's car crunching over the gravel driveway.

"Something's come up," Sloan said through the open window as she pulled next to him. "I need you to come back to town right away."

"What's wrong?"

"I found Wendy Downing."

CHAPTER 45

Cedar Creek, Nevada
Thursday, August 1, 2024

MARGOT PACED THE HOTEL ROOM AND CONTINUED TO GNAW AT her thumbnail. It was a bloody mess by the time she finally heard a knock at the door. She hurried across the room, checked the peephole, and saw Mr. Menendez standing in the hallway. He wore a suit like he had all the other times he'd shown up out of the blue, either at her apartment or at whatever restaurant she was employed. It had taken him only fifteen minutes to get to the Cedar Creek Inn, and Margot tried to figure out why he, too, was in Cedar Creek. She didn't bother asking if he lived there, if he'd followed her there, or if he was in Cedar Creek—like Margot—because the story of baby Charlotte's return was all over the news.

She opened the door as he walked into the room, wheeling a large suitcase behind.

"You alone?" he asked.

"Yeah." Margot closed the door. "I didn't know who else to call. We're all over the news."

"You did the right thing."

"You've seen it, right? The baby Charlotte story?"

Mr. Menendez nodded. "I've seen it."

"Wendy Downing? They know who I am. Or, at least they know the name I used."

"Tell me how you got *here*," Menendez said, tapping his index finger on the hotel room's armoire. "To this town and in this hotel room."

Margot blew out a lungful of air that ricocheted off her bottom lip and fluttered her bangs.

"You're gonna be mad."

"Just tell me, Margot."

"The true crime podcast I follow had breaking news that baby Charlotte had resurfaced. I knew about the story from back in the nineties, so I was interested in the details. Then I heard that baby Charlotte was put up for adoption by a lady named Wendy Downing, and that the FBI was looking for her. That's *me*, Mr. Menendez. That's the name you had me use on the ID you made me."

Margot waited for a response.

"Keep going."

"Anyway, once I put two and two together, my conscience got the better of me. I asked a friend for help, and he figured out where Sloan Hastings was staying in Cedar Creek. So, I drove up from Reno to talk with her."

"You spoke with Sloan Hastings?"

"Yeah. She's the baby you and I put up for adoption, isn't she?"

Menendez did not answer.

"I know she is. I ain't stupid. It's bothered me for thirty years what we done. You said she needed loving parents, and that's what I kept telling myself over the years. But you never told me you *took* her from loving parents. You never told me you kidnapped her!"

Mr. Menendez looked across the room to the closed door. He held a finger to his lips to quiet Margot.

"What did you tell her, Margot?"

"Sloan?"

"Yes. What did you tell her?"

"I told her everything. I mean, everything I know, anyway."

Margot saw Mr. Menendez close his eyes. "You shouldn't have done that, Margot."

"Yeah, well, I'm starting to wish I hadn't. But I saw it on the news and had to get it off my chest."

Margot paused before she asked her next question.

"Did you kidnap her, Mr. Menendez?"

No answer.

"'Cause now I got problems. They're looking for Wendy Downing. Ain't gonna find her 'cause she don't exist. But they're gonna find *me*, and I need help. They're gonna think I kidnapped her, Mr. Menendez, and I need to know what to tell them. After this all occurred to me, all's I could think to do was call you."

"Where is Sloan Hastings now?"

"She went to get her friend. Said he was the sheriff. Stamos, I think she said his name was. She was gonna bring him here so I could tell him what I told her. I started thinking about it, and decided I wanted a lawyer with me before I talk to any sheriff."

Menendez pulled the desk chair into the middle of the room and faced it toward the window.

"Here's what we're going to do, Margot. Sit."

Margot stood from the edge of the bed and sat in the chair as Mr. Menendez paced back and forth in front of the window. He stopped to stare out the window. Margot figured he was looking down at the creek while he drummed his fingers on the windowsill and figured out their next move. Eventually, he reached into the breast pocket of his suit coat and walked across the room, deep in thought, Margot believed.

"I think I know how to handle this," Mr. Menendez said as he walked past her.

"How," Margot asked, suddenly feeling strange sitting in a chair in the middle of the room.

Mr. Menendez leaned down from behind her and whispered in her ear.

"Do you feel better having gotten our secret off your chest?"

"I don't know. I guess."

"Good. You'll be able to rest in peace."

His words barely registered before Margot felt a sharp jolt to her neck, as if a ring of fire had enclosed around her throat. She gasped but no air would enter her trachea. She reached for her neck, digging her fingers into her skin as she attempted to grab the cord cinched around her neck. She tried to twist out of the chair but the pressure from the garrote pulled her backward and firmly set her shoulders against the backrest.

For thirty seconds she clawed at her neck. After another thirty, she thought to open her eyes. She stared at the sunlight pouring through the hotel window until her vision was taken over by a black, inky ring that encroached from the periphery, slowly constricting her world until everything disappeared.

CHAPTER 46

Cedar Creek, Nevada
Thursday, August 1, 2024

Since Ryder had dropped her video to her social channels on Tuesday night, the rest of the media had taken notice. Speculation had spread that baby Charlotte had returned to Cedar Creek, and reporters, hoping to cash in on the story, descended in droves on the small mountain town, hoping to land an exclusive interview, or at least record the first sighting. Ryder noticed the uptick in media presence and was desperate to beat her colleagues to the story.

She sat in her SUV, which was parked in the back corner of the Cedar Creek Inn. Her cameraman dozed in the passenger seat. She rolled her window down when the inn employee exited the back door and made her way across the parking lot.

"She reserved a room earlier today," the woman said when she reached Ryder's open window. "She was with another woman. Older, maybe fifty."

"You got a room number?" Ryder asked.

"Maybe."

Ryder handed over another fifty-dollar bill. It was the third one she'd given the woman. The employee took it and stuffed it in her pocket.

"Three-oh-three. Here's a keycard."

She dropped the card through the window, hurried back across the lot, and disappeared through the back door.

Ryder slapped her cameraman awake.

"Kerry, let's go."

Kerry jolted awake.

"What's wrong?"

"We've got a room number. Grab your camera."

A minute later, Kerry was pointing his camera at Ryder, who stood in front of the Cedar Creek Inn sign.

"I'm in Cedar Creek, Nevada, where it is rumored that baby Charlotte has come to reunite with the Margolis family. My sources tell me that she is at this hotel, the Cedar Creek Inn, and we're about to track her down to get the first interview, or at least the first sound bites from her."

Ryder jogged across the parking lot as Kerry followed. The footage they would later post was not controlled by a stabilizer. Instead, it was rough and raw as the video bounced while Ryder ran to the back door of the inn and pushed through it. In the stairwell, she climbed three flights of stairs while Kerry followed behind, capturing everything. On the third-floor landing, Ryder stopped and turned to the camera. She spoke in a whisper.

"I've got it from a good source that baby Charlotte, aka Sloan Hastings, is staying in room three-oh-three."

Ryder slowly pushed open the door to the hallway, and Kerry moved the camera to capture the room number on the door halfway down the hall. But just as Ryder was about to exit the stairwell, the door to room 303 opened. She quickly pulled the staircase door closed while Kerry adjusted the camera and aimed it through the vertical window in the door. The mesh of the Georgian wired glass blurred the footage. A man in a suit and tie walked out of room 303 wheeling a suitcase behind him. He walked to the far end of the hallway, pressed the call button, and then entered the elevator. Kerry zoomed in on his face just as the doors were closing.

When the man was gone, Ryder hurried down the hallway to room 303. She took one last look into the camera before she inserted the key and opened the door.

"Sloan Hastings?" Ryder called out as the door swung open.

She walked in with Kerry following.

"Sloan Hastings?"

When it was clear that the room was empty, Ryder turned back to Kerry.

"Hurry!" she said as she raced back down the hallway and took the stairs two at a time, Kerry following close behind and capturing footage that was sure to be disorienting and blurred.

When they made it out the back door, they ran into the parking lot and searched for the man in the suit. He was nowhere.

CHAPTER 47

Cedar Creek, Nevada
Thursday, August 1, 2024

Eric HURRIED TO THE PASSENGER SIDE AND CLIMBED INTO SLOAN'S car. The tires spit gravel as she backed down the driveway and brought Eric up to speed on the details of Margot Gray.

"Margot Gray?"

"That's the woman's name. Wendy Downing was an alias."

"But why is she confessing to you. Or to me, or whatever is happening?"

"Guilt. From what she told me, Margot Gray was just twenty-three years old when a man approached her at the diner she waitressed at with a deal she couldn't refuse. The man told her he was an attorney and needed her help with an adoption."

"Guy Menendez?"

"Yes. He told her he needed to cut through red tape in order to get a little girl to a couple who wanted to adopt her. Margot said she needed the money and decided not to ask questions. When recent news broke that baby Charlotte had returned home and that police were looking for a woman named Wendy Downing, she finally figured it out."

"Then, what, this lady tracked you down?"

"Yeah. The podcast she listens to mentioned that I was in Cedar Creek reuniting with the Margolis family. She found me by hacking into the Vrbo database."

"And she's at your rental now?"

"No, I put her up at the Cedar Creek Inn. I figured my rental's about to be overrun by reporters. I convinced her to stay put while I found you. She's very much on edge. It dawned on her that coming clean about her role in my abduction could likely get her in some trouble."

"It will. Unless she can lead us to Menendez and help us figure out what happened to your birth parents. Then there's probably a deal for her."

Sloan nodded. "I'm not sure she knows any more than she told me. Guy Menendez knew what he was doing. He chose Margot because she was an easy target. And it sounds like the guy's been keeping tabs on her for thirty years. She said every couple of years he either calls her or shows up to check on her. Gives her money and makes sure there's nothing she needs or is worried about."

"She's been in contact with him recently?"

"Sounds like it. She gave me his cell number. I'm hoping it'll help us find this guy."

Eric nodded. "My office will be able to trace the number. Let me talk to her first."

Sloan came out of the foothills and into town. She passed the Louis-Bullat Bridge and turned into the parking lot of the Cedar Creek Inn. When she did, her stomach dropped.

"Shit."

"What's wrong?"

"Her car's gone. She had an older model Mazda and we parked right here. It's gone."

Sloan parked in the spot where they'd left Margot's Mazda and grabbed the keycard from her pocket as she climbed out of the car. She and Eric jogged across the lot, entered the inn, and took the elevator to the third floor. Sloan looked up and down the long hallway as she approached room number 303. She opened the door and entered. The room was empty.

"Margot?"

Eric checked the bathroom. "Empty."

Sloan walked to the foot of the bed, where the woman had been sitting when Sloan left her.

Margot Gray was gone.

THE PAST

Cedar Creek, Nevada

Sunday, July 2, 1995
2 Days Prior . . .

SANDY STAMOS TURNED DOWN THE LONG DRIVE AND PULLED TO A stop in front of the cabin. He opened the back hatch of the Suburban and grabbed the long, padded bag that contained the rifle he'd taken from the Harrison County Sheriff's Department. He'd come up with his plan after visiting Tom Quinn in Lake Tahoe, and had made the call on the way home. He opened the door to the cabin and checked the time—4:05 p.m. Company was due to arrive at five, and Sandy was going to make damn sure the man followed directions and came alone.

He'd made a tactical decision by arranging the meeting at his cabin, and there were pros and cons to the choice. The cabin was isolated in the foothills and there was no chance anyone would discover the two men meeting there. Also, the cabin was on his turf, and he knew the lay of the land. If things broke bad, he'd have the advantage. The con, of course, was that he might have invited the enemy into his home, thereby giving away the location of his family's cabin—a closely kept Stamos secret ever since his father had become sheriff of Harrison County decades earlier.

He grabbed a Gatorade from the fridge and headed upstairs with the rifle slung over his shoulder. He opened the window in the main bedroom, stepped over the sill until his boot gripped the shingles of the roof, and then ducked through. He scaled the A-frame roof and made his way to the chimney. He took his position behind the red brick and surveyed the land. From his vantage point he could see the entirety of the valley, and the town of Cedar Creek off in the distance. He also had a bird's eye view of the road that cut behind the cabin and ran adjacent to the gorge his property butted up against. From his perch on the cabin's roof Sandy could also see the wooden bridge that jumped the gorge and arched over the creek below—the lone access point to his cabin.

Sandy pulled the rifle from the soft carrying case and positioned it on a bipod atop the chimney. He checked the site and adjusted the focus so that the reticle was aimed at the beginning of the bridge. Lifting a pair of binoculars that hung from his neck, he trained them on the bridge and waited. Thirty minutes passed before the vehicle came into focus.

The BMW slowly crossed the bridge and turned onto the frontage road. Sandy kept the binoculars focused on the bridge for another minute, waiting for trail vehicles. None came. He turned back to the chimney, twisting the rifle in the process as he placed his eye to the scope. He adjusted the reticle to focus on the long driveway that led from the frontage road. As the car slowed and then turned onto the drive, Sandy set the crosshairs on the driver's side windshield.

When Preston Margolis climbed from the car, Sandy kept the man in the crosshairs.

Cedar Creek, Nevada

Sunday, July 2, 1995
2 Days Prior . . .

"Y OU ALONE?" SANDY YELLED FROM THE ROOFTOP.
It caused Preston to look around for the source.

"Answer the question."

"Yeah," Preston yelled. "I'm alone."

"Stay where you're at and don't move. Understand?"

"What's this about, Sheriff?"

Sandy didn't answer. He left the rifle on top of the chimney and climbed down the side of the roof to where a shed stood next to the cabin. He jumped onto the roof of the shed and hurried over to the side where he'd set up a ladder earlier. He clambered down to the ground, pulled his Glock from its holster, and hurried to the side of the cabin. When he peeked around the corner he saw Preston Margolis in the same spot on the driveway. With his Glock out in front of him, Sandy emerged.

When Preston saw Sandy, he raised his hands.

"What the hell, Sandy?"

"Open the trunk."

"What?"

"Open it!"

"I'm alone, Sandy. Who the hell do you think I'm bringing with me?"

"Humor me."

Preston walked to the back of the BMW and pulled open the

trunk. Sandy came around and pointed his Glock into the back of the empty space. He went to the passenger's side door next and pulled it open. Also empty.

"Feel better?" Preston asked.

"Forgive me for trusting a Margolis as far as I can throw him."

Sandy holstered his gun.

"Where the hell are we?"

"My family's hunting cabin."

"Why did you have me come all the way out here?"

"Because someone's trying to frame your wife for Baker Jauncey's murder, and I need your help figuring out who it is."

Cedar Creek, Nevada

Sunday, July 2, 1995
2 Days Prior . . .

SANDY ASSUMED TWO THINGS WHEN HE CONCOCTED HIS PLAN TO ENlist the help of Preston Margolis. The first was that Preston had nothing to do with the murder of Baker Jauncey and would do everything possible to protect Annabelle. The second was that, as an attorney at Margolis & Margolis, Preston had unprecedented access to files and information that could help Sandy figure out who Guy Menendez was.

"Can I get you a beer?" Sandy asked as they walked into the cabin.

"Maybe a whiskey, instead? It's not every day that I have a gun pointed at me."

Sandy motioned to the kitchen island and for Preston to take a seat. He poured two fingers of Jameson into a tumbler and grabbed a beer from the fridge. Sandy took a stool next to Preston and pushed the whiskey over to him.

Preston took a long sip.

"Okay, Sheriff. Start from the beginning."

"Someone at Margolis and Margolis killed Baker Jauncey," Sandy said, taking a sip of beer.

"What?"

Sandy nodded. "Marvin Mann, Baker's investigator, tracked me down a few days ago to tell me an interesting story. Baker had stumbled across evidence of financial fraud inside your law firm—

money laundering, embezzlement, misappropriation of funds, and more. Baker enlisted his trusted investigator to help him figure out who was involved, and gave Marvin a stack of documents he took from the firm. The next day Baker was dead—the victim of an apparent hit-and-run. Marvin Mann came to me with his suspicions that Baker's death was no accident. He handed over all the documents Baker had given him, and I asked my accountant to take a look at them. The bottom line is that some very shady things are going on at your law firm. Baker Jauncey caught wind of them and was killed because of it."

"Who?" Preston asked. "Who's involved in this fraud?"

"That's why I asked you out here. I don't know who's involved. But I'm hoping if I share what I know, that you'll be able to figure it out since you have easy access to Margolis and Margolis files."

"What did you learn?"

Sandy walked over to a cabinet above the refrigerator and removed a few pages of the files Marvin Mann had given him. These were copies; the originals were still stashed in the Reno safe deposit box.

"This is some of what Baker found at the firm. It's just a taste of what he gave Marvin Mann."

Preston skimmed the pages.

"If this is just some of what Baker found, where's the rest of it?"

"Tucked away somewhere safe for now. And that's all I'll say until I know if you're going to help me."

"Take me through what your accountant found," Preston said.

For fifteen minutes Sandy laid out the complicated puzzle of the fraud taking place inside Margolis & Margolis.

Preston paged back through the documents.

"There're no names on any of these pages. They're all anonymous shell companies and numbered accounts."

"There's only one name in any of the documents. Guy Menendez."

"Who?"

"Guy Menendez."

"There's no one by that name at Margolis and Margolis."

Sandy nodded. "I figured that much already."

"Tell me what this has to do with my wife."

Sandy took a sip of beer. "It was a setup, Preston. Someone killed Baker and then made it look like he was hit by Annabelle's car."

"Why?"

"Your guess is as good as mine. But here's what I'm stuck on. Your family has influence just about everywhere in Harrison County and much of Nevada. The Harrison County coroner's office is under your family's authority, and the coroner's office literally stole Baker's body from Reno in the dead of night and did their own autopsy. The only way that happens is if someone decided to meddle in the case. And when meddling happens around these parts, it usually has Margolis fingerprints on it."

Preston opened his palms. "It obviously didn't come from me."

"That's why you're sitting here, counselor. I need you to help me figure out what's going on. The Reno Medical Examiner's Office came to a wholly different conclusion about how Baker Jauncey died than did the Harrison County coroner. According to the coroner, the official cause of death was head trauma sustained during the hit-and-run. Reno says Baker was hit by a baseball bat. So, best I can tell, someone didn't like the idea that Baker's death was going to be blamed on him being cracked by a baseball bat, and much preferred the official line stating that he died from being run over by Annabelle's car."

"So just to be clear, my wife is no longer a suspect in Baker's death?"

"Not so long as I'm running the investigation."

"What do you need from me?"

"I need you to figure out who's behind the fraud at Margolis and Margolis."

"And you think the answer lies somewhere in the files inside my law firm?"

"I do."

Preston pushed the whiskey away and stood up. "Then I'll go look."

"When?"

"Right now."

Cedar Creek, Nevada

Sunday, July 2, 1995
2 Days Prior . . .

P RESTON WAITED UNTIL NIGHTFALL TO GO TO THE OFFICES OF MARGO-
lis & Margolis. Hours earlier he'd watched the cleaning staff exit
the building, pack up their vans, and pull from the parking lot
after leaving the offices immaculate for Monday morning. He
drank coffee to keep himself alert as he bided his time. When he
was certain the building was empty, without even an eager junior
associate remaining, he climbed from his car and entered through
the rear door. It was close to midnight.

His office was on the third floor, and he quickly sat behind the
desk and fired up his computer. The firm was on the cutting edge
of technology and had digitized all its files over the last twenty-four
months. Margolis & Margolis had been using internal email for
years, but had leaned fully into the new Internet age that was upon
them. Preston was one of the young attorneys encouraging the
transition to digitized files and electronic records, and was the
point man for implementing the firm's conversion into the tech-
nological era. Because of this, he was more than familiar with the
inner workings of the firm's digital files, and even without being a
partner had easy access to everything.

It took just thirty minutes of sniffing to find the name *Guy
Menendez* buried in the files. Once he was onto the scent, he never
lost it. He spent hours digging through the firm's files and diving
deeply into the financial records. The tracks were covered well

enough for the lazy snooper or casual observer to miss, but armed with the knowledge Sandy Stamos had provided, Preston knew what to look for, and found it easily. So obvious was the fraud and theft that Preston wondered how it had gone unnoticed for so long. Unless, he wondered, someone at the top was part of it.

He drank a pot of coffee and kept digging. He spent all night picking through the files and unraveling the web of corruption. At just past 4:00 a.m., with his desk cluttered by computer printouts that carefully detailed the financial fraud and the way it had been covered up, he hit pay dirt.

"Son of a bitch," he whispered, staring at the computer screen with bloodshot eyes.

Despite the obnoxious hour, he picked up his desk phone and punched Sandy's number into the keypad. Sandy answered on the first ring.

"Anything?"

"Everything," Preston said. "I know who's skimming the money."

PART V

Into Focus

Chapter 48

Cedar Creek, Nevada
Thursday, August 1, 2024

Aᶠᵀᴱᴿ Sʟᴏᴀɴ ʟᴇꜰᴛ ᴛʜᴇ Cᴇᴅᴀʀ Cʀᴇᴇᴋ Iɴɴ, ꜱʜᴇ ᴅʀᴏᴘᴘᴇᴅ Eʀɪᴄ ᴀᴛ the sheriff's office. Margot Gray couldn't have gotten far. Eric would put his deputies on the lookout for an older model Mazda and alert the Nevada Highway Patrol. If Margot was still in town, they'd find her. If she were on the road, they'd bring her in. Eric also planned to run the phone number Margot had provided that belonged to Guy Menendez.

In the meantime, Sloan knew it wouldn't be long before the press found her rental house. She'd accepted Eric's offer to lay low at his cabin in the foothills. She needed to pack a few things first, so she headed back to her rental house with a heavy mix of disappointment and frustration. As she pulled into the driveway, the sun was setting, lighting the clouds above the Sierra Nevada Mountains in an eerie glow of crimson that screamed to Sloan that the opportunity to unlock the secrets of her past was bleeding away.

Inside, she grabbed a Diet Dr. Pepper and sat at the kitchen table. She found Special Agent John Michaels's card and called him. Over a fifteen-minute conversation, she told him about Margot Gray, aka Wendy Downing. She gave him Margot's description and the make and model of the car she was driving. She read off the phone number that was believed to belong to Guy Menendez and answered a slew of questions from Agent Michaels.

"Stamos is the sheriff out there in Harrison County?" Michaels asked.

"Yes," Sloan said. "He and I have been . . . not exactly working together, but in close contact since I've been out here."

"Something I need to know about?"

Sloan thought about Eric's father and the mysterious link between Baker Jauncey's death thirty years earlier and the disappearance of her and her birth parents. She wouldn't know where to start.

"Maybe at some point," she said. "But let's concentrate on Margot Gray for now."

"Give me the day. I'll be in touch in the morning. Anything else?"

"Yeah. How did my story leak?"

"I'm launching an internal investigation to figure that out. But right now I'm going to run with the leads you've given me."

"Keep me posted."

"Will do."

Sloan ended the call just as she heard a car door slam outside. She went to the living room window and peeked through the plantation shutters.

"Shit."

A CBS Channel 4 news van was parked outside. The back doors were open, and a man pulled equipment from the van. Before Sloan could look away, another news van pulled down the road and parked across the street. A reporter opened the door and hurried across the front lawn. Sloan snapped the shutters closed as the woman reached the front stoop and knocked on the door.

"Shit, *shit!*" Sloan whispered to herself.

"Sloan Hastings?" the reporter yelled. "Monica Campbell with NBC News. We're hoping to speak with you about the alleged connection to baby Charlotte Margolis and her parents, who are still missing."

Her phone buzzed in her hand and startled her. She looked at the screen and saw that Nora was calling. She walked into the kitchen and answered in a whisper.

"Hello?"

"I just spoke with Tilly. News vans are parked outside her house and reporters are milling around."

"Yeah, here, too. I'm at my rental and two news vans just pulled up. Some lunatic is pounding on my front door as we speak."

"I'm coming over," Nora said.

"To do what?"

"Rescue you. Stay put. I'll be there in a few minutes. And pack your stuff, you're not staying there."

The call ended and Sloan went back to the front window. A third van had pulled to the curb. As the reporter continued to pound on the front door, Sloan heard more knocking at the back door off the kitchen.

"Relentless," she said to herself.

She briefly considered opening the door and giving them the sound bite they were all so desperate for, and the video footage and first live images they wanted so badly. But Sloan knew it wouldn't end with a simple statement. They'd want answers that Sloan did not have.

She ran upstairs and packed her suitcase, emptying the drawers she had filled just a few days before. She cleared out the bathroom and lugged her suitcase down the stairs just as her phone buzzed with a text message from Nora.

"I'm pulling up now."

Sloan watched through the front window as Nora tore into the driveway and screeched to a stop at an odd angle, the front wheels on the grass. She opened the driver's side door and stormed past the reporters who thrust microphones in her face and shouted questions as cameras rolled and recorded everything. Nora kept them at bay with an opened palm and a shake of her head until she was on the front porch, when Sloan opened the door and pulled her inside.

"This is insane," Sloan said.

The weight of the situation was beginning to dawn on her. Baby Charlotte Margolis had dominated the news and tabloids for nearly a year after she and her parents disappeared, and even this many decades later the American public was obsessed with her story. And now they were desperate for the sequel—the return of baby Charlotte Margolis.

"You're like a famous movie star dodging the paparazzi." Nora looked down and saw Sloan's bag. "Good, you're packed."

Nora grabbed Sloan's suitcase.

"Follow me."

"Where are we going?"

"We're getting the hell out of here."

"They'll just follow us."

"Unlikely," Nora said. "Just trust me. Ready?"

Sloan nodded. Nora opened the front door and ran down the steps with Sloan's suitcase in tow and Sloan close behind.

"Sloan Hastings!" one of the reporters yelled. "Are you baby Charlotte Margolis?"

"Where are Preston and Annabelle Margolis?" another reporter yelled.

Sloan ignored the questions as she raced to Nora's car, ripped open the passenger's side door, and quickly climbed in. Nora threw the suitcase into the backseat, sat behind the wheel, and slammed her door closed. The engine was still running, and she dropped the car into reverse, screeching her tires as she backed into the street and scattering the cameramen who had encroached on the vehicle. When she was clear, she put the car into drive and sped off. It took just a moment for the news crews to throw their equipment into the backs of the vans and start their pursuit. But by then it was too late.

As the vans spun around the cul-de-sac, a Ford F150 skidded to a stop at the end of the street, blocking the crews from exiting the neighborhood. The drivers of each of the three vans laid on their horns. When the F150 stayed put, one of the drivers got out and approached the pickup truck.

"Get the hell out of the way!"

The window of the F150 rolled down to reveal Lester Strange, the Margolis family's longtime handyman.

"No can do," Lester said.

CHAPTER 49

Cedar Creek, Nevada
Thursday, August 1, 2024

NORA PULLED DOWN THE ALLEY BEHIND HER STUDIO AND PARKED next to the Dumpster.

"Who was that in the pickup truck?" Sloan asked.

"Lester, our handyman. He's as loyal as they come. I asked him for a favor, and he didn't hesitate. It bought us some time. Come on."

Sloan followed Nora down the alley and through the back door of the photography studio. Inside, Nora closed the blinds.

"You're safe here for now, but the rest of this town is a crapshoot. Reporters believe you're staying at the Cedar Creek Inn, and there are a bunch of news crews there. Now, they obviously found your rental house. Reporters are lurking outside the gates of Tilly and Reid's estate, too. They'll probably go to my house at some point, but my studio is too far removed for anyone to find us here. For a while, at least. We're working on Plan B."

"Maybe I should just talk to them."

"No way," Nora said. "You need a lawyer before you do that. You could get a nice payday out of it if you give the right person an exclusive. Probably pay off all your medical school debt. Plus, I'd talk with that FBI agent you mentioned before you start dishing out interviews. Never know what you can and can't say."

Sloan walked over to the window and peeked through the blinds. "So we're just going to hide at your studio? For how long?"

"Hopefully not long. Tilly said things should be ready in about an hour."

"What things?"

"Until we can help you organize the right journalist to speak with in the right setting, we're getting you out of Cedar Creek."

"And going where?"

"Margolis Manor. The family's winery is the only logical choice. It's only a few hours away, but it may as well be on the other side of the earth, because once we're there no one will find us or bother us. Even if the press somehow tracked us there, the property is massive and impossible for anyone to penetrate. We can stay there until things settle down, or at least until we figure out your best path forward."

"Are you sure? I feel terrible that I've brought all this drama with me."

"Of course. It was Reid's idea. A couple thousand acres of isolated land covered by wine grapes in Oregon? It's perfect. Reid's arranging things now and will call when everything's set. The press outside the front gates of Reid and Tilly's estate are throwing a wrench into things at the moment, but he's figuring that out as we speak. For now, we'll just wait here until we get the all clear."

Sloan rubbed the front of her pants. A buzzing nervousness filled her gut. She needed to find a discreet way to call Eric and let him know what was happening.

"Oh, look at you," Nora said. "You're a nervous wreck."

Sloan forced a smile. "I just feel awful for putting everyone in such an awkward position."

"Listen, there're lots of things about Ellis's family that are hard to swallow. But one thing Tilly and Reid are good at is protecting the people they care about. They'll help you navigate this thing with the media. They have the contacts and the influence to calm this frenzy down and get you in touch with the right people. It'll just take some time."

Nora pointed at the remaining boxes of Annabelle's photos.

"Let's finish looking through the last two boxes," Nora said. "It'll get your mind off all this nonsense."

Through the congestion in Sloan's mind, and the anxiety coursing through her veins, a thought came to her. She and Eric had spent the previous night combing through the details of the investigation into the disappearance of her and her birth parents. The biggest revelation they'd come across was that Annabelle's blood had been found in the kitchen of her home, having been cleaned up in an attempt to hide the evidence. The closets in the home were empty and Preston and Annabelle's clothes were missing, hinting that they'd left of their own volition. Margot Gray's confession that someone had paid her to pose as baby Charlotte's birth mother only added to the confusion. When midnight came, Sloan and Eric had more questions than answers. But perhaps the boxes in front of her, and the photos Annabelle took that summer, held the missing pieces of the puzzle.

"Are Annabelle's photos time stamped?"

"They should be."

Nora walked over to one of the boxes and removed a photo. In the bottom right corner the date was stamped in red. Nora held the photo up.

"Yes. June 22, 1995."

Sloan squinted and lifted her chin. "How close do the photos come to July Fourth?"

Nora looked at the remaining boxes and then back at Sloan, a shade of understanding coloring her eyes. "The day she disappeared?"

"Yeah. You've seen most of these photos. How close do they come to July Fourth?"

"All the way to that morning," Nora said. "If I remember correctly."

"Let's see."

CHAPTER 50

Cedar Creek, Nevada
Thursday, August 1, 2024

SLOAN AND NORA TOOK TURNS CHECKING THE STREET FOR NEWS CREWS. They made it through the second box of photos and found, toward the bottom, an envelope of pictures dated July 4, 1995—the day Annabelle Margolis disappeared with her husband and two-month-old daughter. The day, Sloan knew from the case file, that a large amount of Annabelle's blood had been cleaned up from the kitchen floor.

"Here," Nora said. "These are from July Fourth."

Nora quickly paged through the photos.

"Yeah. I remember developing these. I didn't do it myself. I brought the film to the drugstore to be developed. The rolls of film were among Annabelle and Preston's belongings when we eventually cleared out the house weeks after they . . . and you, went missing."

She handed the photos to Sloan.

"Who's looked at these?" Sloan asked.

"I have, but years and years ago. And the detectives investigating the case wanted to see them. But they never found anything interesting. They gave them back to me, and they've been sitting in my attic ever since. Until Ellis pulled them out for me the other day."

Sloan and Nora removed the pictures—dozens of glossy 4x6s—and spread them across the table. Sloan's fingers tingled with anticipation as she arranged the photos. They revealed the story of her and her birth parents' last day in Cedar Creek, told through the lens of Annabelle's camera. The images began in the morning, with beautiful shots of the sunrise off the back deck of Preston and Annabelle's new home. Then, the photos proceeded to the Split the Creek Gala in town, where the Fourth of July celebration had taken place.

"Here's you in your stroller," Nora said, passing Sloan a photo of baby Charlotte tucked into a stroller and protected from the sun by the overhanging visor. "You were so dang cute!"

There were several photos of baby Charlotte alone, and a few with her in Preston's arms.

"All of these were taken on the Nikon FM10 I gifted Annabelle that summer," Nora said. "She carried that camera everywhere. Kept it hanging around her neck and shot anything that looked photogenic."

Nora removed the last photo from the envelope.

"God she was good," Nora said. "Look how she framed this photo of you."

Nora held up a photo of baby Charlotte lying on a red-white-and-blue blanket positioned on the lawn next to the creek, blurred images of sailboats drifting past in the background.

Sloan took the photo and examined it. The date was stamped in red at the bottom of the photo.

"The Split the Creek Gala for the Fourth," Sloan said. "Is that still a thing around here?"

"Oh, sure. It's been going on as long as I can remember. This past July was the biggest turnout in Cedar Creek history."

"So it's an all-day thing?"

"Yes. Starts in the morning and runs straight through until sunset. A huge fireworks show wraps things up at night."

Sloan held up the photo of herself on the blanket. "So this is sometime in the late morning or early afternoon, based on the sunlight. And this is the last photo in the bunch. Are there more from that day? It's the day we all disappeared. It's worth looking at what Annabelle's last photos were. Unless this is it, and then it doesn't tell us much."

Nora shook her head. "These photos were from the last roll of film we found. We didn't find any other rolls in the house."

"What's in the last box?" Sloan asked, pointing at the lone remaining cardboard box at the end of the table.

"Just random photography equipment that was left at Preston and Annabelle's house. No one knew what to do with the stuff when we were emptying out the house, so I took it."

Nora stood up and walked to the far side of the table. She lifted the last box and carried it over to Sloan. When Nora removed the top, she paused. Her forehead burrowed with wrinkles.

"What the hell?"

"What's wrong?" Sloan asked. "More pictures?"

"No, just this."

Nora reached into the box and, from the random bits of equipment, removed a camera.

"It's Annabelle's. The Nikon FM10 I gave her that summer."

"Why is that strange?"

"Because this wasn't with Annabelle's belongings when we cleared out the house."

"Are you sure? It was nearly thirty years ago."

"I'm sure. I gave it to her as a birthday present, and I wondered where it went. Part of me figured that if Annabelle had gone on the run, she'd have taken it with her."

"We both know Annabelle didn't go on the run."

Nora nodded.

"Then how did her camera end up in the box if she didn't leave it at her house?"

Nora looked at Sloan and then back to the camera, turning it over as if holding an ancient relic. "I don't know."

Nora twisted the camera one last time and then pulled it close to examine it.

"Son of a gun," Nora said. "There's still a roll of film in here."

"In the camera?"

"Yes."

Sloan stood. "Are there photos on it?"

"It shows three shots remain. That means there're twenty-one undeveloped photos in here."

"A continuation of what's here," Sloan said, pointing to the photos that covered the table. "From the day we all disappeared, right? They have to be from the same day."

Nora's lips remained separated, slack-jawed by what they'd discovered. "Let's find out."

Sloan's stomach roiled with anxiety and a foreboding sense that the mystery of her life was about to be uncovered.

"What's wrong?"

Sloan shook her head. "Nothing. I'm just nervous, I guess. To see what's on the photos."

"We don't have to look at these."

"Of course we do. Can we develop them in the darkroom?"

"Yes. But only if you're sure."

"Let's go."

They heard the back door open.

"Nora?" Ellis said as he walked into the studio. "We're ready, but we've got to leave now. The news crews are still outside the house, but my parents are leaving through the maintenance road behind the property."

"I had Sloan pack her things," Nora said, pointing to Sloan's suitcase.

"Perfect," Ellis said, wheeling Sloan's suitcase to the back door. "I'll put this in the car."

"What about Annabelle's photos?" Sloan asked in a whispered voice.

Nora took the camera and stuffed it into her bag.

"I've got a darkroom at the house up north. We'll develop them there."

"At the winery?"

"Yes, from back in the day."

"Ready?" Ellis asked a moment later.

Nora nodded. "Are we all driving together?"

"Not driving," Ellis said. "Flying. My father chartered a helicopter to get us the hell out of here."

CHAPTER 51

Cedar Creek, Nevada
Thursday, August 1, 2024

SLOAN COULD HAVE BEEN IN A DREAM, AND ACTUALLY CONSIDERED that she was, as she held Nora's hand while they ran through the field to a waiting helicopter silhouetted by the still-glowing horizon, its rotors spinning and thud-thud-thudding vibrations through her chest. Ellis followed close behind and when she climbed onboard, she saw Tilly and Reid Margolis strapped into their seats.

"Welcome!" Reid yelled over the pounding of the helicopter blades. "I know we haven't known each other long, but I don't allow anyone to treat members of my family so rudely. That includes the almighty American media."

The copilot assisted Sloan and Nora into the belly of the helicopter and helped them strap into their seats.

"Here you go, ma'am." The young man handed Sloan a pair of noise-canceling earphones. "It's about a two-hour flight, you'll need these."

Sloan tried to smile as she took the headphones and snapped them over her ears. The thudding of the rotors immediately dulled. She looked at Nora, who squeezed Sloan's hand and smiled. How this woman had become such a close friend in only a matter of days, Sloan could not explain. But she was damn happy for the friendship.

Ellis took the seat across from them while the copilot secured the door before climbing back into his seat in the cockpit. Through the headphones Sloan heard the pilot's voice.

"Okay folks. Settle in for a two-hour flight. Weather is clear and skies are calm. Should be uneventful."

Sloan looked out the window as the helicopter lifted off, the grass of the prairie flattening with the downward push from the rotors. Momentum pulled her back into her seat as the helicopter accelerated, heading northwest toward Oregon.

CHAPTER 52

Bend, Oregon
Thursday, August 1, 2024

MARGOLIS MANOR WAS A SPRAWLING ESTATE THAT COVERED TWO thousand acres in Bend, Oregon. It was dark by the time they arrived, and the Margolis home was brilliantly lit from above. Nora pointed out landmarks as they approached—the main home, the guest cottage, the tennis courts, the winery, and the vineyard. When the helicopter landed in a clearing a hundred yards from the pool, Sloan got the impression that this was not the first time the family had arrived at the estate in such a fashion.

The pilot shut down the engine, the copilot opened the door, and they all spilled out. Sloan took Ellis's hand as he helped her and Nora down the steps before turning his attention to his mother, who took the stairs gingerly and relied on her son's assistance. Two men appeared and spoke briefly with Reid before pulling luggage from the compartment. Reid Margolis led them all across the lawn, past the pool and patio, and through the back door of the home. Sloan walked into the kitchen and realized how magnificent the place was—from concrete countertops to cherry-wood cabinets and twenty-foot ceilings, the home was gorgeous.

"Welcome to Margolis Manor," Reid said with a smile.

"Thank you," Sloan said. "I'm sorry, I'm a bit overwhelmed at the moment."

"We apologize for whisking you away like that," Tilly said. "We just couldn't believe the number of news vans parked outside the gates of our home. We knew things would only get worse, and we're not prepared to speak with the media just yet."

"I'm just stunned that there's so much interest," Sloan said.

"You shouldn't be," Reid said. "When you all went missing that summer, it was the biggest story in America. You're learning about today it by paging through recorded history. We lived it. The press was incessant back then, and remained that way for years. It's no surprise your return has caused such an uproar, and we're not about to walk blindly into the media trap we fell for decades ago. It was, excuse me, a goddamn mess. Accusations, conspiracy theories, rumors, and flat-out lies. We're not going to allow that same thing to happen again. We're going to control the narrative this time around, and the best way to do that is to address the media on *our* terms. We've bought a few days by coming here, and we'll take the weekend to figure out the best approach."

It was not hard, Sloan thought, to see that Reid Margolis was the patriarch of the family—the one who called the shots and made the decisions.

"I'm really sorry for any problems this has caused," Sloan said.

"Oh, stop it," Tilly said, coming over and taking Sloan's forearm in her soft hands. "This is not your fault, and we'd have it no other way."

"I'm all for taking a minute to figure out our options," Ellis said. "But we're going to have to speak with the press at some point. Mostly they'll want to hear from Sloan, but all of us will have to make statements. We should get our talking points laid out so we're all on the same page."

"For Christ's sake, Ellis," Reid said. "This is not trial prep. We'll get on the same page tomorrow after I make some calls to the networks and inquire about interviews."

"I'm not sure if this will help," Sloan said. "But my department chair back in Raleigh is the medical consultant for NBC and HAP News. I could reach out to her and see if she could put us in touch with anyone."

Reid nodded. "That's a great start. I'll make some calls of my own and we'll see what comes of it. But that's on the agenda for tomorrow. Right now, after that stressful exit, can I get anyone a drink? God knows I need one."

A few minutes later, two bottles of Margolis Manor cabernet were opened, and they all sat in the living room watching *American Events,* during which Avery Mason recapped the details of baby Charlotte's miraculous resurfacing after nearly thirty years. A quick perusing of the channels told them that every major network, as well as the cable news outlets, were reporting on the return of Charlotte Margolis.

CHAPTER 53

Bend, Oregon
Thursday, August 1, 2024

F OR TWO STRAIGHT HOURS, AND FOUR BOTTLES OF WINE, SLOAN
watched the news coverage with the Margolises. Although Sloan
had dipped her toe into the story of her disappearance by perusing
old news articles and tabloid magazines, the networks took a deep
dive. Old footage from 1995 played across the screen of a fifty-
something Reid and Tilly Margolis answering questions outside the
gates of their estate. Another shot showed old footage of a press
conference conducted by Nevada State Police detectives, during
which Reid and Tilly begged the community to come forward with
any information about their missing son, daughter in-law, and
granddaughter. Sloan watched scenes of detectives pulling boxes
from Preston and Annabelle's home, of Annabelle's car and the
damaged front end, of Baker Jauncey and the idea that the family
had skipped town to avoid prosecution. Reid finally shut off the
television when the news anchors began repeating themselves.

"That's about all I can take," Reid said.

Tilly cried softly as she sat on the couch. When neither Reid nor
Ellis consoled her, Nora and Sloan each took one of Tilly's hands.

"Let's call it a night," Ellis said. "We'll reconvene at breakfast and
talk strategy."

Tilly nodded and allowed Sloan and Nora to help her from the
couch. Reid came over and took Tilly under the arm.

"Ellis, can you show Sloan her room?"

"We've got it," Nora said.

Reid led Tilly out of the living room and into the hallway, where they disappeared into the first-floor bedroom.

"The staff took your bags to the guest cottage," Ellis said. "We thought you'd be more comfortable in your own space."

Sloan smiled and nodded. "That's fine. Whatever works best."

"I'll get Sloan settled," Nora said. "Why don't you go to bed. I'll be up in a little bit."

Ellis nodded and kissed Nora before heading upstairs. Sloan followed Nora out the front door and along a lighted walking path. The guest cottage was bigger than Sloan's apartment in Raleigh. It featured a full kitchen, a large living space, a bedroom with a king bed, and a massive bathroom. The sliding door off the living room led to the pool deck.

"I hope this is okay," Nora said.

"Are you kidding me? It's beautiful."

"Can I get you anything before bed?"

"I think I'm good. Well, there is one thing, I guess. I'm still hoping to develop those photos."

"Of course. We can do it tomorrow."

"You said you have a darkroom here?"

"Yes. Ellis put it in for me right after we were married. We used to come up here every weekend. I needed a place to develop my pictures, so Ellis had Lester convert an old walk-in closet in the cellar into a darkroom. It's in the main house. It's stocked with everything we need. Let's take a look tomorrow?"

"Yeah." Sloan nodded. "Let's do that."

A moment later Sloan was alone in the guest cottage. She watched through the front window as Nora walked back to the main house and disappeared into the darkness. She grabbed her phone and made a quick call to her parents, letting them know where she was and getting an update on the media onslaught back in Raleigh. There were still news vans parked outside their home and at her parents' practice, but Todd and Dolly hadn't uttered a word to any reporters.

Her next call was to Eric.

"Did you make it up to the cabin?" Eric said when he answered.

"I'm still at the sheriff's department, but this town is teeming with reporters."

"No. I'm in Oregon."

"What?"

"News crews trapped me in my rental house. It's a long story, but Reid and Tilly Margolis flew me, if you can believe it, by helicopter to their winery in Oregon."

"You're kidding me."

"No. I'm with Nora and Ellis. Reid and Tilly are here, too, and they're all plotting the best way to handle the press. The plan is to bide our time here for the weekend. Any news on Margot Gray?"

"No. If she's still in Cedar Creek, she's doing a great job of avoiding my deputies. And if she's on the road, no one in the Nevada State Police can find her."

"Great."

"Oh, and the phone number she gave you for Guy Menendez was a burner phone, so there's no way to trace it."

"Damn it!"

"We're not done looking. We'll find her."

"Thanks, Eric."

Sloan ended the call and walked into the bathroom to brush her teeth and prepare for bed. With the water running and her electric toothbrush buzzing, she thought she heard something out in the main room, as if maybe the front door had opened. She twisted the handle on the faucet and turned her toothbrush off. She listened for a moment but heard nothing. She stepped out of the bathroom and walked to the front door. She moved the curtains to the side and peered out into the night. The main house was dark but for a lone window on the second story. A figure appeared beyond the curtains just before the light went out and the entire house stood in darkness.

Sloan reached for the deadbolt and twisted it into place.

CHAPTER 54

Cedar Creek, Nevada
Thursday, August 1, 2024

Marvin Mann turned on the late-night cable news as he packed his pipe tight with tobacco and cozied into his recliner. At sixty-three years old, Marvin was living his best life. Other than an arthritic hip angered by foul weather, and a right eye hazy from a developing cataract, he was in damn good shape. He golfed twice a week and played in a cribbage league on Thursday nights. His children were grown and scattered, and much of his travel schedule involved he and his wife flying around the country to visit them and his four grandchildren—from as far as New York, to as close as San Francisco.

Although Marvin and his wife had considered moving over the years, they'd always found their way back to Cedar Creek. They'd sampled trial runs in Phoenix, Santa Fe, and even an extended six-month stay in St. Petersburg to see what the buzz of Florida was all about. None of the locations suited them quite right, and after years of searching, they decided Cedar Creek was the place they'd live out their years. It wasn't simply *home* or *where he was born*, it was where he'd made his living. His occupation was not something he could pick up and perform in another state. Marvin had spent more than a decade as a legal investigator for Margolis & Margolis, and when his tenure ended with the death of Baker Jauncey, he retired from legal investigation and set up his own private investigation service.

Today, his agency employed twenty-six investigators and, although he'd slowed down over the years, Marvin had yet to retire. In his sixties now, he was no longer doing fieldwork—that was for the kids who could hide in hedges and stay awake all night on stakeouts. His role nowadays was as the face of the agency. He nurtured his network of contacts, which included attorneys, law enforcement personnel, Nevada State Police detectives, and a short list of ex-cons he kept on the payroll when he needed something dicey. The bottom line was that until someone could step up and run the agency more efficiently, Marvin was going to continue working. He didn't mind.

He finished packing his pipe just as a replay of *American Events* came back from commercial break. He heard Avery Mason's familiar voice as she started a segment.

"Now to breaking news," the newsmagazine host said, "out of Cedar Creek, Nevada, a small town in the foothills of the Sierra Nevada Mountains. Of course, many of us are familiar with Cedar Creek because of the missing Margolis family that captured the attention of the nation. In 1995, Preston and Annabelle Margolis disappeared with their infant daughter, Charlotte. For decades there have been no breaks in the case, and the family's whereabouts have remained a mystery. But now, in a stunning twist to the nearly thirty-year-old mystery, baby Charlotte Margolis has been found alive and well living in Raleigh, North Carolina."

Marvin turned his attention away from his pipe, stood from his recliner, and walked slowly toward the television. The picture of a pretty young woman filled the screen.

"Sloan Hastings submitted her DNA to an online genealogy site and learned she was not only related to the Margolis family of Harrison County, Nevada," Avery Mason continued, "but that her DNA profile suggested she was baby Charlotte Margolis, missing for nearly three decades. Sloan Hastings is a twenty-nine-year-old physician training to become a medical examiner under our network's very own medical consultant, Dr. Livia Cutty. Sloan Hastings's adoptive parents, Dolly and Todd Hastings, are dentists from Raleigh, North Carolina. So far there are no details about how the Hastings came to adopt Charlotte Margolis, but our sources assure us that Dolly and Todd Hastings are not suspected in baby Charlotte's disappearance. To this point, there is no word on the whereabouts of Preston and Annabelle Margolis. The FBI is involved in the investigation, and we will keep you up-to-date on any developments. Here with us now in the studio is Dr. Craig Fanning, a genealogist who will help us understand how this remarkable discovery was made using genetic tracing and DNA technology."

Marvin lifted the remote and shut off the television. He stood in silence as the information settled and his mind processed what he'd just heard. He had long suspected that the timing of the Margolis family's disappearance, so closely packed around the deaths of both his old boss, Baker Jauncey, and Sheriff Sandy Stamos, was not a simple coincidence. He knew back then that the events were all connected, but had lacked the courage to try to piece the details together.

He placed the unlit pipe to his mouth and walked into his office. He sat at his desk and opened the top drawer, pulling it as far as it would slide. Taped to the back of the drawer he found the small, yellow envelope he'd hidden there years ago. Inside was a key to the safe deposit box he had opened with Sandy Stamos. For nearly thirty years he had paid the yearly fee on the box, but had never once been back to the Reno bank to look at the contents. He'd read through those documents once, and that had been enough. They had gotten two people killed and Marvin had never been anxious to revisit the documents. Still, he knew enough not to get rid of them.

He pulled the key from the envelope and spun it in his fingers. It was time, Marvin knew, to wake the demons from the past. He'd allowed them to sleep too long.

CHAPTER 55

Bend, Oregon
Friday, August 2, 2024

Sloan woke Friday morning to a steady clinking coming from outside her window. It took a moment to remember where she was. The king-sized bed and its down comforter swallowed her and kept at bay the chill from the air conditioner in the guest cottage. The pounding outside continued. She pushed the covers to the side and stood from the bed, lifting the plantation shutters and squinting against the morning sun.

Out in the field, fifty yards from her bedroom window, was a large, yellow construction machine that looked like a backhoe. Instead of a bucket on the end of the long arm that extended out in front of the machine, however, was a metal post. Sloan watched as the man controlling the machine raised the post high in the air and then drove it into the ground. Once speared into the soil, the machine made the rickety sledgehammer noise as the hydraulics drove the pole into the ground until it was waist high. The noise abated for a moment—long enough for the man to load another post into the sleeve of the machine's extended arm, position it ten feet from the first, and begin the process again.

There was a knock on the door that startled her. She closed the shutters and headed out of the bedroom. When she pulled open the front door Nora stood on the porch.

"Good morning," Nora said. "Did you sleep alright?"

"Are you kidding me? The bed and the comforter are—"

"Heavenly, I know. It's ridiculous out here. I always feel like I'm a million miles away from anywhere. I bet you'd have slept later if it weren't for the racket."

Sloan squinted. "What is that?"

"That would be Lester."

"Lester, the handyman? The guy who blocked the news vans for us yesterday?"

"That's the one. He drove up last night. He's in charge of the property here. That's really his full-time job now—taking care of Margolis Manor and the winery. Reid has him putting in a new fence to keep the mountain lions out of the vineyards. Sorry if he woke you. Lester knows no other gear than go-go-go."

"I needed to get up anyway. Probably would have slept until noon in that bed."

"Breakfast will be ready soon."

"Let me shower and I'll come right over."

CHAPTER 56

Cedar Creek, Nevada
Friday, August 2, 2024

Marvin wasn't sure if it was the weather or the stress of the past screaming at him through the years that caused his hip to ache, but he walked with a slight limp as he headed up the steps of the Harrison County Sheriff's Office. He smiled politely at the woman behind the front desk.

"Hi. I need to see Sheriff Stamos."

"I'm not sure the sheriff is available, but I'm sure a deputy can help you."

"I need to speak with the sheriff. Can you let him know that Marvin Mann needs a word?"

As the owner of the largest private investigation firm in Harrison County, Marvin had a good working relationship with Eric Stamos. He wondered if that relationship would be stronger or nonexistent after today. Marvin placed his PI badge on the counter for the woman to see.

"It has to do with all the nonsense going on around town with the media."

She paused a moment and then nodded.

"Let me check for you."

She disappeared through a door behind the reception desk and Marvin paced the lobby for a few minutes, noticing that his palms were sweaty. He'd kept his secret for nearly thirty years, but the ten minutes he waited in the lobby of the Harrison County Sheriff's Office felt like the longest part of the journey.

"Marv," Eric Stamos said as he came through the side door. "I thought you and the Mrs. moved to Florida."

Marvin smiled. "We tried, but the humidity chased us away. Plus, the mosquitos are the size of plums and they've got geckos everywhere you step. I'm still a working man anyway, and not ready to retire just yet. That's what's brought me in to see you this morning."

"Yeah, what's going on?"

Marvin glanced at the woman behind the desk and then lowered his voice. "Can we talk in private?"

Eric, too, looked at the receptionist and then back to Marvin. "I'm in the middle of something, Marv." Eric pointed outside. "As I'm sure you can tell. Can this wait until next week?"

Marvin shook his head. "I don't think it can, Sheriff. I believe it's waited long enough."

"What's it about?"

"Your dad."

CHAPTER 57

Bend, Oregon
Friday, August 2, 2024

T WENTY MINUTES AFTER SHE WOKE, WITH HER HAIR WET FROM HER shower, Sloan walked to the side entrance of the main house. Nora met her at the sliding glass door and handed her a coffee mug spiraling with steam.

"Thank you," Sloan said.

She walked into the kitchen to the smell of bacon, toast, and coffee. Everyone was around the kitchen table.

"Good morning, dear," Tilly said.

"Morning," Sloan said.

"Did you sleep alright?"

"Yes, the guest cottage is wonderful."

"Let's eat and then get to work," Ellis said.

Reid turned on the television as they ate omelets and toast. The morning news shows were saturated with stories of baby Charlotte's return, photos of Sloan, and the same historic footage they watched the night before.

"I think that, for Sloan in particular, she should have an attorney present when she speaks with the media," Ellis said. "Especially if you give a formal interview."

Sloan shrugged. "Okay."

"We could use someone from the firm, unless you have your own attorney already."

"No. I don't have an attorney. What do I need a lawyer for?"

"To prevent you from walking into an ambush. My brother and Annabelle are still missing. The FBI, as you said, is reopening the investigation. If we all start spouting off at every random question posed to us, a federal agent somewhere will try to use our words against us."

"To do what?" Sloan asked.

Reid smiled. "Ellis is being a bit overprotective. But it's true we don't want to say the wrong thing during an interview. If we all grant interviews, and do so with legal representation present, the chance for misinformation to be spread will be lessened. Unfortunately, we learned that the hard way back when all this happened. The media will twist your words and statements to match whatever narrative they hope to sell. We won't let that happen this time."

Ellis wiped his mouth and stood. "I'll make some calls. Do you have anyone in mind, Dad? From the firm? If not, I'll make the call on who we all use."

"The call's yours, son."

Ellis nodded and hurried out of the kitchen. Sloan got the impression that a vacation for Ellis Margolis involved reading legal briefs and plotting trial strategy. It was a far stretch to imagine the man in a swimsuit lying on the beach.

Reid laughed when Ellis was gone.

"I'm afraid he doesn't have an 'off' switch."

"No," Sloan said. "I'm flattered that he's so willing to help me."

"It's survivor's guilt," Tilly said, taking a sip of coffee.

"Tilly," Reid said in a scolding voice.

"Oh, stop. It's as obvious now as it was back then. He feels guilty that his brother is gone and feels the need to make up for his absence. He's done it at the office for nearly three decades, and constantly tries to prove himself to both of us."

"Perhaps," Reid said. "But it comes from a good place."

"Okay," Nora said, standing with her breakfast plate and heading to the sink. "Let's not talk about Ellis when he's not here to defend himself."

"Defend himself against what?" Tilly asked. "We're not making accusations, just observations."

Nora smiled awkwardly at Sloan, then looked back at Tilly.

"Just the same, let's move on to something else."

"Good idea," Reid said. "I've arranged for a tour of the vineyard and winery. Since this is Sloan's first time here, I figured we'd take our minds off the hectic craziness we just escaped from."

Sloan smiled. The last thing she wanted was a wine tour.

"How does that sound, dear?" Tilly asked.

Sloan pushed a smile onto her face and nodded. "Yeah. Sounds great."

"Excellent," Reid said. "We'll get ready. Let's meet in the tasting room in an hour and we'll get started."

Reid and Tilly disappeared into the first-floor bedroom, leaving Nora and Sloan alone in the kitchen.

Nora smiled. "Sorry. You just got a little behind-the-scenes look at my constant struggle."

Sloan smiled. "I think you handled it well."

"I probably could have done better, but it's early and that's all I had. Before the grand tour," Nora rolled her eyes, "let's head into the darkroom and see what's on that roll of film."

"Now?"

"Sure. We've got an hour."

CHAPTER 58

Cedar Creek, Nevada
Friday, August 2, 2024

Eric walked into his office and pointed to the chair in front of his desk. "Sit and talk," he said to the aging PI.

Marvin Mann was well known in Harrison County. Over the years his PIs had caught cheating spouses, uncovered siblings hiding inheritance money from each other, found employees stealing from their bosses, and everything in between. One of Marvin's investigators had even assisted Nevada law enforcement in solving a Las Vegas murder a few years back. As far as private investigators went, Marvin Mann was as legit as they came. So when the man mentioned his father, Eric was more than curious.

Eric spun his finger in the air as he took a seat behind his desk. "It's early on a Friday morning and my plate is full. Start talking."

"I'll get right to the point. Back in '95, right before your dad died, he and I were working a case together."

"You and my dad?"

"Yes, sir."

"Were working on a case *together*?"

"Yes, sir."

Eric looked up and did some quick math. "Your PI firm hasn't been around long enough for you to be doing PI work for my father in '95."

"It wasn't PI work. And you're right, I didn't even have my agency at the time. Back then I was a legal investigator for Margolis and Margolis. My boss was Baker Jauncey."

Eric sat up straight, as if his spine had turned to ice. "The guy who was killed in the hit-and-run."

"That's him," Marvin said. "Only it wasn't a hit-and-run."

Eric stood up and closed his office door before returning to sit on the edge of his desk in front of Marvin.

"How do you know that, Marv?"

"Your dad told me."

"Why was my dad talking to you about Baker Jauncey?"

"I told you. Baker was my boss. And, the night before Baker died, he told me about some shady things going on inside the Margolis law firm."

"What sort of shady things?"

"Financial fraud, embezzlement, misappropriation of funds, to name a few. Baker took some internal documents from the firm that he thought proved the fraud. He gave them to me for safe-keeping. Then he asked me to look into the fraud to see if I could figure out who was behind it, and to do it very quietly. The next day he was dead."

Eric cocked his head. "What's it got to do with my dad?"

"I was spooked after Baker was killed, and I suspected that the hit-and-run was no accident. I went to your father to tell him my suspicions. But like stink on shit, your pop was already all over it. He told me Baker was killed by blunt force trauma to the back of the head. And it wasn't Annabelle Margolis's car that did the dam-age, but rather a baseball bat."

A lump formed in Eric's throat, and he took a deep breath to contain his emotions. After hearing Dr. Cutty's interpretation of Baker Jauncey's autopsy, Eric had assumed that his father knew the truth for the simple reason that he hadn't arrested Annabelle Mar-golis. To hear Marvin Mann confirm this fact filled him with pride that transported him back to the nine-year-old boy who looked up to his dad.

"The autopsy from the Harrison County Coroner's Office states that Baker died from being struck by a car," Eric said. "How did my dad figure it out?"

"Your dad told me that the Harrison County Coroner's Office re-possessed the body, or whatever it's called when one morgue snatches a body from another. But before Harrison County took the body, the medical examiner down in Reno had a look. That first autopsy report was never formally registered. Instead, the Harrison County coroner determined Baker's head injury was the result of being hit by a car. And we all know who owns the Harrison County Coroner's Office."

"The Margolis family."

"Bingo. With what your dad learned from that original, unofficial autopsy, coupled with the documents Baker had given me, your dad and I knew Baker's death was a direct result of what he had discovered inside the Margolis law firm. And we both knew that Baker had not only been killed because of what he'd stumbled over at Margolis and Margolis, but that the killer was very likely someone at the firm."

Eric stood and paced his office.

"What did my dad do about it?"

"Your dad decided to go toe-to-toe with the Margolises. He went about it quietly and kept his investigation under wraps. No one knew that Baker had taken the documents from the firm, so your dad and I stashed the files in a safe deposit box until we could figure out what it all meant. Last I heard, your dad was going to ask an accountant friend to look at the documents to see if he could make sense out of them."

"Who?"

Marvin shook his head and shrugged. "No idea. The last time I spoke with your dad was that day at the bank when we stashed the documents. About a week later, Preston Margolis and his family disappeared, and that story occupied the town's attention for the next several weeks. Hell, the whole country dropped everything to pay attention. Shortly after the family disappeared, your dad died when he drove his cruiser into Cedar Creek. Supposedly out of his mind on heroin. But I've always known your dad's death was no accident, and was definitely not an overdose."

Eric threw up his hands. "Christ, Marv! How come you've never mentioned this to anyone before now?"

"Put yourself in my shoes, brother! Baker gave me the files and was killed the next day. I gave those files to your dad, and he was dead a week later. I had a wife and three young kids at the time, and I knew two things. One, that no person on earth knew that I had any idea about fraud at Margolis and Margolis. And two, that if the people who killed Baker and your father knew I had seen the documents, I was a dead man. And that's if I was lucky enough for those bastards to come after me alone, and not my family."

Eric nodded and took a deep breath. "So why now?"

"Why?" Marvin shrugged. "My conscience, for one. It's been eating at me for nearly thirty years. And then there's this girl who just showed up—baby Charlotte. I know that whatever happened to her and her parents can't be a coincidence. It has to be connected to your dad and Baker, and whatever got them killed. I just need you to promise me you won't let them go after my family."

"I don't even know who 'they' are, Marv."

"Maybe you will if you take a look at the documents I gave your dad."

Marvin reached into his pants pocket and removed the key he'd retrieved from his desk drawer the night before.

"This is the key to the safe deposit box your dad and I opened all those years ago."

"Where?" Eric asked, walking over to Marvin and taking the key. "Where's the safe deposit box?"

"Reno," Marvin said. "The box hasn't been opened for nearly thirty years."

CHAPTER 59

Bend, Oregon
Friday, August 2, 2024

SLOAN FOLLOWED NORA OUT OF THE KITCHEN AND THROUGH THE long hallway, at the end of which was a door to the cellar. Nora opened it and clicked on a light before starting down the rickety wooden steps. Sloan followed close behind. The staircase was dark and damp, offering a scent of cold and mold. At the bottom was the door to the darkroom. They both slipped inside and turned on the lights. Waiting on the table was all the photography equipment Nora had introduced her to back in Cedar Creek.

Nora placed the Nikon FM10 onto the table and removed the roll of film that had sat dormant in Annabelle's camera for nearly three decades. Nora held it up.

"Wanna give it a shot?"

"Me?"

"Sure. I bet you know what you're doing. Just like Annabelle."

"I can try. As long as you don't let me ruin anything."

"You won't ruin anything," Nora said, handing Sloan the film roll.

A sensation came over her when Sloan took the film in her hand, as if some personification from the past had reached across time, hurtling three decades in the blink of an eye, to place the film in her hands. Sloan shook her head to dispel the sense of déjà vu that came over her.

"Okay, I know that we start with the enlarger."

"Yep," Nora said. "The film gets loaded here, and then we focus the image of the negative onto the easel below and imprint it onto the photo paper."

"Got it," Sloan said. "But first we dim the lights."

"Correct."

Nora turned off the lights, momentarily sending the room into pitch-blackness that blinded Sloan. It was so dark that blinking had no effect on her vision. After a few seconds, Sloan heard a click. The crimson glow of the safelight returned Sloan's sight. Nora helped her load the film into the enlarger and focus the first image onto the photo paper below. After a series of exposures, Nora handed Sloan a pair of tongs.

"Take the paper from the easel and place it into the first tray of liquid," Nora said.

Sloan carefully lifted the blank photo paper and slid it into the tray, submerging the paper. She remembered from her time in the darkroom at Nora's studio that this first tray was filled with developing solution, and that the photo paper remained there for sixty seconds.

"Get ready," Nora said, looking at her watch to gauge the time. "Okay, move it to the stop bath."

Sloan used tongs to lift the still-blank paper from the developing solution and transfer it to the second tray, where it remained for a few seconds before Nora prompted her to transfer it to the final tray—the fixer. It was there, Sloan remembered, that the image slowly came to life on the photo paper.

After a couple of minutes Sloan saw a faint image forming. She squinted through the red glow of the safelight until the image came fully into view. Pictured was a Cooper's hawk taking flight from a tree limb—wings outstretched and ready to soar.

"It's a hawk," Sloan said.

Nora removed the photo and hung it on the drying rack while she studied it. "This was taken . . ." She leaned closer to the photo. "From Annabelle's driveway. Look."

Nora pointed at the photo and Sloan moved closer.

"This is the side of their house and the pool in the background. She had to have been standing in the driveway when she took it."

Sloan pointed to the bottom of the photo. In red block lettering was the date: JULY 4, 1995.

"So," Sloan said as her mind pieced together that fateful day nearly thirty years ago. "The last photos we saw—the ones you had previously developed—were taken by Annabelle at the July Fourth Cedar Creek Gala in town. And these, whatever else is on the film roll, must have been taken once Annabelle arrived home."

"It looks that way, yes."

Sloan had yet to mention to Nora that Annabelle's blood had been found inside the home. Perhaps Nora knew this fact, but didn't have the heart to tell Sloan. Either way, Sloan was looking at photos Annabelle took on the day she disappeared, taken at the home from where she vanished.

"How many photos did you say were on the film?" Sloan asked.

"Twenty more," Nora said.

"Let's see what else Annabelle took photos of that day."

THE PAST

Cedar Creek, Nevada

Tuesday, July 4, 1995
The Day Of . . .

ANNABELLE LIFTED THE NIKON FM10 AND SQUINTED THROUGH THE viewfinder. She twisted the lens to bring Charlotte into focus and snapped off three photos in quick succession as her daughter lay on the blanket. Folks walked past on the sidewalk behind her and smiled while they pointed at Charlotte, who was dressed in an adorable Fourth of July outfit complete with a red-white-and-blue bonnet.

"How adorable," one woman commented on the way by.

"Thank you," Annabelle said, forcing a smile and trying to look as natural as possible. Inside, though, she was terrified.

Since Preston had told her what he'd found at the firm on Sunday night, and what Sheriff Stamos had discovered about Baker Jauncey's death, Annabelle had been a nervous wreck. Preston's plan—to act as normal as possible and get through the Fourth of July and the Cedar Creek Gala without tipping anyone off about their impending escape from Cedar Creek—had her both giddy with excitement and paranoid at the same time. She wanted nothing more than to get away from this crazy town that Preston's family controlled, but she knew it wouldn't be as easy as packing up and leaving. There would be repercussions for Preston attempting to lead a quiet life far removed from the Margolis political machine. But that was a long-term problem they'd deal with at some point. For their immediate plan to work, they needed to make their getaway under the cover of darkness. With July Fourth falling on a Tuesday, and the Margolis & Margolis offices closed for the week, there was no better time to skip town. It would be days before anyone knew they were gone. Preston wasn't due back at the office until the following Monday, and by then most of their plan would not only be set in place, but well under way.

Annabelle looked around. Sailboats cut through the creek and a band played Bruce Springsteen's "Born in the USA" from a stage behind her. Annabelle continued to take photos of Charlotte and the gala. She ran through a roll of film and loaded another into her camera. She hoped the ruse was fooling anyone who might be watching her. The plan was for Annabelle and Charlotte to stay at the gala and make their presence known while Preston slipped away to pack their things at the house. She wondered what was taking him so long.

She spotted Stella Connelly walking her way. Annabelle turned quickly, grabbed the handle of the stroller, and pushed Charlotte in the opposite direction. Narrowly avoiding a run-in with Preston's ex, she took a deep breath to calm her nerves, and then reminded herself that they were leaving tonight. Annabelle hoped they would never look back.

Cedar Creek, Nevada

Tuesday, July 4, 1995
The Day Of . . .

ANNABELLE EXHALED A SIGH OF RELIEF WHEN SHE SAW PRESTON walking down the sidewalk toward her. She was rocking Charlotte in the stroller.

"What took so long?" she asked when Preston came up and gave her a kiss.

"Just making sure we had everything. Every suitcase we have is packed full, and just about every drawer in our bedroom is empty. You head home now and make sure I got everything that's essential. I'll stay here and make sure people see me."

Annabelle nodded. "Okay. Charlotte's sleeping. I'll bring her home with me. She'll need to eat when she wakes up."

Preston kissed her again. "Remember, we don't need everything. At some point we'll come back and collect it all, but right now we need the essentials. It might be a while before we're back here."

"I can pray," Annabelle said.

"Go. I'll stick around here for an hour or so. Then, as soon as I get home, we'll hit the road."

Annabelle tried to smile but tears welled in her eyes instead.

Preston hugged her and whispered in her ear. "It's almost over."

"Promise?"

"Promise."

Cedar Creek, Nevada

Tuesday, July 4, 1995
The Day Of . . .

ANNABELLE PULLED INTO HER DRIVEWAY AND PARKED. SHE OPENED the trunk of the BMW in anticipation of stuffing it with luggage. As she turned from the car, she took a moment to admire the house where she was supposed to raise her kids and grow old with her husband. Despite the forced design, it was a beautiful home. She looked to the still-unfinished three-car garage with Lester's ladder tilted against the side. She saw the tread marks in the grass, left by the bulldozers and backhoes that had dug the hole for the pool. Waiting at the corner of the driveway were chest-high stacks of pavers meant to line the side of the house and lead to the back patio and pool deck. Part of her was sad that she'd never see this home completed the way she and Preston had planned. Another part of her was ready to run like hell and never look back.

In the distance, positioned high in the branches of a lodgepole pine, a Cooper's hawk sat. The bird released a long crow that echoed into the afternoon. Annabelle squinted her eyes at the beautiful sight, lifted the camera that still hung from her neck, and snapped off a photo of the bird just as it took flight—its wings outstretched and the colorful underbelly visible. The bird was gone in just a few powerful strokes of its wings and Annabelle hoped the single shot she'd managed to get off had captured the beauty of the animal.

She collected Charlotte from the baby seat and hurried through the front door. Several suitcases waited in the foyer. For the first time, she allowed herself to believe her family was actually leaving. She climbed the stairs to the second floor. In her bedroom she placed Charlotte in the bassinet next to the bed and walked into the bathroom to wash her face. Things had been spiraling out of control ever since her car was found abandoned on the side of the road where Baker Jauncey's body had been discovered. In her postpartum confusion, and suffering from sleep deprivation over the last two weeks, Annabelle's mind had spun with possible explanations—even conjuring the possibility that she had taken her car out that night during a forgotten moment of delusion. She secretly wondered if she had been the one who ran Baker Jauncey down, only for her sleep-deprived mind to block out any memory of the event.

She had become sick with these thoughts until Sheriff Stamos invited Preston out to his hunting cabin to break the news that Baker Jauncey had not died from injuries suffered when Annabelle's car struck him, but had instead been killed by a baseball bat. And, Sheriff Stamos added, whoever killed Baker Jauncey was likely behind the fraud happening inside Margolis & Margolis. Preston had spent all of Sunday night at the office digging through the firm's files and looking into the fraud. When he came home early Monday morning he told Annabelle about everything he had found. It was then that they had decided to leave Cedar Creek. Annabelle was not so naïve to think that they could escape this godforsaken place without interference from Preston's family. She only hoped that she, Preston, and Charlotte were far enough away when the rest of the Margolis family figured out their plan.

Annabelle cupped cool water in her hands and splashed her face. She soaked a washcloth and rubbed the coolness into the back of her neck. Finally, she took a deep breath and walked back into the bedroom. Charlotte was sleeping in the bassinet. She opened the dresser drawers to make sure Preston had packed everything she needed. She was about to check the armoire when a car door slammed outside.

Annabelle hurried to the bedroom window, hoping Preston was ahead of schedule and that they might get an early start on their stealth exit from Cedar Creek. But when Annabelle pulled the window curtain to the side, it was not Preston she saw.

"What the hell?" she whispered to herself.

Annabelle's breath caught in her throat. Although she wasn't sure why—intuition, maybe, but a premonition more likely—she lifted the Nikon FM10 that still hung from her neck, placed her eye to the viewfinder, and snapped several photos as she stood at her bedroom window, capturing the person's movements as they walked across the driveway and to the front door. Annabelle's stomach dropped when she heard the doorbell chime.

She thought briefly about not answering, but her car was in the driveway with the trunk open. It was obvious someone was home. She took a deep breath, lifted the camera strap over her head, and placed the Nikon in Charlotte's bassinet. She grabbed the handle and carried her daughter down the stairs.

CHAPTER 60

Reno, Nevada
Friday, August 2, 2024

Eric and Marvin made it to the Reno bank in just over an hour. Eric pushed his 4Runner during the drive, topping 100 mph in spots because he knew he was up against the clock, and had unintentionally placed Sloan in danger by encouraging her to burrow her way into the Margolis family. Eric believed his father's death was related to Baker Jauncey's hit-and-run, and that someone inside the Margolis family possessed information about it. But until Marvin Mann offered his amazing story, Eric hadn't considered that a Margolis family member was responsible for his father's death. If it were true, Eric had sent Sloan into the lion's den.

He pulled into the bank's parking lot and hurried Marvin along as they walked through the revolving doors and into the lobby. They rode an elevator to the lower level where Marvin showed his ID to the gentleman behind the desk.

"Marvin Mann. I've got a safe deposit box that I'd like access to."

The man tapped his computer and checked Marvin's ID before disappearing into a back room. He was gone for some time, leaving Eric to wonder if the PI was telling tales. The man finally walked back through the door and slipped a piece of paper across the counter. On top was a photocopy of Marvin's driver's license.

"Sign here," the man said, and Marvin obliged.

"Follow me, sir. I'll show you into the vault."

The man came around the counter and led Marvin and Eric into a large atrium where a locked gate protected the vaulted room.

"I can only allow named persons into the vault," the bank employee said, looking at Eric. "But you're welcome to wait out here."

"Do you have a private room where we can take the box?" Marvin asked.

"Yes, sir, we have several."

The man walked to one of several doors off the atrium and unlocked it. Inside was a chest-high table in the middle of the small room. No chairs.

"You can wait here," the man said to Eric.

Eric nodded and walked into the room. He watched the bank employee unlock the gate to the vault. Marvin Mann disappeared inside.

CHAPTER 61

Reno, Nevada
Friday, August 2, 2024

A FEW MINUTES LATER MARVIN MANN EMERGED FROM THE VAULT CAR-rying a thin safe deposit box. He walked into the small room where Eric waited and placed it on the table. He lifted the top of the metal box to reveal a stack of papers inside. Marvin removed the documents and slipped on his reading glasses.

"Yep," he said. "These are them."

Eric took the first stack of pages and read through them. They looked to be financial statements. He noted a couple of pages indicating the creation of a limited liability corporation, another page was a spreadsheet of financials, and the third was a list of deposits made into a numbered account. Eric picked through each page until he reached the end of the stack. He then removed the final bundle of documents from the safe deposit box and fingered through the re-maining pages. Each page was the same gibberish—account num-bers, financial spreadsheets, and names of corporations.

He reached the end of the stack and turned to the final page. There, stuck to the last page, was a yellow sticky note that carried his father's familiar handwriting.

"Holy shit."

Marvin peered through his cheaters to read the sticky note. "I'll be damned."

Eric ran from the private room and raced up the steps, bolting across the reception area and through the front doors. As he sprinted for his car, he fumbled for his phone to call Sloan.

CHAPTER 62

Bend, Oregon
Friday, August 2, 2024

WITH TREMBLING HANDS SLOAN SECURED ANOTHER PIECE OF PHOTO paper in the easel and set it below the enlarger. She fed the film into the machine and pressed the button to set the exposure. The process took just over a minute before Sloan transferred the blank paper through the three trays of solution. As it floated in the fixer, the final tray, she waited. Painstakingly, a form began to take shape on the paper. Sloan used tongs to lift the photo out of the solution. She clipped it to the drying rack next to the photo of the Cooper's hawk. In the glow of the red safelight, the image materialized.

Blurry crossbars in the foreground told them that the picture had been taken through a window.

"These are curtains in the foreground," Sloan said. "And the blurry lines are window grids."

The angle of the photo was on a downward trajectory, clearly taken through a second-story window. Nora moved closer to the photo.

"That's Preston and Annabelle's driveway. And their BMW. This was taken through Annabelle's bedroom window."

As the image came into sharper focus, a person emerged.

"Who is that?" Sloan asked.

Nora lifted the photo from the drying rack and took a closer look.

"It's Ellis."

THE PAST

Cedar Creek, Nevada

July 4, 1995
The Day Of . . .

ANNABELLE WALKED DOWN THE STAIRS WITH CHARLOTTE IN THE bassinet, took a deep breath, and opened the door.

"You know the trunk on the BMW is open?" Ellis said before anything else.

Annabelle repositioned the bassinet, transferring the weight to her hip. She nodded. "Yeah, Ellis. I do."

"Whoa!" Ellis walked through the doorway and into the foyer, staring at the suitcases that filled the space. "You guys going on vacation?"

Annabelle's pulse quickened. Their chance at a stealth exit was slipping away. Annabelle closed her eyes, turned from the doorway, and carried Charlotte into the kitchen. She placed the bassinet on the kitchen table as Ellis followed.

"Seriously," Ellis said, letting out what Annabelle considered a nervous laugh. "Are you and Preston going somewhere?"

"Yes," Annabelle said, opening the refrigerator to grab a bottle of water.

"Where?"

"As far away from this place as possible."

Annabelle surprised herself with the edge to her voice. Pent-up frustration from the past year with the Margolis family was finally finding its way to the surface, and the recent revelation that Ellis had been stealing firm money and was possibly involved in Baker

Jauncey's death had her at a breaking point—and scared to death that she was alone with her brother-in-law.

"So . . ." Ellis said with a deep furrow to his brow, as if trying to work out the scenario. "You're going to skip town when you're a suspect in the hit-and-run death of a Cedar Creek resident? I'm not sure the police would approve of that move."

Now it was Annabelle who laughed. She came around the kitchen island and smiled in Ellis's face.

"No, no, Ellis. I guess you haven't heard. Baker Jauncey wasn't killed by my car. He was dead before the hit-and-run."

The furrow left Ellis's forehead and genuine confusion came over his face. The reaction caused Annabelle to smile bigger.

"The autopsy—" Ellis started to say, but Annabelle cut him off.

"The autopsy is wrong. But don't take my word for it. Talk with Sheriff Stamos. He's the one who told Preston and me about it. You see, someone took my car that night and tried to make it look like I killed Baker Jauncey. But here's where it gets interesting." Annabelle smiled again. "Sheriff Stamos thinks the same person who killed Baker Jauncey is also embezzling money from Margolis and Margolis."

Annabelle lowered her voice.

"You wouldn't know anything about that, would you, Ellis?"

A long pause.

"No, I would not."

Annabelle turned and slammed the bottle of water onto the counter.

"We know, Ellis! Preston and I know everything. He went through the computers at the firm. He went through *your* computer, Ellis. Preston knows about everything you've been doing. So, I take back what I said earlier. Don't ask Sheriff Stamos. You won't have to. He'll be tracking you down to ask *you* a few questions."

Ellis stepped backwards, the fingers of his right hand sliding over the granite countertop as he inched away. Annabelle saw him swallow hard, turn, and slowly walk through the front door. She heard his car start as he pulled out of the driveway.

CHAPTER 63

Bend, Oregon
Friday, August 2, 2024

T HE DARKROOM GLOWED AN EERIE CRIMSON AS SLOAN AND NORA stared at the photo of Ellis.

"What was Ellis doing at Annabelle's house that day?" Nora asked.

The question came in a whisper and Sloan got the impression she was asking herself.

"Let's see what else is on the roll of film," Sloan said.

Nora looked at her and nodded. She hurried to feed the film into the enlarger and worked to see a preview of the negatives.

"The next several are blurred," Nora said.

"What's on them?"

Nora shook her head as she tried to decipher the images. "They're too blurry to make anything out."

She kept feeding the film through the enlarger.

"Here," she said, squinting at the tiny image and trying to make sense of it. "It's . . . two people. Let's develop this one."

They ran through the process again, exposing the image onto the photo paper in the easel, and then transferring it to each of the three trays of chemicals—the developing solution first, then the stop bath, and finally the fixer. Nora started the timer and after the paper was in the last tray of liquid for a minute, she lifted it out with tongs and clipped it to the drying rack. Sloan squinted through the darkness to make out the image that was slowly evolving.

"Here it comes."

In the photo were two people facing each other. Their shapes sluggishly took form.

"It's Annabelle," Sloan said. "But . . . how?"

Nora moved closer to the photos and waited another few seconds until the image took hold.

"That's . . ." She paused, as though allowing the print to come into fuller form, to make sure she was correct.

"Tilly," Nora finally said. "That's Tilly standing with Annabelle in the kitchen."

After another few seconds the colors came through, and a clear image formed. Sloan saw Annabelle and young Tilly Margolis standing in front of the kitchen counter.

Sloan looked at Nora. "All the pictures we've developed to this point were taken by Annabelle."

"Yeah?" Nora asked, not understanding.

Sloan pointed at the photo. "So, there's Annabelle in the photo. Who the hell's taking this picture?"

THE PAST

Cedar Creek, Nevada

July 4, 1995
The Day Of . . .

A SENSE OF URGENCY FLOODED HER SYSTEM AFTER ELLIS LEFT. ANNA-belle ran into the foyer, grabbed one of the suitcases, and hauled it to the car. She ran back to the house, grabbed two more pieces of luggage, and wheeled them out. One of them caught on the cob-blestone walkway and tumbled over. She left it where it lay and con-tinued, throwing the lone suitcase into the back of the BMW. One more trip and the foyer was empty but for a single duffle bag and her purse. As Annabelle was heading back inside, she heard a car pull into the driveway. When she turned, she saw Tilly's white Cadillac.

Annabelle slumped her chin to her chest. She and Preston should have skipped town the day before. Now, their exit would be messy and filled with drama. She didn't bother to wait for Tilly, or close the front door. Instead, Annabelle walked into the kitchen and started to clean one of Charlotte's bottles. Charlotte was start-ing to fuss and needed to eat.

"What's going on outside?" Tilly asked as she walked into the kitchen. "Preston's car is packed full like you're leaving forever."

"Tilly, I'm right in the middle of something with Charlotte. Can you come back tomorrow?"

Annabelle continued to scrub the bottle as the kitchen sink ran.

"Where's Preston?"

"He's on his way home from the gala."

"I'll help you with the baby while we wait for him."

Annabelle closed her eyes. She just wanted to climb into the car with Preston and Charlotte and get as far away from Cedar Creek as possible. Running on very little sleep, she had no energy to deal with her mother-in-law.

Tilly came over to the sink and reached for the bottle Annabelle was cleaning. Annabelle pulled it away.

"Tilly, I can't do this right now. I was up all night with Charlotte and just don't have the energy to fight with you."

"Who's fighting?"

Annabelle finished rinsing the bottle and then went to the cupboard and removed Charlotte's formula.

"Where are you going, Annabelle? With all your bags packed and so late in the afternoon?"

The condescension sent Annabelle over the edge. She turned around to face her mother-in-law as they stood in front of the sink.

"We're leaving, Tilly."

Tilly let out a patronizing laugh. "Who's leaving?"

"Preston and me. We're leaving this house and this town and all the crap that's attached to it."

"Oh, that's silly. If you'd like to leave, that's fine. It's welcomed, actually. But my son? You think you're going to take my son away? Who do you think you are?"

"His wife! I'm his wife, Tilly. Do you even hear yourself? You talk about your thirty-year-old son the same way I talk about my infant daughter. Preston is a grown man, and grown men make their own decisions. They don't do what mommy tells them to do."

"And you think Preston wants to leave Cedar Creek?"

Now it was Annabelle's turn to laugh. "You think you control everything that goes on, but you know so little. And when you find out, your perfect little world with all your money, and the cookie-cutter houses you make your kids live in, and your country-club lifestyle, it's all going to crumble. And the sad thing is, you don't even know it's about to happen."

Charlotte began to fuss. The rising tone of Annabelle and Tilly's exchange caused her to cry and squirm in her bassinet.

CHAPTER 64

Bend, Oregon
Friday, August 2, 2024

"I HAVE NO IDEA," NORA SAID IN RESPONSE TO SLOAN'S QUESTION about who was operating the camera in the photos of Annabelle and Tilly.

"How many negatives are left on the roll?" Sloan asked.

Nora went to the enlarger. "Four."

"Let's go. Let's see what's on them."

A frantic energy filled the darkroom. As Sloan and Nora stood in the red glow of the safelight, they both sensed they were on the precipice of solving a decades-old mystery, even if they could not comprehend what they were about to uncover.

Nora worked expertly now. She was no longer a teacher taking Sloan under her wings. She was a master, running through the developing process like someone who'd done it thousands of times before, pointing and giving orders that Sloan followed without hesitation. Nora exposed the negative onto the photo paper in twelve-second increments to make sure they'd have a clear image. Then she ran the blank photo paper through the developing baths. This time, though, as they waited while the image sat in the final tray, Nora got busy working on the next negative. By the time she had the photo submerged in the developing solution, the first image was ready to come out of the fixer.

While Nora prepared the next negative on the roll, Sloan clipped the photo to the drying rack and then she used tongs to move the second image to the stop bath. Her movements were rushed, but under Nora's guidance, each step of the process was done correctly. Finally, they had four photos hanging on the drying rack, each in different stages of development.

The first image, still dripping with fixer solution, had come to life. Slightly blurred, it showed Tilly with a handful of Annabelle's hair and Annabelle's head pulled down from the force.

"They're . . ." Sloan pulled the photo off the drying rack. "Fighting."

Nora removed the second photo from the drying rack, and they stared at it. The seconds passed at a snail's pace as they waited for the image to form. Finally, the color came through and they witnessed Annabelle pinning Tilly against the kitchen counter with outstretched arms.

Nora grabbed the third photo from the drying rack. She and Sloan were breathing heavily, the pictures were a portal to the past that put them both in the middle of the battle being waged inside Annabelle Margolis's home nearly thirty years earlier. Nora blew on the blank photo to hurry the developing process. As the image visualized, she gasped.

"Oh my God."

Sloan looked at the image in Nora's hand. In it she saw Tilly Margolis holding a long butcher's knife.

THE PAST

Cedar Creek, Nevada

Tuesday, July 4, 1995
The Day Of . . .

"WHAT'S WRONG, TILLY?" ANNABELLE SAID, HER FACE CLOSE TO her mother-in-law's. This confrontation had been a long time in the making. "For the first time in your life, you've got nothing to say?"

"Oh, I have plenty to say. And you're going to listen. You may hold a spell over my son, but you possess no such effect on me. I know the game you're playing. You're white trash out for a payday, and you've completed the trap. I'll give you credit there. I don't take Preston as a fool, but I'll be damned if he's not a complete buffoon when it comes to you. Here's the offer. Reid and I will pay you to go away. You'll be well taken care of, and so will your child."

"*My* child?" Annabelle said with a laugh. "You mean your son's child, too, right? And your granddaughter?"

"I'm under no illusion as to what that child represents. She was a way for you to trap Preston into a life of servitude. And I admit, you've won. Reid and I will readily grant you the victory and give you what you want. You'll see that the package we've put together is more than fair."

Annabelle laughed again. "You and Reid are offering me, like, a severance package to go away?"

"*Like*, exactly. We can have the marriage annulled, and we'll pay you a monthly stipend until the child is eighteen. You'll see that the offer is more than fair."

"For fuck's sake, Tilly! Are you still running that crazy idea through your warped mind? I don't want your money."

"No, you want Preston's. But what you don't understand is that Preston has no money. Not the kind you're after. If he goes through with this nonsense, Reid and I have warned him that he will be excommunicated from the family."

"Excommunicated? Has Cedar Creek turned into the Middle Ages?"

"Cute," Tilly said. "Preston will be cut off if he continues this nonsense with you."

Annabelle shook her head. "With the way you keep them on such tight leashes, it's no wonder your own son is stealing money."

The comment, Annabelle noticed, went straight over Tilly's head. She truly was clueless.

"Cut off means Preston gets no more family money. He'll be fired from the law firm. He will not be allowed to work anywhere in Harrison County."

"You promise?" Annabelle said. "Please, Tilly, promise me that everything you just said is true. Promise me that you'll let Preston leave this godforsaken place and never look back. He'll be here soon. Will you please tell him what you just told me?"

Annabelle took a step closer to her mother-in-law.

"You think idle threats like that will scare him, but in reality they'd set him free. It wasn't my idea to leave this place. It was Preston's. He can't wait to get the hell away from you."

"You little tramp!" Tilly yelled, startling both Annabelle and Charlotte.

Charlotte began to cry in earnest now, kicking her legs and flailing in the bassinet. As Charlotte squirmed, one of her kicking feet struck the button on Annabelle's camera, which rested near the edge of the bassinet. Charlotte's heel connected with the button, snapping off a photo just as Tilly exploded into a fit of rage and grabbed Annabelle by the hair. The two women wrestled but Annabelle was unable to break free from the woman's grip as Tilly pulled her head down and spun her around.

Annabelle charged forward in a bull rush and she and Tilly crashed into the kitchen counter and cabinets. The impact was jarring and caused Tilly to lose her grip on Annabelle's hair. Annabelle pinned Tilly against the counter until she could safely back away from her. When her mother-in-law turned around, her right hand gripped a long, serrated knife from the butcher's block. Annabelle was so shocked by the sight of the knife that she had no chance to react. Tilly plunged the blade into her midsection. Annabelle let out a cry, more from fear than pain. Strangely, she felt nothing at all until Tilly pulled the knife from her gut. Then Annabelle felt the warm flow of blood pour over her hands as she grabbed at her stomach.

Lightheadedness quickly descended and Annabelle was only peripherally aware when Tilly plunged the knife into her a second time. A moment later Annabelle collapsed onto the kitchen floor. The house would have been eerily silent but for Charlotte's wailing. As Charlotte's legs flailed, her heel activated the camera again, firing off another photo, this time of Tilly holding the bloody knife.

Cedar Creek, Nevada

July 4, 1995
The Day Of . . .

WHEN PRESTON PULLED UP TO THE HOUSE, HE SAW HIS MOTHER'S car in the driveway.

"God damn it!"

He saw the trunk to the BMW open and suitcases piled inside. He had hoped to escape Cedar Creek without confronting his mother. And God help him tonight if his father was inside. Preston shut off the engine and opened the car door. As soon as he did, he heard Charlotte crying from inside the house. Not simply crying, though; his daughter was screaming in a way Preston had never before heard. He ran to the house, took the front steps two at a time, and rushed through the front doorway. He jumped over a duffle bag that lay in the foyer, and when he made it to the kitchen he saw Charlotte in her bassinet, positioned on the kitchen table. His daughter was kicking and squirming and unleashing a blood-curdling scream that colored her face fire-engine red.

He took a step into the kitchen and the story unfolded. Anna-belle lay on her back, one leg bent backward at the knee, arms crumpled at her sides, and a pool of dark red blood encircling her body. Standing next to Annabelle's body was his mother. She held a serrated kitchen knife smeared with blood in her right hand. When Preston looked at her, she dropped the knife and it clattered to the floor, the noise momentarily overcoming Char-lotte's screams.

"She attacked me, Preston," his mother said. "You must believe me. She attacked me and I defended myself."

Charlotte continued to wail in her bassinet.

"What did you do, mother?"

"It was self-defense."

Preston reached his hands to his head and grabbed his hair as he stared down at his wife and the blood and the knife. "Oh my God, oh my God, oh my God."

"She attacked me, and I defended myself," his mother said again, this time with anger in her voice.

Preston shook his head and reached for the phone, lifting it off the wall jack.

"What are you doing?"

"Calling an ambulance."

"No," Tilly said. "You can't do that."

Ignoring his mother, he began to dial. Tilly ran over and swiped the phone from his hands. It skidded across the floor.

"You can't. She's already gone. It's over, son, and it's better this way."

Preston's eyes filled with rage, and he shoved his mother backward. Tilly stumbled and fell onto the floor next to Annabelle, barely missing the pool of blood. As the anger bubbled from him, Preston climbed on top of his mother and placed his hands around her neck.

"What did you do?" he said through clenched teeth as he violently gripped his mother's neck. "Did you kill her in front of my daughter?"

Preston saw his mother's face turn a deep purple. She opened her mouth, but nothing came out.

"You hated her. Even though I loved her, you hated her. I'll kill you like you killed her!"

He spat the words out in a craze-filled scream before he heard a loud crack and felt the concussion of something striking the back of his head. The blow took the strength from his arms, like a spigot had been opened that bled all the energy from his body. Although he tried to continue squeezing his mother's neck, his hands and arms would no longer cooperate. After a second, Preston slumped to the floor and, just before his eyes closed, saw Ellis standing over him. There was a baseball bat in his hands.

Charlotte screamed and Preston looked at the child. Her feet continued to flail, her right heel striking the camera a final time.

PART VI

Soaring

CHAPTER 65

Bend, Oregon
Friday, August 2, 2024

SLOAN AND NORA STARED AT EACH OTHER AS NORA HELD THE PHOTO showing Tilly with a knife in her hand.

"She killed her," Nora said. "Tilly killed Annabelle."

Sloan swallowed hard and looked back to the photo, trying to process what she was seeing, how these photos came to be, and who had taken them.

"I'm still . . ." Sloan said, shaking her head. "Who took these photos?"

"And what happened to Preston?" Nora said. "And you. What happened to *you* that night?"

Slowly, as if the answer dawned on them at the same time and from the same place, they looked to the drying rack and the final photo that hung there. Enough time had passed so that the image was clearly formed. Nora pulled it off the clip. With her mouth agape, she reached over to the wall and clicked on the overhead light. In her hand the photo showed Ellis eerily staring into the lens of the camera and holding a baseball bat. Sloan's mind made the connection to Dr. Cutty's impression of Baker Jauncey's head wound, which she believed had been caused by a baseball bat.

"Nora!" a voice yelled from somewhere outside the darkroom.

It was Ellis.

"Nora!" he yelled again, this time his voice was louder and closer.

Nora and Sloan looked at each other with panicked eyes. They'd left the cellar door off the kitchen opened and footsteps pounded down the steps. They both startled when Ellis pounded on the darkroom door.

"Nora, are you in there?"

Nora held her finger to her lips for Sloan to stay silent. But when Sloan placed her trembling hand onto the table to steady herself, she knocked over one of the trays containing the developing solution. It fell off the table and crashed onto the floor.

"Nora," Ellis yelled. "Open the door!"

The door shook as Ellis pounded from the other side.

CHAPTER 66

Cedar Creek, Nevada
Friday, August 2, 2024

Eric drove at close to 100 mph as he raced north out of Reno and away from the bank where he and Marvin Mann had discovered his father's message—a sticky note written in his father's cursive that was now affixed to his dashboard. It read: *Guy Menendez = Ellis Margolis.*

"Call her again," Eric said to Marvin Mann as they raced north toward Cedar Creek.

"It's going straight to voicemail," Marvin said. "Her phone is either off or she has no service. Even an old man like myself knows this."

"Just try!" Eric said, knowing that Sloan was at Margolis Manor with Ellis, and in grave danger.

Marvin tried again.

"Voicemail."

"Text her. Same message."

Marvin worked his fingers over the keyboard of Eric's phone, retyping the identical message he'd sent numerous times since they'd left the bank.

Ellis Margolis is Guy Menendez. Find an excuse to leave and call me!

"Done," Marvin said.

Eric ran a hand through his hair as he thought.

"Look up the number for the police department in Bend, Oregon."

"Where?"

"Just do it, Marv!"

Marvin used Eric's phone to search.

"Got it."

Marvin dialed and handed Eric the phone.

"Bend Police Department," a woman said on the other end.

"Hi, my name is Eric Stamos. I'm the sheriff down in Harrison County, Nevada. I've got an emergency and need to speak with someone up there. Your chief or someone in charge."

"Do you need to call 9-1-1?"

"No, the emergency is up by you. I need to speak with someone in charge up there."

"And what was your name, sir?"

Eric took a calming breath. "This is Sheriff Eric Stamos from Harrison County, Nevada."

"One moment please."

An eternity passed before someone returned to the line.

"This is Chief Mortenson, who am I speaking with?"

"Hey Chief, this is Eric Stamos. I'm the sheriff down in Harrison County, Nevada and I need your help."

"Sure thing, Sheriff. What's up?"

"I need you to get some uniforms over to Margolis Manor."

"The winery?"

"Yes, sir. I've got a situation developing. If you could go out there and check on things, I'd consider it a personal favor."

"What's the issue out at the winery, Sheriff?"

"It's a long story, and we don't have time for me to give you all the details. I've got a friend out at the winery, and I think she's in danger. I can't reach her by phone, and I need you to go check on her."

"What's this friend's name?"

"Sloan Hastings."

"Sloan . . . the girl in the news?"

"That's her, yes."

There was a short pause.

"This phone number you're calling from is the best way to reach you, Sheriff?"

"Yes, sir."

"I'll head out there myself and let you know what I find."

"Thanks, Chief. If you can make it a priority, I'd appreciate it."

"I'm headed there now."

CHAPTER 67

Bend, Oregon
Friday, August 2, 2024

"SHIT," SLOAN WHISPERED AS THE TRAY CRASHED TO THE FLOOR.

"Nora! Is Sloan with you? Open the door!"

Ellis pounded and the doorframe shook. They both looked again at the photo of Ellis eerily staring from the photo, a baseball bat in his hands. They heard heavy footsteps as Ellis walked away from the darkroom door and bounded up the steps. Moments later he was back. They heard jingling.

"Keys?" Sloan whispered. "Are those keys?"

"No," Nora said. "The lock is not key activated. It's a deadbolt."

When they heard hammering, they understood. Ellis was going to dismantle the lock one way or another.

"He's coming in, Nora!"

"Follow me," Nora said, running to the far side of the darkroom.

Sloan hadn't noticed the other door. She'd only been in the room for a moment originally before Nora had cast the space into darkness. Then, the room had been lit by the glow of the red safelight. But now, with the overhead lights ablaze, she saw it. A heavy wooden door, rounded on top and with thick wooden planks creating an ornate X across the front.

Nora twisted the lock and pushed the door open. The hinges protested in a high-pitched screech until the door came to a halt. Based on the franticness of his hammering, Ellis had heard the door open.

"Nora! Stay in the darkroom. Something's happened. It's not safe for you to leave."

Sloan saw Nora hesitate, and sensed her doubt. Sloan knew she wanted to believe her husband. She grabbed Nora's hand and pulled her through the doorway and into the darkness beyond.

"Where are we?" Sloan asked.

"The caves of the winery."

"Caves?"

"Where they keep the wine while it ferments and ages."

Their voices echoed in the dark, damp tunnel. They turned and hurried through the corridor until the light from the darkroom lost its reach. After another few steps they were in complete darkness.

"I left my phone in the guest cottage," Sloan said. "Do you have yours?"

"No," Nora said. "It's in the kitchen."

They half jogged through the cavernous space, placing their hands on the wine barrels that lined the tunnel for guidance. Finally, they emerged into a large atrium of the tasting room. Nora felt for a light switch and clicked it on. Strings of bulbs lined the ceiling in long lines and blinked to life.

The circular atrium had three tunnels leading from it, each lined with oak barrels of fermenting wine. In the middle of the vestibule was a mahogany bar used for tastings. Massive double doors were closed but Sloan could imagine them open with sunlight pouring through and wine enthusiasts filling the space.

Sloan ran for the double doors that would take her from the caves and lead her out into the vineyards, but Nora's scream stopped her cold. When she turned, she saw Nora standing by the bar. On the ground, creeping from behind the bar, appeared to be a puddle of red wine, as if cabernet bottles had shattered. Sloan took a hesitant step toward the tasting bar, and then another and another until she stood next to Nora and looked behind the mahogany. On the floor lay Tilly and Reid Margolis. In each of their foreheads was a gaping hole. A still-expanding pool of blood was spilling across the floor.

The images Sloan and Nora had developed in the darkroom

flashed through her mind—Tilly holding the serrated knife, Ellis gripping the baseball bat. The tabloid covers of Annabelle and Preston cradling their newborn daughter also clouded her mind. The crime scene photos she'd reviewed with Eric. The flashes and thoughts came too quickly to comprehend. As her eyes refocused on the carnage in front of her, something else stole her attention.

"Help."

Sloan looked at Nora.

"Help."

The voice was feeble, and Sloan could not decipher its source. She felt Nora grip her hand, fearing, Sloan knew, that perhaps Reid was still alive. But another glance at the wound to the man's forehead confirmed he was dead. Sloan had seen enough gunshot wounds during her rotation through emergency medicine to know that a hole through the forehead was not survivable.

"Please, help me."

They both looked toward the tunnel to their right. The pleas were coming from the darkness within.

CHAPTER 68

Bend, Oregon
Friday, August 2, 2024

ELLIS MARGOLIS HADN'T FELT THIS OUT OF CONTROL SINCE THAT fateful summer in 1995 when things had begun to fall apart. Back then it was Baker Jauncey who had set off the cascading dominos. With some luck, and some difficult decisions back then, Ellis had navigated his way through that situation. His mother had become his unwilling accomplice after she killed Annabelle during a rage-fueled altercation. Their relationship had never been the same since that night. His mother hated Ellis for killing Preston, even though he'd done it to save her life. At least, that's how the story played out.

The truth was, that after Annabelle had revealed to Ellis that Preston knew about the fraud at the law firm, Ellis had no choice but to kill them both. But when he returned to Preston's house on the Fourth of July, his mother had already taken care of Annabelle. And when Ellis saw Preston choking his mother, he knew there would never be a better opportunity to solve all his problems.

That night at Preston's house had drawn Ellis and his mother to-gether in a way they had never before known. They'd never been closer. To hold another's secrets brought people together more powerfully than even unconditional love. Their livelihood depended on the other staying quiet about that night, and for twenty-nine years they both had. Then Sloan Hastings showed up.

Ellis had been running through his options since the day Nora told him that baby Charlotte had turned up in North Carolina. It was a scenario Ellis had never considered. His biggest loose end over the decades had been Margot Gray. But he had kept her content over the years. Only recently had she gone off the rails with guilt, when the Sloan Hastings story broke, and Margot put things together. Ellis managed to quiet her just in time, but Margot Gray was just one of several problems. The world was closing in around him, but he'd found a solution that would solve all his problems.

Back on that fateful July night, he had loaded Preston and Annabelle's bodies into his truck and cleaned up Annabelle's blood from the kitchen floor using pool chlorine diluted in water. Still, it wasn't enough to stop the investigators from finding traces of her blood on the floor. But the detectives had never come close to figuring out what happened in that house, or where Annabelle and Preston's bodies had been hidden. Late at night on July 4, 1995, Ellis had driven up to the winery to bury the bodies far out in one of the vineyards. So many years had passed that Ellis couldn't remember the exact location.

Then, he'd driven baby Charlotte across the country and found Margot Gray. He paid her handsomely to take care of the baby for a few months and then pose as Charlotte's mother during the makeshift adoption. It had gone off without a hitch and allowed Ellis to avoid the impossible task of having to kill his infant niece. In retrospect, however, killing the child would have prevented the turmoil he was going through today. More hard decisions lay ahead. But he could weather the current storm only if he went through with them. No one would suspect that he was responsible for the carnage at Margolis Manor. Not when the perfect fall guy was in his midst.

He used the hammer to pound the handle of the screwdriver. With one final effort he drove the tip of the screwdriver into the lock, splintering the door. When he pushed the door open, the darkroom was empty. But laid across the table were photos that stole his breath. They brought him back to that night at Preston's house. In one photo he saw his mother fighting with Annabelle. Another pictured his mother holding the long, serrated knife.

How, Ellis wondered, had these photos come to be? Who had

taken them? How were they possible? On the table next to the enlarger, Ellis saw an old Nikon FM10 camera. In a flash he remembered finding it in the child's bassinet. After the cleanup, he'd taken the camera and stashed it in his attic.

Finally, Ellis's gaze fell to the last photo. It was an image of himself, staring straight out from the picture, the baseball bat he'd used to kill his brother in his hands. Confusion flooded his system at how these photos could exist. But his bewilderment was overcome by guilt, as if seeing himself in the act made it all real. He was a master at compartmentalizing his actions, but the photo allowed the memories of that night to seep from the part of his mind that he had locked them in. He remembered walking into Preston's home with the baseball bat, prepared to use it on Annabelle. He remembered seeing Preston on top of his mother, his brother's hands around her neck. He remembered the dull thud of the bat connecting with Preston's temple.

He blinked several times, working to free his mind from the grip of the troubling memories. Then he looked to the far end of the room and saw that the door to the caves was open. He took off in a dead sprint.

"Nora!"

CHAPTER 69

Bend, Oregon
Friday, August 2, 2024

"H ELP," THE VOICE SAID AGAIN.

"It's coming from the tunnel," Nora said.

They wanted to leave the caves, to push through the doors and run for their lives through the vineyards. But the soft pleas had captured their attention. Both women slowly walked toward the darkened tunnel. A few feet into the cave, just beyond the light from the atrium, they found a man on the ground.

"Please," the man said. "Help me."

"Lester?" Nora said, crouching on the ground. "What are you doing in here?"

"Please, he's going to kill me."

Sloan crouched next to Nora and saw the face of Lester Strange, the Margolis family's handyman. His left wrist was handcuffed to the metal rack that held the wine barrels. His face was badly beaten.

"He's going to kill me. He's going to kill everyone and make it look like I did it. Please."

Lester pointed down the cave.

"There's a sledgehammer down there. I use it to rack the wine. Please."

Sloan didn't hesitate. She stood and ran into the darkness. After a moment of searching she found the sledgehammer and carried it back to Lester.

"Look out," she said to Nora.

Lester pulled his handcuffed wrist away from the metal rack, removing all slack from the handcuffs. In one swift motion, Sloan brought the hammer down and obliterated the cuffs. Lester's hand sprang from the rack, the shattered cuff hanging from his wrist.

"Nora!"

Ellis's voice echoed from the far end of the cave that led from the darkroom. All three ran through the tasting room, bright sunlight searing their eyes when they pushed open the double doors.

CHAPTER 70

Bend, Oregon
Friday, August 2, 2024

THEY RAN FROM THE CAVES AND INTO THE VINEYARDS. A GUNSHOT rang out into the morning and echoed off the mountains. Sloan ducked but kept running, following Lester as he bolted through the vines. With her heart racing and breaths coming heavy and loud, she didn't notice that Nora was no longer by her side. She slowed and looked back down the path that ran between the vines. There, thirty yards back, Nora lay on the ground. Sloan doubled back. Nora was holding her right leg, bright red blood covering her hand and the ground, spilling across the dirt like slow-flowing molasses.

"Oh my God," Sloan said as she crouched by Nora's side.

Falling back on her training, she quickly assessed her patient and found the source of the blood. A gunshot wound to the back of the right leg, with an exit wound in the front.

"Okay, that's good," Sloan said.

"What?" Nora grunted through gritted teeth.

"The bullet went in and out."

"That's *good?*"

"Yes. We don't want it to ricochet inside of you. This is much cleaner. And based on the amount of blood, it missed your femoral artery."

"Nora!"

They heard Ellis yell from a couple paths over.

Sloan looked around. In front of her were vineyards as far as she could see. Behind her, a couple hundred yards away, were the guest cottage and the main house. On the nightstand in the guest cottage was her phone.

"Can you walk?" Sloan asked Nora.

Nora attempted to push herself up off the ground but as soon as she put weight on her leg she collapsed. She shook her head.

"Okay," Sloan said as she thought.

She stood up and pitched onto her tiptoes, attempting to locate Ellis. She saw his head bobbing a couple of paths over, heading deeper into the vines. She grabbed the bottom of her blouse and ripped the fabric, tearing off a strip from the bottom. When she broke it free, she had a thin length of silk two feet long. She crouched down and secured the fabric around Nora's leg, cinching it close to her groin.

"Ouch," Nora said when Sloan set the knot, which dug into Nora's skin.

"It's a tourniquet. Well, the best I can do at the moment. It needs to be tight for it to work."

Sloan stood up again and tried to find Ellis.

"He is heading into the vines. My phone is back at the guest house."

"Don't leave me here."

Sloan smiled. "Not a chance."

She leaned over Nora as if Nora were a kettle bell.

"This is going to hurt," Sloan said. "Grunt and groan, but don't scream, okay?"

Nora nodded.

Sloan grabbed Nora under the armpits and lifted her like she was performing a kettlebell clean. She got Nora to her feet. Nora hopped on her left leg. Sloan bent down and placed her shoulder to Nora's hip, then lifted her over her shoulder. Compared to the weights Sloan was used to lifting, Nora was light. She took off in a controlled jog, heading back to the main house.

"Hang in there," Sloan said as she ran.

CHAPTER 71

Bend, Oregon
Friday, August 2, 2024

Sloan was breathing heavily as she came to the edge of the vineyards, her quads burning worse than during any CrossFit routine. But she ignored the pain. She had a singular goal to get to the house and call for help. At the edge of the vineyard, she paused. The cover the vines provided gave her a sense of protection, and she was hesitant to exit from them. She looked left and right while Nora continued to groan as she lay over Sloan's shoulder. Between the edge of the vineyards and the back of the guest cottage were a hundred yards of field.

Sloan took off in a jog, Nora bouncing on her shoulder as she ran. Halfway through the field another gun blast sounded and brought Sloan to her knees. Nora tumbled from her shoulder and cried out in pain as she rolled onto the ground. Sloan took inventory, feeling her body for a wound or blood. She found neither, and felt no pain. Another gunshot rang out. Sloan crawled over to Nora, the cattails of the field enough to give them partial cover.

Lying on her shoulder, Sloan looked over the cattails to see Ellis charging across the field to where they were lying.

"He's coming," Sloan said. "We have to go!"

"I can't," Nora said. "You go. Get to the house and call for help."

"I'm not leaving you."

Nora shook her head. "He won't kill me. I'm his wife."

Sloan remembered the image of Tilly and Reid Margolis, lying dead in the tasting room, and had a different thought about that. She couldn't leave Nora, and knew in an instant that she would either die defending her, or kill to protect her. She grabbed Nora under the arms and dragged her to the edge of the large machine that stood in the middle of the field. It was the yellow tractor-looking machine she had seen Lester using earlier in the morning to drive fence posts into the ground. It wasn't much, but it was more protection than lying in the grass.

She dragged Nora around to the front of the machine and peeked around the edge. As soon as she did, another shot rang out. Sloan dropped back to the ground. Ellis was close, and even if Sloan were willing to leave Nora, running for the house would mean getting shot. To lie there and wait would mean the same.

CHAPTER 72

Bend, Oregon
Friday, August 2, 2024

Ellis Margolis ran from the edge of the vineyard and saw Sloan Hastings carrying Nora over her shoulder. He fired off another round that caused the women to tumble into the prairie grass. He continued his pursuit and saw Sloan stand from beneath the cattails. He fired again. Running as frantically as he was, there was little chance of hitting his target. The shots were intended to pin them down and prevent them from getting to the house. He'd kill them when he reached them.

He was desperate for this day to be over. He wanted to put an end to it all, call the police, and tell them what he'd discovered— that Lester Strange, the family's loyal employee, had brought bloodshed to the very family that had supported him over the years. The only explanation, Ellis knew, would be that with the emergence of Sloan Hastings, Lester went on a killing spree to cover his tracks from decades earlier. Ellis would emerge as the lone survivor and fill in any holes the authorities had trouble understanding.

The truth, if he could pull it all off, would remain hidden as it had for the past three decades. Ellis had been embezzling funds from Margolis & Margolis for years to cover his opioid addiction. In recent years, his drug abuse had bled into a gambling problem. He had believed, nearly thirty years before on that fateful Fourth of July evening, that the deaths of Preston and Annabelle would forever keep his secret safe. But now Sloan Hastings promised to uncover it all, to dig up the secrets Ellis had buried a lifetime ago. The bloodshed at Margolis Manor was the only way to keep it all hidden. He would find a way in the coming years to compartmentalize even this terrible day.

As he approached the large EVO1 fence post driver, he slowed. The women were here somewhere, and he wasn't going to allow himself to get close enough for either to attack him. He'd seen the Hastings woman's muscled physique and would leave nothing to chance. He circled around the big yellow machine, approaching from the front. He heard a moan and recognized Nora's voice. After another step he found the women lying in the cattails huddled against the machine. A white fabric of some kind was wrapped around Nora's leg.

"Please, Ellis," Nora said. "Stop this madness."

He looked at her with pity. Killing his parents had been difficult. Killing his wife would be the hardest thing he did.

"Did you shoot them, Ellis? Did you shoot your parents. Please, tell me it wasn't you."

"Where did the pictures come from, Nora? In the darkroom. Where did those photos come from?"

"Annabelle's camera. The one I gave her that summer."

"But who took them, Nora?"

Nora never had the chance to answer. Sloan sprang from the ground and charged at Ellis, putting her shoulder into his midsection. The collision knocked the wind from his lungs and the gun from his hand.

CHAPTER 73

Bend, Oregon
Friday, August 2, 2024

Sloan drove her shoulder forward, lifting Ellis off the ground and driving her legs like she was pushing the heavy sled at the gym. In a final effort she lunged upward and threw Ellis to the ground, landing on top of him. With Ellis on his back and Sloan straddling his chest, she dug the thumb of her right hand deep into his left eye socket. Ellis released a guttural moan as a sickening popping noise came from his eye. Sloan rolled to the side and looked for the gun in the tall cattails.

She ran back to the spot where she had originally tackled him and searched while Ellis moaned. She spotted the black handle first, then the silver metal of the barrel. She reached for it just as she felt a hand grab her ankle. She screamed as she fell forward, Ellis pulling her leg backwards. She reached for the gun but as her fingers brushed the handle, Ellis dragged her backwards through the tall grass. Sloan kicked her legs and tried to crawl forward. The gun was just out of reach, but her body moved in the wrong direction as Ellis rose first to his knees and then to his feet, gaining traction with each movement.

Sloan flipped onto her back, breaking her ankle free from Ellis's grip. She pulled her knee to her chest and then exploded forward in a powerful kick to his groin that connected with full force and brought the man to the ground. Sloan scrambled back to the gun as she heard sirens in the distance. She found the gun again, this time taking it in her hands and turning to Ellis. But he was no longer doubled over from her kick. He was standing over her, his left eye swollen shut and sunken, with blood flowing down his cheek.

Sloan's back was against the giant yellow machine and she pointed the gun at Ellis. She knew instantly from the deranged look in the man's only remaining eye that she would have to shoot him if she hoped to stop him from killing her. Her right index finger began to depress the trigger, but before she did, she heard a rumble like a car backfiring. For a moment Sloan believed that she had fired the gun, but she felt no recoil. Her back, however, began to vibrate as the fence post driver roared to life. She saw Ellis look up at the big machine just as the driver shot a fence post down onto his head. The weight of the post, and the power of the driving machine, sent the post into his skull and through his chest. The machine echoed in the redundant clinking that had woken her that morning, and then went silent. It took Sloan a moment to understand the physics of what had happened, but as she looked at Ellis Margolis standing stiff and upright, she realized that the ten-foot fence post had been driven through his body and into the ground, killing him instantly and riveting him into place.

Sloan lowered the gun and slowly turned. When she looked up into the big machine she saw Lester Strange sitting in the operator's seat, his hands on the controls.

CHAPTER 74

Bend, Oregon
Thursday, August 15, 2024

NEARLY TWO WEEKS AFTER HER HARROWING ORDEAL AT MARGOLIS Manor, Sloan was back in Oregon. The FBI had summoned her. For the past ten days, since Agent John Michaels and his task force had reviewed the photos Sloan and Nora discovered on Annabelle Margolis's camera that told the story of the night she and Preston disappeared, the FBI had used ground penetrating radar to explore the property around the winery. The day before, they zeroed in on three specific locations where the ultrasound showed foreign objects deep underground. Experts were brought in to confirm that the soil had been disturbed and relaid years before. Knowing Ellis Margolis had access to earth-moving equipment stored on the property suggested that the bodies had been buried deep in the ground. Cadaver dogs were brought to each of the three sites and offered a positive response to one of them. Excavation was underway.

Agent Michaels met Sloan at the front gates and escorted her in a golf cart to the digging site far out among the cabernet vines. The area was cordoned off by yellow crime scene tape. Backhoes and front loaders roared as their hydraulic arms clawed into the earth and lifted massive amounts of soil to deposit into waiting dump trucks that beeped when they reversed out of the area.

Agent Michaels pulled up to the site and Sloan exited the cart. Crews of agents stood by while others watched a large monitor powered by a gas generator that told the operators of the earth-moving machines how deep to dig.

"That's it," one of the agents yelled as the front loader lifted its final bucketful of soil from the deep hole in the ground.

The agent came over to Michaels.

"We're at about three feet away. We've gotta go by hand now."

A ladder was lowered into the hole, which was eight feet deep, and three agents scaled down. Once they were in the hole, other agents tossed shovels down and the digging continued.

"How did you find this specific location?" Sloan asked Agent Michaels. She looked out at the vast property that went on for thousands of acres.

"We had a team of a hundred agents walk the grounds with radar looking for anything under the ground. Got a bunch of hits but narrowed them down to a couple. Then we brought in the experts and the sonar. They were able to distinguish the objects underground that were of interest versus the nonsense. Once we had a few specific locations that looked promising, we shot hydraulic piers down to the foreign objects and then brought them back up. Cadaver dogs sniffed the piers to let us know if we were on the right track. The dogs went crazy in this location."

Agent Michaels paused.

"We're pretty sure this is it."

Thirty minutes later one of the agents yelled.

"Got something down here, doc."

The FBI's forensic anthropologist climbed down the ladder and Sloan watched as the man knelt in the hole and worked diligently. Finally, one of the agents who'd completed the final dig climbed up the ladder and approached Michaels.

"Sir, they're bones. The doc confirmed they're human remains."

Agent Michaels looked up, exhaled a lungful of air, and placed a hand on Sloan's shoulder.

"It took nearly thirty years," Sloan said. "But we found them."

Agent Michaels turned to Sloan. "*You* found them."

CHAPTER 75

Raleigh, North Carolina
Friday, September 6, 2024

SLOAN SAT IN HER PARENTS' LIVING ROOM. TWO CHAIRS, WHICH DID not belong to her parents but had been brought in by HAP News, were set in the center of the room perfectly positioned in front of a portrait of Sloan and her parents. The portrait had hung above the fireplace for as long as Sloan could remember. This morning it was on the side wall of the living room. Producers had asked if they could move the portrait so that it was on display in the background during the interview because it so perfectly embodied the theme and feel they were striving for—baby Charlotte returns *again*.

Three cameras stood in the room. One positioned directly in front of the two chairs; the other two off to each side. Studio lights were mounted on tripods and white backdrops surrounded the chairs. Microphones hung from long boom poles. Sloan had decided to give her exclusive interview to Avery Mason and *American Events*. The decision came after a long conversation with Dr. Cutty, who knew Ms. Mason and promised she'd be fair in both her questions and the inevitable spin that Sloan's story was generating.

Sloan had put off the interview for the last month, but ever since forensic anthropology confirmed that the bodies found buried at Margolis Manor were, indeed, Preston and Annabelle Margolis, she could wait no longer. Sloan needed to set the record straight and fill in the details the public was desperate to learn.

Margot Gray's body had been discovered in a Dumpster on the

north end of Cedar Creek. Eric Stamos and the sheriff's office had been able to piece together surveillance footage from the Cedar Creek Inn that showed Ellis Margolis arriving at the inn with a large suitcase and taking the elevator to the third floor. Moments later, footage showed him wheeling the same suitcase out of the building. Together with the footage Ryder Hillier had provided, it was clear that Ellis Margolis had exited room 303 wheeling a suitcase behind him. Margot Gray's body was suspected to have been inside.

Since Sloan had refused to speak with Ryder Hillier, the podcaster had instead set her sights on telling the story of Margot Gray and the woman's role in the baby Charlotte saga. With footage Ryder had captured at the Cedar Creek Inn, the Margot Gray podcast proved to be one of her most popular.

The photos Sloan and Nora developed from Annabelle's camera were the only mystery that remained about the disappearance of Annabelle and Preston Margolis. No one could explain how the photos had been taken or who had been operating the camera the night Annabelle and Preston were killed. This lone mystery fueled the true crime community and produced dozens of conspiracy theories, the worst of which was that Nora Margolis had taken the photos that night in a demented attempt to document the murders for posterity's sake. Sloan planned to shut those rumors down during her one-on-one with Avery Mason.

"Five minutes," the producer yelled.

Sloan smiled at her parents, who offered encouraging nods.

She took a seat in one of the staged chairs, glancing briefly at the portrait that looked so out of place hanging on the side wall of the living room. Avery Mason took a seat next to her.

"Are you ready?" Avery asked.

Sloan took a deep breath and nodded. "Ready."

A producer held up his hand and counted down. "Three, two, one."

The world tuned in, and Sloan Hastings told her story.

CHAPTER 76

Raleigh, North Carolina
Friday, June 27, 2025

T HE FOLLOWING SUMMER, SLOAN STOOD AT THE FRONT OF THE CAGE at the Office of the Chief Medical Examiner in North Carolina. She looked out at a standing-room-only crowd, bigger than any she'd seen for the other fellows who had given their end-of-the-year presentations. She wasn't surprised. Her story had gone viral over the last year, and the return of baby Charlotte Margolis was as big a news event today as was her disappearance thirty years before. This time, though, Sloan provided the answers that had eluded the media, law enforcement, and true crime fanatics who had chased the story for three decades.

She exhaled a calming breath and looked out at the crowd awaiting her presentation. Dr. Cutty was in the front row and had been integral in helping Sloan fine-tune her presentation. Her parents were in the back, and next to them was Eric Stamos, who'd made the trip from Cedar Creek. As a late arrival, Sloan saw Nora walk through the cage's doorway. Nearly a year after a bullet ripped through her leg, and three surgeries later, Nora used a single crutch but managed without issue as she took a seat. She offered Sloan a subtle wave and a smile.

The room quieted and the lights dimmed. Sloan clicked a button on the remote and the SMART Board lit up with the title of her presentation.

Advancing the Science of Forensic Genealogy

"My name is Dr. Sloan Hastings, and over the next four hours I am going to detail how forensic genealogy allowed me to solve a thirty-year-old cold case—the disappearance of my birth parents, Preston and Annabelle Margolis."

CHAPTER 77

Raleigh, North Carolina
Friday, June 27, 2025

Aftern the presentation Sloan spoke with a few of the attending physicians who were riveted by her research and the story she had to tell. She introduced her parents to Dr. Cutty, who promised to take good care of Sloan during her final year of training. Todd Hastings made a final push for Sloan to consider forensic dentistry.

When the crowd thinned, she found Eric in the back of the cage.

"You didn't have to come all the way out here," Sloan said.

"Are you kidding me? I wouldn't have missed it. You were great, by the way. Everyone in the room, or the cage—whatever this place is called—was hanging on your every word."

"Thank you. And really, Eric, it means a lot to me that you came. How long are you in town?"

"Heading back tomorrow."

Sloan nodded.

"Listen, Sloan . . . thanks for everything you did for me."

"It wasn't just me."

Eric cocked his head. "None of it would have happened without you. I'd still be looking for answers about what happened to my dad. Now I know."

"I wish we could have found those answers while your grandfather was still around."

Eric smiled. "Me too."

There was a long stretch of silence.

"I've got an early flight in the morning," Eric said. "But I'm wondering if you'd let me take you out to dinner tonight. To celebrate."

Sloan nodded. "I'd love to. You want to come by my apartment at seven?"

"Yeah, perfect."

"You still remember how to get there?"

"How could I forget?"

"I'll leave the Mace in my desk drawer."

"Appreciate it," Eric said with a smile. "See you tonight."

After Eric left, the only people remaining in the cage were her parents. Sloan looked around but Nora was gone.

Sloan drove home with the weight of the world lifted from her shoulders. Two weeks of downtime sat between her and the start of her second year of fellowship. She was ready to get away from research and into the morgue, and sensed that she was one year away from fulfilling her dream of forensic pathology. With the baby Charlotte case on her résumé, Sloan would have no problem finding a spot on a homicide task force.

She pulled into the parking lot of her apartment complex, grabbed the box from the backseat that contained her year's worth of research, and carried it up the steps. When she made it to the third level, she found two things waiting for her. The first was a package wrapped in brown paper propped against her front door. The second was Agent John Michaels, who leaned against the wall much like Eric Stamos had a year before.

"How'd your dissertation go?" he asked when Sloan made it up the stairs.

"I think it went well. But best of all, it's over."

"Big relief?"

"The biggest."

Sloan walked to her door.

"What's with the house call? Something new come up?"

"No. I'm here to make you an offer."

Sloan pointed to the package leaning against the front door. "This yours?"

"Nope. It was there when I got here."

Sloan looked at the package and then back to Michaels.

"What kind of offer?"

"The Bureau needs some fresh blood in the forensics unit. We could use someone like you once you're done with your final year of training."

"The FBI?"

"Yes, ma'am."

"I was thinking about a homicide unit."

"You're thinking too small. Rumors are already starting to spread, and people are talking. You're in high demand, and you're not made for a homicide unit. The Bureau is a bigger platform, and our task force is a much better fit for your skill set. You'd be working in the FBI laboratory in forensics, helping solve crimes and cold cases from around the country."

Sloan inserted her key into the front door. The offer was everything Sloan had hoped to do.

"Can I think about it?"

"Sure. You've got a year to decide."

Agent Michaels handed her a business card.

"Keep in touch."

Sloan smiled. "I will."

"And good luck in the morgue."

"Thanks."

A moment later, Sloan watched over the third-story railing as Agent Michaels drove away. When he was gone, she looked down at the package still leaning against her door. It was the size of a wall hanging and contained no address label or postage to suggest it had been delivered by a formal courier service. She looked around the complex, as if the person who left it would still be in the area. Seeing no one, she opened her door, dropped the box of research onto the kitchen floor, and lifted the package to carry it into her apartment. When she did, she noticed a second, smaller box that had been set behind the package. She took both inside.

In the kitchen she used scissors to cut the crisscrossing rope on the smaller package, popped the cardboard top, and opened the box. Inside was Annabelle's Nikon FM10 camera and a new package of film. Sloan smiled as she turned the camera over in her hands.

Placing it on the table, she reached for the larger package—the wall hanging—and slowly peeled away the brown paper to reveal a framed photo. Once she had the paper removed, Sloan turned the frame around to admire the picture. It was an enlarged image of the Cooper's hawk taken by Annabelle as the bird took flight outside her home—the picture Sloan and Nora had developed at Margolis Manor. The hawk, lighted by the afternoon sun, was majestic with its wings fully outstretched.

A white envelope was taped to the bottom of the picture. Sloan set the frame flat on her table and opened the envelope, pulling out a card. She read the message and smiled.

> You will soar to great places.
> —Nora

ACKNOWLEDGMENTS

As usual, a big "thank you" to everyone at Kensington Publishing who continues to believe in me and support my books so enthusiastically. I'm grateful that, years ago, my first manuscript swirled around New York and somehow landed on John Scognamiglio's desk. It's been a pretty good run since then, and one I hope to continue for many years.

To Amy and Mary, always my first readers.

To my agent, Marlene Stinger, who has told me so many times that "it only takes one book." Here's to many more of those in the years to come.

To Claire Ammon for answering my questions about genealogy, online ancestry websites, DNA, and forensics. I'm sure I didn't get everything in the world of forensic genealogy correct, but Claire helped me get close. Any errors are mine.

To Carrianne Hornok for helping me with darkroom photography.

To Kelly Witt for sharing her enthusiasm of CrossFit so that Sloan Hastings could be such a badass. I would have included all your suggestions about CrossFit, Kelly, but they would have run the book to 600 pages, so I had to pick and choose!

To the bloggers, influencers, and readers who have read my books, written reviews, and put my books on the map through word of mouth. I'm forever grateful.

Postscript:

Although geographically you can look at a map and see where Cedar Creek is *supposed* to be located, you won't find it. Cedar Creek, Nevada, does not exist. Nor does Harrison County. Much like my first novel, *Summit Lake,* I created Cedar Creek to suit my needs.